ADVANCE PRAISE FOR
HONOR CODE

"*Honor Code* explores the harsh reality of victim shaming and how too often the very institutions designed to protect us are the ones to silence those who dare come forward. Tragic, gripping, and very important."

—Amy Giles, author of *Now Is Everything*

"Feminist and furious, *Honor Code* will have your heart racing and your blood boiling up to the last twisty page."

—Emma Berquist, author of *Devils Unto Dust*

"Relentless, twisting, raw, and incredibly human."

—Kate Brauning, author of *How We Fall*

"Not the private school book you've been prepping for—*Honor Code* weaves a seductively dark web and then burns the whole thing to the ground. Breathless, gritty and thrilling."

—Kendra Fortmeyer, author of *Hole in the Middle*

"Raw and rage-inducing, *Honor Code* will make you question what is right, what is real, and what we tell girls about their value in this world."

—Rebecca Barrow, author of *You Don't Know Me but I Know You*

honor code

KIERSI BURKHART

carolrhoda LAB
MINNEAPOLIS

Carolrhoda Lab™
An imprint of Carolrhoda Books
A division of Lerner Publishing Group, Inc.
241 First Avenue North
Minneapolis, MN 55401 USA

For reading levels and more information, look up this title at
www.lernerbooks.com.

Cover and interior images: Nata Kuprova/Shutterstock.com (letters); Gordan/
Shutterstock.com (border).

Main body text set in Janson Text LT Std 10.5/15.
Typeface provided by Linotype AG.

Library of Congress Cataloging-in-Publication Data

Names: Burkhart, Kiersi, author.
Title: Honor code / by Kiersi Burkhart.
Description: Minneapolis : Carolrhoda Lab, [2017] | Summary: Fifteen-year-old
    Sam contacts a reporter, hoping to expose a fellow student at elite Edwards
    Academy for rape, but the reporter tells her parents and soon, she is facing him
    in court.
Identifiers: LCCN 2016034413 (print) | LCCN 2017007086 (ebook) | ISBN
    9781512429961 (th : alk. paper) | ISBN 9781512442755 (eb pdf)
Subjects: | CYAC: Rape—Fiction. | Preparatory schools—Fiction. | Schools—
    Fiction. | Reporters and reporting—Fiction.
Classification: LCC PZ7.1.B88 Hon 2017 (print) | LCC PZ7.1.B88 (ebook) | DDC
    [Fic]—dc23

LC record available at https://lccn.loc.gov/2016034413

Manufactured in the United States of America
2-45310-23503-1/12/2018

TO AMBER J. KEYSER—
FRIEND, MENTOR, MOM, SISTER . . . AND THE
OTHER HALF OF MY BRAIN.
EVEN A THOUSAND MILES APART, WE ARE
STILL ALWAYS TOGETHER.

ACT ONE

CHAPTER ONE

http://privateschoolnewb.tumblr.com
Aug. 30, 2017

Sorry if this first post is weird. I'm writing on my phone in the car. We drove through some enormous stone gates earlier, but we still haven't gotten to the school. It feels like the campus goes on forever, just grass and trees and big brick buildings.

My parents are about to drop me off for my first day at a fancy-pants private boarding school. No, I won't tell you which one. That would defeat the purpose of an anonymous blog, wouldn't it?

Before I got here I always wondered what it was like. I bet a lot of other people have, too. So I thought it would be cool to relay my authentic experience. Show the world what the inside of one of these places is like. For all the other wonderers out there.

I'll post more when I'm settled in. Hopefully I get some followers before then so somebody will read this drivel. Not that it really matters—I'm also doing this for me. To keep myself accountable. I know how these places can suck you up, mold you around, and spit you back out in a totally different shape than when you started.

I need to stay me. But do stick around, ask me questions, whatever you want. Who doesn't like having an audience?

It's two in the afternoon, and a loose crowd of First Years—me among them—snakes toward the towering stone cathedral at the center of campus. I walk right behind a pod of chattering Second Years who are all finding their old friends in the salmon stream, catching up on what they did over the summer.

I wonder if I'll make it to my second year. When I got accepted to Edwards Academy, Dad made me commit to one year before he'd write that first tuition check, the *Titanic* of expenditures. The deal is this: I can't back out before one year is up, the way I backed out of guitar, soccer, and mock trial back in middle school. No matter what.

"And if you don't like Edwards Academy after giving it a whole year," Dad had said, "then fine. Experiment over, no hard feelings."

The conga line of students and faculty finally reaches the double doors of St. Joseph's Cathedral, or what I've heard called "Cath." The tops of the cathedral towers, far overhead, are made of stone and glass and good old wood. As we enter through the massive doors, the quality of sound suddenly changes—the chatting and giggling of students fills up the air around me, echoing, multiplying. It feels like there are a few thousand people here instead of just a few hundred. A vaulted ceiling yawns over us, flanked by enormous buttresses that hold it up, like the ribs of a blue whale. The light streaming in through stained glass windows turns everything yellow and pink and glowing.

If I were the religious type, it would be easy to believe a higher power resided here. Cath feels alive. Will I really get to come here every single morning? I can't imagine ever getting used to this—to the marble pillars that mark the aisles, or the delicate gold molding, or the vibrant colors of the glass panels.

Up ahead, the Fourth Years slip into the front-most pews. Behind them sit the Third Years, then Second Years. And finally, us lowly Firsties, standing at the very back while we wait for permission to sit.

I'm busy looking for somebody. There, that must be her— in the very first seat of the very first pew, across the aisle from Provost Portsmouth himself. That must be the Head Girl.

Last year, all the prefects from all the houses got together and voted her as the best of them. And even luckier for me? She's the Head Prefect of my house, Isabel House.

Edwards has . . . a patchy background. It was boys only for over a hundred years. The school opened up to female students in the '80s, but this is the very first time they've had a Head Girl.

Maybe I could be voted in as Head Girl in my Fourth Year if I stick with this. That would be admission to Harvard in the bag, and a straight shot from there to Harvard Law School.

Up in the front pew, the Fourth Year girls greet each other by kissing each other on the cheeks, like Europeans. Weird. I've never seen people do that except on TV.

Kissing on the cheek? Will I have to kiss people on the cheek?

The faculty member who led us into Cath stops at the back-most pews, calling out, "Sit in alphabetical order, please!"

Crap, I've fallen out of order. I glance around for the two kids who'd been standing on either side of me earlier—but I think they've gone to sit down. I'm already lost and school technically hasn't even started yet.

Eventually I spot their two vaguely familiar faces and push toward my seat.

Just in time. The full, thick, reverberating notes of the organ start to spill out. The First Years all sit silent and ram-rod straight. The whole cathedral takes on an immensity as the haunting voice of the organ saturates it, and the old guy playing it closes his eyes and starts really getting into it as he strikes the two keyboards. The Second Years sitting in front of us start giggling as the combed-over threads of his white hair whip back and forth over the bald part of his head, which looks a lot like a fried egg sunny-side up. I close my eyes and just try to listen.

After the organ, the chaplain recites something. Then Provost Portsmouth comes up to the high marble altar, which has been converted into a podium.

He starts his opening remarks talking about old Dr. Edwards. When Morgan Edwards started his school, Portsmouth tells us, back in 1870-something, he'd lamented how his older sons had received only "half of an education." Just book learning, he'd said, not life learning. Arithmetic was necessary, of course—but so were ethics. Morals. Poise.

And so he created Edwards Academy as a place to educate and groom a truly wise, well-rounded young man. The young women came later—long after the old doctor had died.

"That's bullshit," the girl sitting next to me whispers.

I tilt toward her. "What is?"

"This place is so closed off from the real world, how could you learn anything about life here?" She shakes her head. She has long, black hair that she parts severely down the middle, and light brown skin like topaz. "By 'life learning' he means how to be rich, white, and successful."

A Second Year prefect turns around and shushes us. We both fall silent.

After the opening ceremony is over, I get a better look at the skeptical girl. She's tall, stick-thin, and built like a dancer. Her dark brown eyes are big.

"Hey," she says. "I'm Gracie."

"Hey. Sam."

"Nice to meet you, Hey Sam."

It's the most inane Dad joke ever, and I let out a noise that's between a groan and a laugh.

We must be in the same house—all the houses were corralled and seated together in Cath. Cool. My awesome new school comes with a built-in friend.

―――――――――――

After the ceremony, we're freed to go unpack and settle in. I cross the rolling green campus at a quick clip, glued to my campus map. There are so many little walkways that branch off the main brick path, I wonder how I'll ever memorize where they all go. The trip back to my dorm winds me through emerald lawns of a meticulously uniform height, encircling red brick buildings with white stone finishes that remind me of movies set in England. There's a lake on my map, which I don't really believe is as big as it looks until I get to it.

The water is clear and dotted with lily pads. As I circle it, approaching what I think is Isabel House just on the other side, an enormous koi fish with gold scales darts under the surface.

I can't believe I get to live here.

I feel like my whole body is vibrating as I spot the giant stone sign that reads ISABEL HOUSE. I'm going to meet my new roommate soon. When my parents helped me carry up my things earlier this morning, she wasn't there—but there were pieces of her already arranged around the room. A crisp gray bedspread and wrinkle-free pillowcases with curling embroidery, that reminded me of a hotel room. Her shiny, new, extra-large laptop sat on the desk, a small tablet lounging next to it. A polished, black leather messenger bag hung off the back of the chair.

I can tell that my roommate's a real upper-class girl. We're going to spend the whole year together, probably become best friends. We'll stay up nights talking in the dark about people we like and don't like, boys, homework, our favorite music. Go to all our meals together. My mom says her maid of honor when she married my dad was her college roommate. What if we went to college together? We could live in a big college house. We could be friends for the rest of our lives.

Inside Isabel House, a prefect sitting at a desk leans forward over a clipboard and stops me. She's chewing gum and has milky, unblemished skin.

"Gotta check in," she says. "What's your name?"

Once I'm signed in, I follow the stairs up to the second floor. My room is at the end of the hall, and there are shadows moving under the door. I'm buzzing.

She's here.

I push open the door. Inside, arranging her already-perfect pillowcases, is Gracie.

Her head darts up, and she smiles when she sees me. "Oh, it's Hey Sam." I walk in and drop my backpack on my bed. "So we get to be next to each other in Cath, *and* we're roomies?" She smiles a funny half-smile, like paint of slightly the wrong hue used to cover up a hole in the wall. "What's the chance?"

I glance at the little black name label she has painstakingly placed on the rear side of her laptop, a label I didn't notice earlier. It says GRACIE CALEZA.

Caleza. Barker.

"Maybe the chance is greater than you think," I say. I point at the label on her computer. "I'm Barker."

"You're a barker?" she says. "You don't look like a dog to me."

What is with this girl's humor? It's so off-key I have to laugh. It's like she gets the concept of jokes, but doesn't quite know how to put one together.

"Barker is my last name," I say. "Yours is Caleza. They paired us up because we're next to each other in the alphabet."

"What? No way." She looks at the label. "That whole form I filled out with my sleeping preferences, my hobbies, my level of cleanliness?"

"All ignored in favor of the much simpler Alphabet Game," I say.

"That's stupid," Gracie says. "But still kinda rad, since we already met and seem to get along."

Rad? Are we in the 1980s? Okay, so she's a quirky goth with a Morticia Addams hairstyle going on, but at least she's up front about things. That will make living together easier.

"But how do you know from just one conversation?" I ask, unpacking the new laptop I got for my birthday last week on my bed, then setting my favorite sketchbook on top. "I could be a serial killer."

She raises her eyebrows. "Are you?"

"Would a real serial killer just admit it?"

Gracie picks up my sketchbook and starts leafing through it. "Oh, yes, these lovely drawings of trees—I can tell, you're definitely a serial killer."

"Serial killers might also like trees."

"You're right." She turns the notebook sideways. "Maybe the tree is so big and green because someone buried a body under it."

I laugh and grab the sketchbook back. "That's so dark! I'm gonna be a lawyer, not a serial killer."

She quirks an eyebrow at me. "A lawyer?"

"You know. The legit way to fight bad guys. Get justice. I want to do pro bono work for innocent people."

Gracie outright laughs. "What? That is the weirdest dream I've ever heard. *I want to be a lawyer who works for free.* What about paying your bills?"

I turn back to unpacking my bag. It stings a little. "Don't we have to unpack before dinner?"

"Oh, no," she says, getting up. "Sorry if I hurt your feelings. I was just kidding. I think that sounds cool. Really, like . . . honorable."

"Running around in a mask saving people isn't realistic," I say. "Lawyer is the best I can do, since I don't have superpowers."

"Yes, you do." She points at my head and grins mischievously. "Right there. That brain is your superpower."

I'm blushing, I know it. "Come on," I say, batting her hand away. "Let's unpack so we can go get dinner."

"Jeez, it's only the first day and you're already a tyrant," she says. "Or are you just hungry?"

"Anytime I'm not eating, I'm hungry."

She laughs. "That explains a lot."

After we've had some time to fill up our closets and meet the neighbors, our House Mother—who tells us brightly, "Please, call me Jean!"—ushers us all to the second-floor lounge, where she surprises us with pizza for dinner.

The lounge is a tacky mixture of its 1980s construction, some old-world Victorian furniture, and dramatic oil paintings in elaborate gold frames. Third and Fourth Year girls are scattered around the room on couches and chairs, looking cozy. We, the First and Second Years, are confined to scratchy pillows on the floor. The TV off to one side plays visualizer effects for the light pop music that underscores the girls' chatter. I nab a seat on a pillow next to Gracie.

Once the pizza is finished and the boxes are cleared away, Jean moves to the front of the room. I'm expecting her to give some sort of speech, but instead she calls the Head Girl up to the front.

"I'll leave it to you, Hayden," Jean says to her. "Ladies, don't do anything you don't want me to hear about later."

"Yes, Jean," the Head Girl says. Jean grins a motherly grin and heads out of the lounge, leaving us alone.

I'm confused. One of the big selling points of Edwards to parents is that no student is ever unsupervised, unless it's nighttime and your door's closed.

I am simultaneously excited and uneasy. What will we be doing on the first night of school without an adult around? The girls around me are whispering to each other about what's coming. Hayden, with her bouncy brown hair, stands with her arms crossed, like she ought to have a lectern in front of her.

"All right, Firsties," the Head Girl says, gesturing for us to quiet down. "My name is Hayden. Jean has passed the duties of initiation on to me, the Head Prefect of Isabel House."

She's pretty, dressed in a high skirt and collared shirt like I imagine Prep School Barbie would be. Her presence is as big as the room.

"Just think of us as your official Welcome Wagon," she says, as two other girls with nice tans get up to flank her. One is blonde, one is brunette. Their outfits are as picture-perfect as Hayden's. "It's our duty to help make your transition here as smooth as possible. Jean left you with us because there are just some things that only another Edwardian can teach you. I take this duty very seriously, so we've made up a handy list of important information."

The blonde prefect starts passing out packets of paper from a stack. She's wearing a sticker name tag that says MANDA.

"Faculty like to pretend that we're all good boys and girls here," Hayden says, "but we all know that's not true. And if you're going to do it, the organ room in Cath is your best bet for privacy." A few nervous laughs from the assembled audience.

The top sheet of the packet reads: *Isabel House Rules & Suggestions*. Below that is a long list of boys' names, divided into two columns labeled *Naughty* and *Nice*.

"Hopefully this list will save you some time," Manda says, "so you don't have to make the same mistakes we did. Stick to the 'nice' ones."

"Don't complain to us later if you go out with a 'naughty' guy and it doesn't go the way you want," Hayden says.

She points us to the Calendar of Events on the next page and launches into extolling the virtues of the upcoming Inaugural Mixer.

"It's a perfect way to get to know people," she says. By *people*, I think she means *boys*.

"Only the Third and Fourth Year boys can ask," Manda says, "so don't go getting cocky and thinking you can just walk up and ask some hottie Fourth Year to go with you."

A couple girls laugh. But I can't imagine having that kind of gumption. Definitely not here, and not with those tall, grown-up-looking boys I saw at the opening ceremony in Cath.

"Feel free to flirt," Hayden tells us. "Let them know you're interested. But be subtle!"

Manda butts in. "You'll notice the calendar contains a lot of other important events for Isabel House girls." It's an exhaustive list: Inaugural Mixer. Homecoming Water Polo Game. Home Weekend. Prefect Nominations. And those are just the big ones before the Christmas vacation. It's a lot to remember, but it sounds like an exciting year. Always something to look forward to.

"But most importantly," Hayden says, reclaiming the spot in the middle of the floor, "the thing that will help you the most in getting adjusted at Edwards is the honor code. Next page, everyone."

The third page of our packet reads: *The Edwards Academy Honor Code.*

"This is the most important text to know," she says. "This wasn't written by teachers or deans or the provost. The honor code was written by us."

"All of us," Manda says, gesturing around the room. "Every Honor Code Committee for the last hundred and fifty years has edited and added to it."

A whole hundred and fifty years.

"It's evolved over time," Hayden adds. "And of course, it has to be approved by the faculty every year. But get to know the honor code, and you'll get it so much faster."

The way she says "get it"—like attending Edwards is a paradigm shift I have to reach the other side of before I understand what I'm even doing here. As I read through the honor code, I hope I can "get it" fast.

> *We are all more than the shine on our shoes, or the pennies in our pockets. Our actions show who we are.*
>
> *Anyone can come to Edwards. What we must prove is that we have the heart, determination, and loyalty to stay.*

It's not long, but it's weird. There are a lot of expectations. Maybe "getting it" will be like the way I switched from thinking boys were gross when I was eleven, to having crushes on them when I was twelve and I finally "got" what all the fuss was about.

"Okay now," jumps in Manda, clapping her hands. "It's time for the games!" She gestures at all of us to stand up. "Up, up, up!" she says, and I imagine we are about to do jumping jacks or maybe make a pyramid. Is that what private school girls do when left alone? Gracie and I exchange a baffled look as we get up. Manda grabs a pen and clipboard from a table and calls, "Clothes off!"

What?

I glance at the other First Years to see if I heard her right. They all look like deer staring into headlights.

"We're just conducting a quick survey," says Hayden, gently pushing Manda aside. "As your house prefects, we're here to mentor you, to offer experience and wisdom. Boarding school is different from what you've experienced before, and we know that."

She walks up to me so her face is right in mine.

Oh, no. I'm first.

She grabs the hem of my t-shirt and pulls it up over my inert arms, revealing my belly and chest and the ugly, nude-colored bra I never expected anybody to see when I put it on this morning.

I am standing only in my bra in front of every girl in Isabel House. My skin is ice cold. Then Hayden gestures to my pants.

Oh, please, no.

"Those, too."

My hands wobble wildly as I do what I'm told. Every undulation of my flesh, every one of my bumps and wrinkles and fat mounds, is now completely visible as I strip off my jeans and leave them in a pile on the floor.

"Hmm," Hayden says, crouching down in front of me like I'm a science experiment. She eyes my cleavage, then my belly.

"Good tits," she says. She plucks the strap of my bra. "But this is so old, it should be in a Goodwill box. Makes you look saggy. Shouldn't have the boobs of a forty-year-old at your age."

I want to die.

I want to become dust, and be blown away in a wind, and never, ever come back.

"Survey says?" asks Manda.

Hayden ignores her, pinching the fat around my waist, just over my hip bone. "This needs a lot of work. You know, Edwards has top-tier sports teams. You should sign up for one, get some cardio conditioning. Improve that bad posture." I try to straighten my shoulders, but she's already moved on, saying,

"There's soccer, racquetball, basketball . . ." She continues her way up my body, poking my fat, squeezing me like I am an avocado at the grocery store and she's testing whether I'm ripe.

I can't speak. Everyone is staring at me. But I'm not the only one anymore, as the girls standing on either side of me have started taking their own clothes off. They are thinner, with fewer mounds for Hayden to squeeze. Next to me Gracie is skinny and stone-faced, staring straight ahead.

"I'm waiting," says Manda. "What's the score?"

"I do love this wild hair," Hayden says, threading her hands through my auburn curls. "And your skin is all right. Take care of it, lotion every day."

"Still waiting."

Hayden keeps on. "But this flab," she says, squeezing my stomach. "This muffin-top thing, it's gotta go. No definition. A very roly-poly kind of look—no guy's gonna want to get on top of that." She sighs, as if my existence is a great disappointment. "Considering the hair and the nice tits, I give her a *Needs Improvement.*" Hayden finally steps away from me, and I realize I'm shivering. "Tame the curls, use better conditioner. And for god's sake, relax. I'll check back in with you in a few weeks and I expect you to have signed up for some kind of physical activity by then—and in the meantime, buy yourself some new clothes."

She wipes the hand she used to touch me on her pant leg, like I'm filthy. The First Year girl to my left has clearly tried to learn from my survey and is sucking in her stomach, straightening her shoulders, exposing her chest.

Hayden stands in front of her, rubbing her chin. "Another good chest," she says as I kneel down and pick up my shirt. It's amazing I haven't burst into flame yet from my humiliation.

"You should get a professional bra-fitting, though, so you're not popping out all the time. Gives an unappealing shape under the shirt when your bra is too small." She pats down the girl's sides like a security guard patting someone down to enter a concert. "And don't do these empire waist cuts. They look terrible on girls with your shape."

I grab my t-shirt and put my arms through it, but my hands are shaking so much it's hard to pull it back on.

"And ditch the hip-huggers," Hayden adds, dragging her foot through the girl's jeans, which lie on the ground in a heap. "They're giving you a muffin top, too. Waist-highs for girls like you who have big, high hips."

"Th-th-thank you," the girl says, her eyes shining with unshed tears as Hayden steps back.

"Just doing my job," she says. Noticing the tears, she adds, "Don't take it too hard. Everyone comes in with some work to do because Edwards has higher expectations than your average school. But I believe in you." She turns to Manda, the score-keeper. "Give her a re-dress. She needs a new wardrobe."

"*Re-dress*," Manda echoes, scribbling on her clipboard.

Next, Hayden turns around to face Gracie. Gracie's eyes are obsidian—sharp and hard and black—as Hayden starts feeling her up.

"You need some toning!" Hayden says, pinching the skin around Gracie's middle and making her squirm with pain. "And maybe an extra portion at dinner? The guys here like a little bit of curve."

"So, what?" says Manda, laughing. "Some aren't skinny enough, and now she's too skinny?"

Hayden flashes a wolf grin. "Like I said! It's good to have some curves." She pushes aside Gracie's straight bangs. "And do something about this haircut. I can't even describe how much of a turn-off it is."

"Verdict?" asks Manda.

Hayden snaps Gracie's bra strap. "Wear a push-up bra. You have good material to work with here—it just needs a little spit and polish."

"*Spit and polish*," echoes Manda. "Is that your final score?"

"That's my final score."

After Hayden moves on, Gracie just stands there, her clothes in a puddle on the floor. I sit down with my clothes back on, wrapping my arms around my knees, and try not to listen to the rest.

CHAPTER TWO

http://privateschoolnewb.tumblr.com
Aug. 31, 2017

Boarding school looks like:
Cool morning walks in the graveyard—and spotting some marvelous wildlife.

I couldn't sleep after getting back to our room last night. Lying in bed, the sound of my own breath was deafening. I replayed what had happened over and over—standing practically naked in front of everyone, getting unsolicited advice about all the things that are wrong with me.

It was like going to class in a nightmare, where my body was the final project waiting for a grade.

I gave up on sleeping, packed my sketchbook, and went on a walk. Besides, I didn't know if I could look my roommate in the eye after the body survey. Neither of us said a word to each other about it the whole night.

Whatever, though. Like I'm the first person ever to get hazed. I just have to try to forget about it.

Instead I focused on how beautiful the campus is, drenched in early morning sunlight. The towering old trees, the ticking white clock tower, the vines crawling up the sides of buildings. I walked all the way across campus to the famous old graveyard, thinking about what I wanted to draw. The graveyard isn't too far from the medical museum. Are corpses buried here that were first autopsied by weird founder doctor-man himself? I heard people had to rob graves for science back in the old days.

Graveyards are lovely. Nobody goes there because most people are creeped out. You almost never run into another person in a graveyard.

Usually.

But I did see someone. Deep down in the graveyard, there's a gazebo that looks over a long, shallow reflecting pool.

And a guy was standing in the middle of the pool.

Must have been an upperclassman—he had clearly outlined pectoral muscles and drawn-on abs. He did these slow, graceful, purposeful motions, lifting his knee into the air, spreading his arms in front of himself, like a swan. Or an eagle. Some regal bird. I'm pretty sure it was tai chi.

Then he turned his head and caught me staring. I couldn't believe it. I thought about taking off, but he just kept doing his peculiar exercises as if I weren't there.

So I kept watching, as if I weren't there, too.

The morning sun lit his perfect profile. His flop of wheat-colored, wavy hair tilted forward and back as he moved.

I've never seen someone so beautiful in real life.

I wish I had thought to draw him so I could show you how magnificent he was. But this story will have to do instead, because I forgot to draw anything.

Gracie and I are both late to morning room inspection, returning from our showers just as Jean knocks on the door. She glances over the clothes on my side of the floor, then the unmade bed on Gracie's side, and lets out a sigh.

"A demerit each," she says, marking something on her clipboard. I feel an almost physical pain. A demerit on my first day?

"You both know the expectations for Level One, right?" she asks.

We nod. *No debris on the floors. Desks neat. Beds made.* It's supposed to teach us personal responsibility: if you're good for one whole semester, you clear Level One and they leave you alone for the next three and a half years.

I thought Gracie would be neater, but the body survey last night must have gotten to both of us. We didn't mention it last night, and we don't mention it now—almost like if we do, we've given it power. We've allowed it to be real. If we never bring it up, maybe we can pretend it never happened.

Except I can't pretend. I can't forget.

Hayden was right. I do have a muffin top. My hair frizzes out all over the place as soon as it dries, no matter what—I've tried. I'm not built like an athlete. Dad used to tease me and call me "The Brain" because I refused to go out for soccer when all the other kids did and asked him instead if I could try out for the Science Olympiad.

"This ugly nickel I found for your thoughts?" Gracie asks, as we walk across campus to Morning Prayer. She holds out what is indeed an ugly, flattened nickel, like somebody ran over it with a truck.

I take the nickel and shake my head. "My only thought right now is that I don't want to be late . . . and I'm wondering where the heck you found this." I toss it into the bushes.

She snickers. "Such a square. We won't get a demerit for being a little late on the first day." A look of doubt crosses her face. "Actually, I wouldn't put it past them, after that run-in with Jean earlier."

We get to Cath just in time. I almost fall asleep during Morning Prayer despite the swelling organ and the eerie, echoing voices of the choir.

Then it's on to breakfast. I slouch in the buffet line behind Gracie, feeling bulldozed. Last night was the worst night of my life. I don't know if I'll ever be able to stop thinking about it and feeling humiliated all over again.

Once we have our food, it's time to figure out where to sit. We could join a table of kids we don't know and probably look pathetic, or sit by ourselves and . . . well, also look pathetic.

Gracie takes the initiative and heads for a table that's half empty, down from some other girls who look like Firsties but aren't in Isabel House. Thank god.

Gracie looks over her schedule while I push around the hard, dry scrambled eggs and burned bacon, and nibble on my toast.

Needs Improvement.

That means improvement is possible, right?

Then I'll commit to improving. Commit like I committed to coming to Edwards Academy. I put down the buttered toast

I'm halfway through eating, thinking of Hayden squeezing my "muffin top," and just drink some orange juice instead.

Soon a bell rings. Time for my first class.

I am upbeat, I say to myself.

Actually, no. I *tell* myself.

I am more than upbeat. *I am excited.* I am ready to learn.

Besides, this is what I'm here for. A good education. That's why Dad cashed out part of his 401(k), and I convinced Mom it wouldn't be so bad that she couldn't help me pick out my dress for Homecoming, or bake brownies for school fundraisers.

"Complete academic saturation," the website had said. And that sounded perfect. Not like my middle school, where people in the back whispered over the teacher and everything was a competition for who could act like they cared the least.

My first class is in Mackenzie Hall, but I can't figure out the map. Gracie and I pass an exhibition hall, an observatory, an art studio. Science buildings. Humanities. A music conservatory. The medical museum, which I hope to never enter. Mom and I went to Body Worlds once and I almost fainted at the first exhibit.

It feels like this school goes on forever. Still no Mackenzie Hall.

"There," Gracie says suddenly, looking at her map and pointing to a building on the other side of a huge lawn. "That's you."

I groan with relief. "Thank god somebody can read this thing."

"See you after class," Gracie says, waving goodbye to me in an exaggerated fashion. She smiles that weird half-smile of hers. "If you don't get lost first."

Finding Room 105 is a lot easier than finding Mackenzie was. Inside, I slide into an open desk and try not to look obvious admiring the new chairs, or the solid wood teacher's desk, or the big touch screen hanging at the front of the room.

Other kids arrive, but it seems like they already know each other. I took a bunch of tests to get placed into my classes, and I got put with Second Years. I thought that would be cool . . . except that it means nobody here is out to make new friends.

They're not talking about fancy cars or vacations—the kind of stuff I expected from rich kids. And they don't really look like "rich kids," if rich kids have a *look*. On TV shows it's real obvious. But everyone here is wearing t-shirts and jeans, cardigans, tunics over leggings. Standard fare. Okay, so they have nicer backpacks, use better hair products, generally look more fit. But that's it.

Then the kid next to me pulls a mechanical arm out of the side of his own desk. A tablet folds out and he starts playing around with it right away.

Whoa.

There's an arm inside my desk, too. But I don't understand the mechanism for releasing it, and I frantically pull at it before our teacher comes in.

When he does, my hand slips, and that's when the desk arm releases.

Mr. Jordan is ravishingly handsome, like he should be on the cover of a romance novel. He has sharp amber-hazel eyes, deep oak skin, and black stubble. His shirt is very tight and he looks barely out of college.

"Hello!" Mr. Jordan says.

Oh, wow.

We have a brief orientation on how to use the tablets, the rules, what he expects from us over the course of the year. It's like any other class I've ever had. He sets out some basic terminology, and as he's lecturing about the fundamental purpose of law and government, my heart swells with thrill.

This is what I'm here for. Law. Justice. Truth. As I flip through the syllabus on my tablet, I stop to read the subheadings for "Due Process" and "Equal Protection." We're going to get in depth about constitutional rights—exactly what I need to get on the fast track to my dream job. Mr. Jordan has even listed Supreme Court cases in italicized letters as required readings.

I'm ready.

Class is over almost as soon as it started. I'd hoped to find Gracie waiting outside for me to help me get to my next class, but I have to make it alone. I'm so disoriented by the enormous campus that I only get to math one second before the bell rings.

I'm frantically searching for an open seat when I spot Gracie sitting in the back row—saving a seat next to her. I fly into it.

"Is this for me?" I ask. I figure out how to release the tablet right away this time.

"Who else?"

"How'd you know I had this class, too?"

"You showed me your schedule, doof."

"Oh, right."

"So you had Mr. Jordan?"

My neck and cheeks feel like a fire's been lit underneath them. Gracie's face breaks into a smile.

"Oh my god," she says. "You're blushing so hard. He's hot, right? I was told he was hot."

"He's hot," I confirm.

"Can we switch first periods?"

"It did put some sunshine in the day to have him for my first morning class," I say, trying to sound over-the-top dreamy, and Gracie laughs at me.

The rest of the week looks mostly the same as the first day: stuffing dirty clothes into our closets and throwing the duvets back on our beds before inspection, rushing to Morning Prayer, then rushing to breakfast, then sitting through seven hours of classes before—finally—freedom.

It's the beginning of September, so the sun gazes down warmly at us as we walk from class to class, and it sticks around until late in the day.

I could get used to this. I could get comfortable here.

Gracie and I spend our afternoons out on the quad in front of Isabel House, absorbing the autumn sunshine, gazing over the pristine, glittering surface of the lake. We doodle in our sketchbooks, do homework, talk about our old schools. We're always hypothesizing about the guy who was doing tai chi out in the graveyard. I've been keeping an eye out for him—blond, hot as a Texas day. One day we think we spot him walking down the main path, but he's too far away for us to know for sure.

"I feel like I know him from somewhere," Gracie says, tilting her head. "But I can't remember how."

"Maybe you were married in a past life," I joke. "You could be soul mates!"

While we're fantasizing about our respective futures with

Tai Chi Guy, some girls lie down near us in shorts and tank tops, basking on towels in the warm September sun.

"It's perfect, right?" I say to a Second Year girl I recognize from Isabel House. She turns her head and pulls down her sunglasses.

"Yeah," she says, noncommittal. "Perfect."

As she looks at me, I feel like I can see a memory churning in her head—the wrinkled flesh of my stomach, my ugly granny bra, Hayden pinching my skin.

Needs Improvement.

The two girls don't say anything else to us, and after only a few minutes they pack up their towels and leave.

I'm not even good enough for a polite conversation.

Gracie puts a hand on my elbow. "Hey, you okay?"

"Why won't any of them talk to us?" I try not to sound whiny, but it comes out like that anyway.

"Because they're snobby bitches trying to haze you," Gracie sighs. "Why does it matter?"

"How can you not care?"

She shrugs, flipping some of her straight black hair out of her face. "I've known girls like that my whole life. It's all a game to them. You have to clear so many hurdles before they'll give you the time of day. Do your hair like this, wear your clothes like that, do the activities they do—then, maybe, they'll let you in."

So it's a game. And games, if you try hard enough, can be beaten. It just takes a couple of tries to figure out what works and what doesn't. Middle school was like that, too.

"But trust me," Gracie says, reading my face. "It's not worth it once you get in. Nothing changes. They're just as shitty as they were before."

I don't say it, but I doubt that. Everyone is different once you get to know them. Even Hayden, I'm sure, is totally different with her friends. She was just giving us tough love, trying to thicken up our skin for the rest of our school career. You'd have to be something special to become Head Girl.

What if I became Head Girl? Would I do the same thing to the First Year girls that Hayden did to me?

Maybe. But I'd be benevolent. Lift them up instead of tear them down. I know Hayden's just trying to do what's best for us—and wouldn't I do the same for my charges? Protect them. Teach them how to fit in, stay safe, do well.

But that's not going to happen unless I figure out the game's rules. I remember a line I read out of the honor code, which is also printed in the back of the student handbook:

> Everything worthwhile takes time, work, and sacrifice.
> The sacrifices asked of us are often greater than we
> expect, but they are what make us true Edwardians.

With some hard work, time, and sacrifice even I could become Head Girl someday.

———

On Thursday, our relaxation session on the quad is cut short by the first Family Dinner. We have to go inside and dress up—the dress code is formal. Gracie tries on a hundred outfits until she settles on a black button-up and gray pencil skirt, like we're headed to a business meeting. I settle on a knee-length green dress with a leather belt around the middle, and feel fancy.

We don't get to pick where we sit at Family Dinner. We're seated according to a chart with students from other dorms, one teacher per table to oversee us. In the brochures, Family Dinner is called "enrichment," to "encourage mingling." It's supposed to help you build connections outside your dorm.

Everyone has to eat in the main cafeteria—Hamilton Hall. It's the first time I've had a meal without Gracie.

Walking into Hamilton Hall is like traveling to a Viking banquet. Once you come through the anteroom, fifty-foot solid wood tables span the length of the cafeteria. Chandeliers hang from exposed raw wood rafters, casting all the plates and cutlery in a dim orange glow. At my table, I find the place settings already waiting with three different kinds of forks. I don't know what that tiny one's for, but it's cute.

I'm ready to make some school-sanctioned friends over an elaborate meal.

Once we're all seated, the faculty member assigned to our table asks pointed questions to get the conversation started. Her icebreaker is: "What's your favorite planet?"

Must be a science teacher. We each have to provide an answer. Almost everyone says "Pluto."

The teacher talks too fast, like she rehearsed her icebreakers a lot just to sound natural. I guess this is as awkward for her as it is for us. The older kids say that they heard the meal tonight was steak, and I'm drooling while the conversation goes on around me. Steak at the most exclusive private school in the Northeast?

Can't wait.

But when the meal arrives, the steaks are gray slabs on stark white plates, a pinch of wilted parsley on top, rimmed with crusty mashed potatoes and squishy carrots.

The steak is cooked well-well-done and tastes like peppered rubber.

At least they peppered it, I guess.

I knew Saturday Session would be a thing, but it's different in person. It feels exactly like the previous five days, except we get to wake up an hour later and there's no Morning Prayer.

After breakfast, my schedule drops me into a classroom with fifteen other kids I've never met before. I was expecting something academic, but Saturday Session ends up being an hour of studying, bullshitting around, and talking about yearbook while our "advisor" pulls us aside one at a time to discuss our aspirations for college.

Guess that's the academic part.

After advising, we're ushered into Cath along with the rest of the student body. This must be why they let us skip this morning—they were planning something bigger and grander later on.

Provost Portsmouth, all shivering jowls and red, patchy cheeks, climbs up to the podium.

"I hope you've had a good first week," he says into the mic. "Before we get too much farther, I want to do our annual review of the honor code together."

This honor code keeps coming up. Do they really care about it that much here? I mean, my middle school had a motto and a code of conduct. But nobody read it. And certainly nobody actually acted by it.

But the provost is intent on making sure we all know it, and starts reading the entire thing out loud.

I think this might be the entire point of the assembly. Gracie is shaking her head.

Up in the front pews, the older kids start chanting the words of the honor code along with him. "*No one has to prove they belong at Edwards,"* the provost booms into the mic.

"What one must prove is that they deserve to stay," they echo back.

Is that why the Head Girl grabbed my boobs? To prove I belonged here? That I deserve to stay?

"When we have conflicts and disagreements, we will talk directly to each other first," the provost says.

"And we will respect each other even when we cannot agree," the students chorus.

Goosebumps run up and down my arms.

"We have no siblings here, so we must be each other's brothers and sisters."

The voices of students swell, filling the high ceiling of the cathedral.

"We have no parents here, so we must parent each other."

After a few more verses, the honor code ends with one resonating, repeated line:

"Keep this community sacred."

It sounds like a prayer.

CHAPTER THREE

http://privateschoolnewb.tumblr.com
Sept. 4, 2017

Boarding school looks like:
Never getting a word in edgewise.

Every day here is like getting ready for a ball. Get up early. Put on my school face. Root around for an outfit I haven't already worn that week. Listen. Take good notes. Wonder if someone in class will talk to me. (They never do.)

I've tried to participate in my classes, but one thing I'll say about private school kids: they are aggressive over-achievers. While the M.O. back in middle school was to sit around and do your best not to be the first one to talk, now it's all about who can talk most. It's impossible to get even a single thought across. These private school kids talk over you like it's a competition to see who can get their noses the farthest up the teacher's butt.

It feels hopeless contributing anything useful in group discussions—or connecting with anyone at all.

And as much as I love doing everything with my roommate (I do) . . . there must be a way to meet people here.
People like me. People who don't understand what this
is all about. People who don't "get it."

This campus is so huge, there has to be a place I can
meet some people who are more like me.

But, honestly, I'm probably giving up. I'm not even
sure if those people do exist at all.

I don't want to give up.

One afternoon, my last class gets out early and I head to the
quad to lounge while I wait for Gracie. I leaf through the packet
the Welcome Wagon gave us.

What did Hayden say that first night? Aside from telling
me to try out for a sport—which, let's get serious, is never going
to happen—she made it sound like activities are where it's at.
That's how you "get it."

I finally get up the courage to go to an extracurricular I'd
seen listed in our packet: Drawing Club. Might not be a bad
idea to find an activity to do instead of lying around on the
quad. When Gracie appears, I tell her where I'm going.

"There's a club for drawing? Why do you need a club?"

"It's not about the club. It's to meet people."

"Why do you need to meet people?"

I struggle not to let out an exasperated sigh at her. "I just
want to feel like . . . I don't know. Like I belong. Why don't
you come with me?" I pick up her sketchbook and dangle it. "I
mean, you're twice the artist I am."

She takes the sketchbook back. "No, thanks. But go, enjoy

your socializing." She flops down in the grass. "I'll be out here sucking up rays."

I don't like leaving her behind, but at some point I have to make my own way. And artists, I've found, are good people. They're thoughtful, and they don't talk much when they're working. Perfect place to look for . . . well, my place.

The sign inside the art building says the drawing rooms are on the third floor. I make my way up two long flights of stairs.

I peek into the first room. Students with easels sit in a circle, sketching. And sitting in the exact center?

It's Tai Chi Guy. He has that wavy hair like slightly cloudy sunshine, a jaw straight from a magazine, and he's bare chested. He looks like a Roman sculpture on the stool, set in a come-hither pose. He's obviously been posed by the teacher, because he looks both perfectly handsome and also slightly ridiculous.

He notices me as soon as I walk into the room, but can't turn his head or risk breaking the pose. I just stare at him, and he turns his eyes as far as they can go to stare back.

A teacher sitting by the window stands up and approaches me.

"Can I help you with something?" she says quietly, like we're in a library.

"Do you have space in your club?" I manage to ask, peeling my eyes away from Tai Chi Guy. "For a new member?"

"It's kind of late to join, and we're looking pretty full." She glances back at the packed circle of easels. "Show me something of yours. Today's the intermediate level club, so if you're good, maybe we could work it out."

I dig a sketchbook out of my backpack and show her some

sketches I've done of a copse of trees, of the Edwards clock tower, of Gracie.

She pauses on this last one, then holds the notebook out to me.

"Is this your friend?"

"Roommate."

"It's really good. She has a nice smile."

I'd used a photo as a reference. Looking at it now, I unconsciously fixed her weird half-smile while I drew it. My version of Gracie looks symmetrical and bland.

"Thanks," I say, taking the sketchbook back and shoving it into my backpack. She's not even complimenting the real Gracie. It's an untrue Gracie.

"You can join the intermediate club," the teacher says, smiling now. "But you'll have to dig up your own chair. I don't have any more."

I do, luckily, locate a chair in the closet, and an extra easel. I get my station organized and place my tiny sketchbook on the lip of the giant easel.

Now I have a chance to look at him, really look at him. His eyes stay on mine as I start to draw him. Up close I can admire the silky-looking texture of his skin and get sucked into his blue-green eyes. Little tendrils of hair trail down his chest all the way to his hips.

The forty minutes of club race past as he changes positions a few times. The teacher announces it's time for one last five-minute drawing.

"I want you to stress motion in this one," she tells us.

Tai Chi Guy puts one arm in the air and leans forward on one knee, like he's about to fly off and save the world.

After it's over, he quickly puts his shirt back on. I bend

down to put my sketchbook in my backpack, trying to look casual even though my heart is racing at what I drew.

"Can I see?" a voice asks. I look around, thinking he must be talking to somebody else. But Tai Chi Guy is standing next to my easel, staring right at me.

"Uh, yeah?" I take the notebook back out and clasp it tight. I don't want him to see how I've drawn him.

"I've already seen the work of the other kids here. You're new."

I hold the sketchbook facedown, thinking of how to distract him from looking at it. "You model often?" I ask.

"Since I was a Second Year. It's meditative for me." He stands there, waiting. He's clearly not going to forget about his request, so I hand over the sketchbook.

We did ten gesture drawings, but the last one is my favorite. From my position in the room I got the profile of his valiant pose. Once I drew it, he was begging for a cape, so I added one. Then it demanded a mask over his eyes, because no hero goes around fighting crime without one.

My first session of Drawing Club, and the hottest guy in the room catches me goofing off and drawing superheroes.

"Wow." Tai Chi Guy stares at this version of himself, eyebrows rising. My head fills with blood. He's going to hate it. "I love it. A lot." His eyes connect with mine. "Thanks for showing me. You like superheroes?"

"I guess," I manage to say. "For a while I thought I'd go into comics."

"But not anymore?"

"Yeah, I dunno. It's hard to make it in art." And once I'd grown up a little, I'd realized what I wanted was to be a superhero, not draw one. That's when Dad suggested I should become a lawyer. *It's the only way to actually take on the bad guys,* he'd said. *In court.*

"That's true," Tai Chi Guy says, passing my sketchbook back. "Well, I hope you find what you're looking for." He extends a hand. "It's nice to meet you. I'm Scully."

"I'm Sam." We shake, and his grip is warm and powerful.

"Hey, Sam," he says, and I can't help thinking of the first time I met Gracie. His skin feels like lightning as he lets my hand go.

I'm electrified.

———

I have to tell Gracie. Over dinner that night, I spill the beans that Tai Chi Guy models for Drawing Club.

"You should join!" I tell her. "Come ogle him with me."

"Hand me that sign-up sheet and I'll write my name in blood," she says. "Did I tell you that I remembered where I know him from?"

"Where?"

"Some garden party when I was a little kid. I think we grew up in the same neighborhood."

Wow. It's almost like they were meant for each other. I feel a little left out, but that's nothing new.

She gets into Drawing Club without even trying—her work's probably even better than mine. We spend our days going to class, studying, and drawing. The exception is Sunday, which is divided between morning free time and a long, super-vised afternoon study session. Every week we go to Drawing Club, hoping Scully will be there again, and try not to openly gawk at him when he does get on the model's stool.

I mark time by the meals they serve in Hamilton Hall. We're always waiting for Wednesday: grilled cheese day.

"Wednesday Best Day," Gracie calls it.

One Saturday, though, I get so tired of waiting in line for the standard buffet that I suggest we ditch the cafeteria and go to the Encore Grill across campus. There we can just order whatever we want, including grilled cheese. No need to wait for Wednesday Best Day.

"Grilled cheese on Saturday?" Gracie asks, eyes sparkling. "I've never even been to the Encore. It's a chore just not getting lost on this campus, and I try to minimize my risk by not broadening my horizons at all."

"We'll go together," I say. "Two heads are always better than one."

So we take a map and head toward the Conservatory, turning left for the Grill, and order up our perfect dinner. Sure, it takes twice as much out of my account as a buffet meal, but it's worth it. I'll skip lunch sometime to make up the difference.

"Do you get the sense," says Gracie over our sandwiches, "that you're always being watched?"

"It's not a sense," I say. "There is a pen-and-paper record of every single time one of us has checked in and checked out of Isabel House."

"You haven't even tried to enter a boys' dorm yet," she says. "It was a police-level interrogation when I had to go to Ernest House for a group project. *What are you studying? For how long? With whom? Leave the door open!*"

Ha. Like going into a boy's dorm is anywhere on my to-do list. Even that one awkward Third Year guy known for wearing sweatpants around campus every day and never washing his hair is out of my league.

Two Third Year girls at the table next to us are leaned in, talking in hushed voices. Gracie, in usual fashion, tilts her head to eavesdrop while she sips her slushie. Then she leans back to me.

"God, no one will stop talking about this stupid Inaugural Mixer. What's the big deal with dances? Why does everyone care so much?"

"Jean made it sound like the Mixer is Edwards's version of Homecoming," I say. "You know how Homecoming is usually right after the first football game of the year?"

"Sure."

"Except our football is water polo. I saw on the calendar that the first polo game's the day after the Mixer."

"Who cares about water polo?" Gracie sighs into her drink, making it bubble up.

"It could be fun," I say. "I've never seen it before. We should go to the game and find out." Maybe we'd make some friends. It couldn't hurt for Gracie to try a little.

"Hard pass," she says. "So what if we don't get a date to the Mixer? Do we just not go?"

"I doubt 'not going' would go over that well with Hayden."

"So, what, we wallflower all night? We should make our own separate dance party. Except instead of dancing, we should stand around sipping spiked punch and snarking about every-one's outfits."

"Spiked punch?" I ask, laughing. We aren't in college yet, where I imagine people get away with stuff like that. But I can picture us a few years from now, living together in Boston, me going to Harvard and Gracie at the art and design school nearby, sipping on coffees and snarking on all the too-hipster outfits everyone else is wearing.

"What, you think someone would catch us if we did spike it?" she asks. "Just two harmless flowers on a wall?"

"Maybe not," I say. "They're always watching us, but most of the time it seems like they don't actually see anything. Definitely not me."

I didn't mean for this conversation to turn into a pity party.

"I do," Gracie says, turning serious. "I see you, Sam."

And she does. She might be the only one, but she does.

So maybe we're both invisible. But not to each other.

At least I have my government class, and Women's Art History after lunch always revives my spirit. We talk about all the famous—and often overlooked—great women artists and painters. I get to write my big paper for the semester on a Renaissance artist, Artemisia Gentileschi, whose work was usually attributed to her father. X-rays of her paintings have revealed that she often revised her pieces to be less violent and in-your-face, probably because her male colleagues criticized her for being too aggressive.

I want to go back in time and slap them for her. Tell all of them they won't be remembered even a fraction as well as my Artemisia. Some days I feel like her, studying and scribbling where no one can see, being overlooked, quietly yearning for some kind of truth.

What is the right answer to all this? What's the secret to belonging? She probably asked herself these questions every day as she toiled in the dark.

On my way to class, my backpack loaded with books, I spot Hayden talking with some of her friends under an enormous oak tree. They look like something from one of my artist's paintings—sunshine dappling their skin as it falls through the leaves; a gentle, caressing breeze giving their perfect hair just the right amount of movement.

Just as I'm approaching them, Hayden's gaze locks onto me. My heart starts pounding as she decidedly turns in my direction and starts jogging toward me.

"Sam, right?" she says, smiling.

I nod just as a spurt of adrenaline shoots through me. I can't tell if I'm afraid, excited, angry—or all three.

"Going to class?" she asks.

I nod again, considering every possible reason Hayden would want to chat with me.

"Can I walk with you?"

"Uh, sure," I say. I clench my hands into fists so she won't see them shaking, and start walking again, quickly, because I'm going to be late. Hayden keeps up easily.

"Have you thought about any of the suggestions I gave you?" she asks.

She remembers that? I thought I was an inconsequential, blubbery stain on the Welcome Wagon's opening night.

Of course I've thought about her suggestions—they consume me. But I don't want to play soccer, or racquetball, or any other stupid sport. I want to draw and go to my classes and eat grilled cheese whenever I feel like it. Except that attitude is probably exactly what's holding me back.

"I've, um, thought about them some."

Hayden makes a *tsk* sound. "I know you haven't signed up for a sport."

How does she know that? Actually, no, it makes sense. It's probably the Head Prefect's job to check in on us, make sure we're engaged in campus life. How well we do reflects on her as our prefect.

"I joined Drawing Club," I say, to show that I have been trying. "But none of the sports caught my interest—"

"Have you thought about the Inaugural Mixer?" Hayden asks before I can finish talking. "I think I have a match-up for you."

"A what?" Is she running some kind of matchmaking service?

"Go sign up for a sport, any sport, and we'll talk more. Okay?" Hayden tucks her hair behind one ear and waves at me. "Bye, Sam!"

Then she's slipped off back to her friends.

I walk briskly to Art History, backpack bouncing. I'm going to be late, but going any faster than a walk would be like a flashing neon sign over my head saying NOT IN CONTROL. And the one thing I do get about Edwards so far?

Nobody ever lets it slip that they're not *completely* on top of things.

I make it to class just before the bell and take my usual seat at the round Harkness table, close to Dr. Winegard so I can hear. She talks so quietly that you have to strain to understand her. In Dr. Winegard's class, we're supposed to take ownership of the discussion and guide it ourselves. She gives us prompts and then it's up to us to keep the conversation going.

While she's starting the discussion, Hayden pops back into my head. What did she mean by a "match-up"? Like, for the Inaugural Mixer? I'd thought the Third and Fourth Year boys would ask if they were interested.

But . . . maybe not?

Sign up for a sport and we'll talk more. About what? My date?

For some reason the guy from Drawing Club pops into my head.

Scully.

I clandestinely reach into my backpack and pull out the packet Hayden gave us the first day of school. I search for Scully's name on the *Naughty* and *Nice* lists.

But . . . his name's not on here at all. I was sure that he was an upperclassman, with a body like that. But maybe he's not?

I put the packet away. As if Hayden would "match" me up with someone like that. Nah, it's probably that guy who always walks around with greasy hair and sweatpants on.

If I did go to the Mixer with Scully, though . . . I wonder what he'd wear. Maybe we'd color-coordinate. Which colors would he look even better wearing? Probably green or blue, to match his eyes. Everyone in the school would see our arms linked together when we walked into Hamilton Hall. It wouldn't matter then how dumpy or frizzy I looked. People would be falling over themselves to talk to me and be my friend.

"Sam?" Dr. Winegard calls my name. Twice.

"Yes?" I say, shooting forward in my chair.

"Sam, didn't you choose Gentileschi for the topic of your research paper?" she says. "Do you have any insight on why she revised this painting?"

I cough. "Oh, yeah."

I explain to the class how the women in the original painting are violently resisting a pair of creepy, lecherous men. But Artemisia Gentileschi's colleagues didn't like it. The male painters thought women should be complimented by the attention; they should just *playfully* bat away creepers who were attracted to them, not fight them.

The class moves on and I sink back into my chair. Maybe Scully asked Hayden about me after seeing my superhero portrait of him.

No. I couldn't have made that much of an impression.

But maybe . . . I mean, that sort of thing happens in books and romantic comedies all the time. The hot guy falls for the girl who *Needs Improvement*. He helps her get into shape, makes her beautiful, and shows her off at the big dance.

The best stories are all based on real life, right?

CHAPTER FOUR

http://privateschoolnewb.tumblr.com
Sept. 19, 2017

What happens in boarding school . . . stays in boarding school.

Today some First Years on our hall got caught smoking pot in their room. A Second Year noticed first, some goody-goody who throws her hand up at every question in the one class I have with her. She likes to talk over Firsties whenever she can, just to show us we're trash.

She was walking by a closed door and heard laughing. Nobody's supposed to keep their door closed before lights-out, so she got suspicious. When the Second Year girl looked under the door, she found a wadded-up towel. It was a dead giveaway to Second Year Overachiever.

Like the honor code says, though:

We have no parents here, so we must parent each other.

We vow to keep each other accountable, because we have no one else.

So Second Year Girl knocked on the door like a Big Boss, and the laughing stopped.

"I know what you're doing in there," she said. "Come out, right now."

She wasn't a prefect, but she was a Second Year, and she was gonna throw it around.

The girls went silent and pretended like they weren't home, probably because they were stoned.

"If you don't open the door," she told them, "I'm going to tell."

Still nothing. Second Year Girl decided she'd done her duty according to the honor code, and petulantly went to tell the House Mom.

As expected, House Mom came to the room and knocked.

"It's me!" she said in that sing-song voice she uses when she's trying too hard to be your mom. "Why don't you open up?"

At this point the girls gave up and opened the door, letting all their pot smoke out into the hall. House Mom took all the paraphernalia from them, reported them to the administration, and then gave them each a cookie from her stash to help quell their munchies. None of us could believe that part.

I heard the First Year girls were punished with extra chores around the dorm, and detention for a week.

But I bet not even their parents will hear about it. This story will never leave the school, except through this blog.

Keep this community sacred.

Every night from eight until nine is Twilight Study Hour, when we're supposed to be doing our homework under the watchful eye of an assigned proctor.

Yep, even our study time is supervised.

Usually I spend Twilight Study Hour doodling. I don't have any afternoon activities except Drawing Club on Tuesdays, and usually I've got my homework knocked out long before eight. So I come to Study Hour prepped with a textbook to slide over my sketches, in case the proctor decides to stroll the aisles.

I've put off telling Gracie about my strange conversation with Hayden, because she'll sneer down her nose. Or maybe she'll be upset that she didn't get matched, too. But I decide to tell her during Study Hour, and now I sort of hope she sneers so when I'm inevitably matched up with Creepy Sweatpants Guy, I can be like, *Remember how we both thought this was really stupid? No way I'm going.*

But the news rolls off her like water off a goose. "Oh, right, the match-ups." Usually I forget her dad went here, until she magically knows some insider information that I don't.

"Enlighten me?" I ask.

"If you're lucky, your prefect matches you up with an available Third or Fourth Year boy." She tilts her head as she looks at me. "No offense, but, like . . . why'd she pick you?"

Of course I can't take offense. It doesn't make sense that Hayden picked me out of all the pretty, popular First Year girls. Unless I'm really matched with Creepy Sweatpants Guy.

Then it makes total sense.

"I'll try to get you a date, too," I say, now that our wall-flowering plan is under the rails.

"I'll pass on the misogynistic, older-men-only, boys-ask-girls 1800s throwback dance."

"No, please, Gracie." I'm annoyed by how whiny my own voice sounds. "I can't go to this thing by myself."

"Isn't the whole point of this conversation that you got a date to the Mixer?" Gracie asks.

Except that my date will be so disappointed when he talks with me that he'll wander off to hang out with his own friends halfway through. Then I'll have no one.

"I'll just find you a date, too," I tell her. "Then we'll both have reasons to go." I don't know how I'll pull it off, but I need Gracie to be there with me.

She gives me a look like she can't tell if she finds me endearing or pathetic. "Okay. If you can pull that off, I'll go."

The proctor raises his head and glares at us, motioning for us to be quiet. I pull out my Welcome Wagon packet again and look over the list of available sports. Gracie gives me a questioning look.

"Hayden says I have to join a sport to find out who my match-up is," I whisper. "So I looked at the list of everything available, and tennis should be the easiest."

"Fine," Gracie whispers back. "You'll like it. Tennis is all about coordination and you've got tons of that." Then she girlishly cups her hands under her chin and raises her voice an octave. "But what sport should *I* do, Sam? You know, to get this imaginary, perfect guy you've picked out for me?"

I laugh as quietly as I can.

"You should do tennis with me," I say. It would be way more fun with her. And besides, we need to get out more if we're ever going to make new friends.

"Hitting something hard? I'm no good at that." Gracie

squeezes her skinny, bony arms. "Maybe theater? I think I'd make a good actress."

"Theater isn't a sport," I say.

Gracie crosses her arms. "Irrelevant."

I cough a laugh into my sleeve. "Well, whatever," I say. "Hayden didn't say *you* had to do a sport. She just told you to buy a new bra and put on some weight."

Gracie's eyes meet mine and they are ice and stone. She doesn't speak. Out of pure shame, neither do I.

I can't believe I brought it up. We've always acted as if those few hours of our lives were lasered off the face of the planet like unwanted armpit hair. Evaporated. Lost in the unclaimed airline baggage room of the universe.

"You should join tennis with me," I whisper, hoping to undo what I've done. But before she can reply, the proctor glares at us and says, "Shh!"

We don't talk for the rest of the hour.

The next day, I go by the administration office after class and write my name down for tennis.

"Just in time," says the registrar. "Tryouts start in a couple days."

Yikes. That doesn't leave me much time to enjoy my freedom.

I walk back to Isabel House with my heart somewhere under my tongue. I hope Hayden is working check-in so I don't have to go looking for her.

Thankfully, she's the one sitting behind the counter, reading from a textbook.

"I put my name on the list for tennis," I say proudly. "So I've got a sport and a club now, like you said."

I can't dare hope.

"Oh, right," Hayden says, glancing up. "I'm glad you've finally decided to deal with that muffin-top issue." I grit my teeth at the reminder. "I guess you've earned hearing about this great match-up I have planned for you. Your match-up is . . ." she trails off dramatically, like we're in a game show. "With Scully! Scully Chapman. You've met him, right? He's a Fourth Year."

Scully Chapman.

I've been matched up with the hottest guy in the history of Earth for a dance. And he's an upperclassman, to boot.

"I've met him," I squeak out.

"Great. I hope you'll take this as an opportunity to work on yourself." Hayden tilts her head. "Are you excited?"

I must look like a ghost who's seen another ghost.

"Oh, yeah. Definitely. I'm also totally stunned!"

This is the answer she wanted.

"Awesome. Good." She looks victorious, like my *Needs Improvement* score was instantly bumped to a *Somewhat Improved*. "Since you're just a First Year, there are probably some things I should tell you."

———————————

I'm buzzing with secrets as Gracie and I head across campus for dinner. A brilliant sunset slathers the mossy brick buildings, trees, and paved paths in fiery orange light. It feels like Edwards Academy is throwing a party for me. Like I was chosen.

When we get to Hamilton Hall, the chefs surprise us with ravioli, one of the few things the kitchen does well. The cheese-filled dough squares drizzled with steaming hot red sauce put us both in a fantastic mood. The bread they serve is warm and buttery, even though it tastes like cardboard. I know Hayden would frown on me eating it, but god, it tastes good. And the wilted spinach in the salad bar is so depressing.

Ravioli night is as good a time as any to give her the news. *Hey, you know that guy we're both drooling over? Yeah, that's my date.*

"I found out my match-up today," I say, just as she shoves a bite of food in her mouth.

"What? Who?" Gracie leans forward. I hope she doesn't get mad. I nod at where Scully sits two tables behind us, laughing with his friends.

"Him."

Her mouth forms a perfect O. "No way! Scully Chapman?"

I nod, trying not to look too amped up about it. "Yep. Him."

"And he had Hayden ask you out for him?" She stabs one of her ravioli. "Couldn't he have talked to you in Drawing Club like a normal person and asked you out himself?"

"It's not a real date," I say, trying to head off any romance fantasy she might be imagining. I repeat to her what Hayden was careful to explain to me—that the Mixer doesn't mean anything. It's a get-to-know-you kind of event. He's not asking me out.

Clearly, other girls had made this assumption. Hayden didn't want me to make the same mistake.

"I still don't understand why it's necessary," Gracie says. "Or normal, for that matter. This whole match-up stuff is actually kind of creepy."

"Like this place is normal in any conceivable way," I say, and Gracie laughs. "Anyway, I could try to find you a cool guy, too. Scully has a really hot friend."

"The tall one with black hair?" asks Gracie.

"Yeah. He seems nice." Maybe.

She shrugs. "He also has a girlfriend."

Oops. But as we resume our dinner, it seems that everything is still okay between us.

Still, I sneak looks at Scully whenever Gracie might not notice. But she's sneaking looks at him, too.

The movie that started running in my head yesterday during Art History plays again: Scully and I, dressed to the nines, waltzing in Hamilton Hall on each other's arms. The whole school looking at me. Admiring me.

Envying me.

Except Gracie is there, too, looking on with her arms crossed and her lips twisted up like she's swallowed a lemon.

The fantasy ends as soon as it started.

———————————

All day the next day, I'm anticipating my first day of tennis. It feels like the school is unwinding, opening up to me as a flower blooms. I'm going to the Mixer with Scully Chapman—easily the most popular guy on this entire campus.

Me. *Me.*

As I approach the enormous green shell of the tennis dome, lingering on the edge of campus like some giant turtle, I'm ready to make magic with my fingers and hit those tennis balls.

The first person to greet me inside is the junior varsity captain. Her name is Bex, which I think is short for Rebecca. She's a Second Year, maybe a Third Year. Right away she invites me to free play.

Tryouts are in three parts: one day of orientation, a second day of practice, and then we compete for the available spots on varsity and junior varsity.

With this and Drawing Club, I'll have most of my activity blocks filled. There goes all that extra study time.

I am, unfortunately, not a natural at tennis. Bex laughs at my feeble initial attempts to get to the ball. Though once I do manage to connect with it, I wallop it across the court. It bounces off the wall of the dome and hurtles back down to the tarmac, nearly taking off Bex's head.

"Nice power," she says, hopping over the net. "Let's work on your stance, though."

There's one faculty member here overseeing us, but that's all. For the most part, orientation is student-driven. All around me seasoned players are showing First Years proper technique.

When we rotate partners, I spot Gracie at the other end of the dome, trying her hardest to hit a ball—and missing spectacularly.

"Gracie!" I shout. "What are you doing here?"

When she spots me, she gallops toward me, laughing. "You thought I wouldn't go out for an actual sport, I bet!"

"Yep. You caught me."

"Good! My surprise worked." She slings her racket over one shoulder. "I figured that if joining the tennis team gets you a date with Scully Chapman, I ought to give it a try."

Afterwards, Bex and some other members of the girls' tennis team invite us to dinner with them. They're chatty and goofy—and nothing like the rude girls on the quad.

Bex's best friend, Eliza, apparently holds some sort of tennis state record for our division. Lilian is quiet and stiff, until she gets something to eat in her —then she comes to life like a possessed marionette and has tons to say. They all love each other.

I like them immediately.

But soon I'm drifting away from the conversation and glancing around Hamilton—casually looking for Scully.

I find him sitting one table over. We see each other at the same time, and he gives me a small wave. I smile back. Then I wave for good measure and Bex says, "You know Scully?"

I whip around. "N-not really. I got matched up with him for the Mixer."

Bex's eyes widen. "Whoa. How'd you score that?"

"He models for our Drawing Club," Gracie says. "Sam drew him like Batman and he got all goo-goo for it."

"Hey, you're pretty goo-goo about him, too," I say. But at the look on her face, I wish I hadn't.

"You guys get to see Scully Chapman topless?" asks Eliza.

"Just for life drawing," I say.

"Hot and actually not a bad guy," says Bex. "Unusual combo."

"Yeah, but his dad's one of Edwards's biggest donors," says Lilian.

"My dad always said the Chapmans were okay," Gracie says. "For Wall Street people."

"The point is that he's rich enough to do whatever he wants," says Bex. "It's a bonus that he's not a terrible person."

Lilian laughs. "Not like Waldo."

In unison, all the girls say, "Ugh, Waldo!"

"Who's Waldo?" I ask. Gracie just shakes her head.

"Only the biggest tool at Edwards," says Bex. "Did you hear he got a new car over the weekend?"

Lilian snorts. "Yes! And then the school refused to give him a pass for it because he bombed finals last year. He tried to pay double the permit fee but they wouldn't budge."

"Why would you bring a car if you had nowhere to put it?" I ask.

"And who just, like, gets handed a car?" asks Eliza.

"Waldo Wilson does, I guess."

"So what did he do with it?" Gracie asks. Stupid rich kids is one of her favorite topics. "With the car?"

"I don't know," says Bex. "It was a big fuss the other night over at Thomas House. Waldo was trying to get his House Dad to park it in the faculty housing part of campus, where he wouldn't need a permit. But it's not like he's allowed to drive it around."

Eliza bursts into laughter. "So it would just sit there in front of Barry's house?"

"How pointless," Gracie says, shaking her head.

When the conversation moves on, Lilian asks, "Where did you two come from? I've never seen you around before."

Gracie grins. "We're ghosts. We only appear when somebody says our names three times."

Eliza cracks up. "Can we keep them?" she asks Bex, who seems to be more or less their leader.

Bex waves her hands around. "Don't ask me like I'm their mom. If you want a play-date, ask yourself."

I didn't expect how good this would feel. To sit at a table with real Edwards students, to have the kinds of conversations I feel like I only ever overhear other kids having.

I giggle, feeling giddy. "We're only available for play-dates on Sundays."

http://privateschoolnewb.tumblr.com
Oct. 3, 2017

Boarding school looks like:
Seeing your crush everywhere.

One lovely reader sent me a message, asking about whether I saw Him again.

Well. I'll tell you. We bumped into each other yesterday after dinner, stacking our plates on the dirty dish rack. Not the most romantic location ever, but it was the first time we'd exchanged a word since I found out we were going to be at the dance together.

It was a nothing conversation, but *what a nothing*. Everything-nothing. I wanted to keep every word locked up inside me forever.

Then we were outside, and I really should have waited for my roommate the way she waits for me. But His dorm is right next to ours, so there was no reason not to walk with Him.

I guess some guy in His group of friends was going on about how he was missing some big League of Legends tournament, because the school doesn't allow online multiplayer games on their network.

"Come to our water polo game instead!" He had said to the guy. "Come cheer for us. We're here in person. We could really use your enthusiasm."

I didn't know He played water polo. Not that I knew much else about Him, either.

And then—as if He couldn't get any more . . . well, hot?—it turned out He's the captain of the team.

It doesn't surprise me, not after I was looking over the available tutors and saw His name there, too. He models for life drawing, captains the polo team, and still has time left over to tutor people who need extra help? He really is some kind of superhero.

So I'm going to make a point of seeing one of His games. Cheer for Him, like He wants. Even if polo isn't my thing, it doesn't hurt to see a bunch of topless dudes wrestling in the water.

The first game is after the Mixer. Since the Mixer is off the table, that's the perfect opportunity to make my move.

―――――――

Before we can really settle in to our new social group, Home Weekend is upon us.

I've never been away from my parents for this long. And while I had desperately missed them for the first few weeks of school . . . now I'm not so sure that I'm ready to leave. I know my way around campus—finally. I have a group of friends. I feel like I'm finally fitting in, "getting it," as Hayden would say.

On my way out to meet my parents at the curb, I stop by Hayden's room. Doesn't look like she's left for the weekend yet—her computer is still sitting out, her open bag on her chair. But she's not here, either. It's perfect.

I write her a note saying what I need, then head down to the pick-up area out in front of Hamilton.

My folks are thrilled to see me. I've grown so used to the unfamiliar, to the strange and new and different, that as I hop into the station wagon, the normal comes crashing down around me, the way a curtain drops after a play and all the lights come back on.

I'm actually thrilled to see Mom and Dad, too. The familiar is like letting out a breath I've been holding since I got dropped off on the first day of school. Even though we've spoken on the phone every week, they still have tons of questions. What's dorm life like? How are my classes? Do I like my teachers? What about my friends?

"And that awful Morning Prayer thing?" asks Mom. It was a challenge to get her accustomed to the idea of me attending a school that used to be religious. "In the big cathedral?"

"We don't have to pray like you thought," I tell Mom. "It's just a musical assembly, and people make announcements."

"But in a cathedral? It's so last century."

"Everything there is last century."

"I just can't believe in this day and age this is acceptable."

"It's nice, Mom. There's a choir. And we have Sundays off unless we really want to attend a service."

Dad's interest lies in my classes. I dish out everything I can—teachers I like, teachers I hate, the subject matter, the course load.

"I didn't realize you'd have so much homework," he says, his pleasure obvious.

"Yeah, it's a real time suck," I say.

"But that's why they schedule out a study time for you every day, right?"

I actually find Twilight Study Hour and Sunday Study kind of humiliating—like I can't be trusted to manage my own time.

"Yep," I say. "Right."

It's a two-hour drive to get home, underscored by Dad's terrible taste in soft rock and Mom's nonstop questions.

But it's nice to see them. And by the end of the drive, I realize it's just one weekend—I'll be back at school in no time.

CHAPTER FIVE

The first thing I do when I get home is take a long, hot shower in my own bathroom. I pat my see-through shower curtain with the cute little neon fish, reminding myself of their squishy texture against my fingers.

I get into my own bed, with its pillow-top mattress cover, and snuggle each one of my stuffed animals before falling asleep.

My first obligation the next day: visit my middle school friends.

We get together in my old best friend's basement. Things are exactly how I remember them—the old TV propped up on crates, the sunken couches with broken springs. This place used to feel like a sanctuary—but now it feels like a dungeon.

All they want to talk about are kids at their new high school, what they're wearing, what dumb stuff they do in class to avoid paying attention. Maybe I'm just as much of a snob now as I used to imagine Edwards Academy students would be, but everything they say seems trivial and boring.

Why can't we talk about something more interesting, like my Women in Art History class? I mention the paper I'm doing, but they just want to gossip, so I conjure up an excuse to leave early and beat it before they can disappoint me more—and before I disappoint them.

Maybe Edwards has changed me more than I thought.

Sunday I kick around the house with my parents instead of socializing. Mom throws on an episode of *Project Runway* and asks me about the big dance. Edwards parents receive a monthly update from the school on what's happening, so she already knew all about the Mixer.

"You going with anyone?" she asks casually, like the answer doesn't really matter. But I know her. She used to watch *Days of Our Lives* when I was at school, and her bookshelf is dominated by romance novels. She lives for this stuff.

"Yep."

"Who?"

"Some guy who's a friend of a friend," I say. Just enough truth that she won't notice how much is missing. The feminist in her would hate this whole "match-up thing." "I like him, and he's, uh, pretty popular. But . . ."

"But what?" Mom asks, her eyes keen with interest. I've never told her about my school crushes before.

"But I'm nervous. What if I say something stupid? He's older than I am—"

"How much older?" she interrupts.

"Just a year."

Another lie. But Mom doesn't even look suspicious as she says, "That's pretty normal, I think, for high school." She nods, completely buying it. I'm on a roll. "Well, I'm happy for you. But don't do anything you wouldn't want to tell me about." Her expression morphs into Mother Bear face. This is her Mama Bear Who Will Kill You For Even Touching Her

Cub face. "I know what the pressure is like after school dances to, you know—"

"Mom, he's a gentleman."

"What about your roommate . . . what was her name? Gracie, you said? Are you going together?"

She never cared about my social life this much back in middle school. It's kind of charming.

"I'm working on finding her a date, too."

"That's cute. A girl and her best friend going to the school dance."

Best friend? I guess so, since it turns out all my old friends are tedious. "Any other friends going?" Mom asks, turning down the volume on *Project Runway* once the judging ends.

"Uh . . . I don't really have any besides Gracie." I wouldn't exactly call Bex and crew my "friends" yet.

"How can that be?" Mom asks. "You're the most intelligent, sweet girl I know."

"Thanks," I say. "But it's not about how intelligent or sweet I am. I'm a First Year. I'm flabby and I'm not rich."

Her face goes dark. Oops. That was the wrong thing to say.

"So what?" Mom says, squeezing the arms of the chair with her nails. "I knew that school was a mistake. I told your dad, 'All this praying in school business, and those snob kids, Sam won't fit in.' And I was right, wasn't I?"

"They're not snobs." And there's not any praying, but it's pointless to repeat that.

"Yes, they are." Here she goes. "You're not rich enough for these kids? You worked hard to get into that school."

Plenty of other kids worked hard to get into Edwards. But nothing I can say can convince her she's wrong.

"They're jerks, Sam," she says definitively. "Forget about

them. You've got one great friend, and she's your roommate to boot. That's what I call good luck."

But they're not jerks. Bex proved that Edwards kids are perfectly nice and friendly—once you get in with them.

It's just that "getting it" part that still needs more work.

———————————

We go to a movie. People of all shapes and sizes move around, living their lives, driving cars and eating fast food. This is the real world—and yet it still feels like a dream. I can't wait to get back to the Edwards world of huge old trees and fantastical brick buildings.

I miss Gracie. I miss my dorm room.

I miss Scully.

Seeing him around campus. Looking for him as Gracie and I eat dinner in Hamilton Hall.

The weekend finally ends. When I get back to campus, everything is glittering and magical. In the two days I was gone, all the leaves have turned a handsome orange-gold, just a preview of the autumn transformation to come—as if the wide arms of Edwards are welcoming me back.

When I walk into our room carrying my duffel bag, Gracie's already there.

"Sam!" She jumps to her feet and hugs me. No one's ever been so excited to see me.

We spend the rest of the night catching up on our weekends, as if it was a whole summer. I only part ways with her to go brush my teeth.

While I'm spitting into the sink, somebody says over my shoulder, "I found a date for your friend."

I jump. Hayden's standing over me in the mirror. I'd almost forgotten about leaving her that note, asking if she could help Gracie get a date.

"Calm down," she says, leaning against the dispenser that hands out free tampons, pantyliners, and even little baggies for throwing away used ones. This school has been the least troublesome place to get a period in my life. "You know Britt Walhausen?"

"Uh, no." I don't know anybody, really.

Hayden lets out a sigh. "He's a good match. I heard he didn't have a date to the Mixer, so I offered him Gracie. He was thrilled."

Did she just say that she offered up my friend like a . . . prostitute?

I close my eyes for a brief second.

"Thank you," I say, but it comes out flat.

Hayden tilts her head, like she expected a bit more pomp and fanfare.

"Just doing my job as your prefect," she says coldly, stepping back. "It's not like just anyone would take Gracie."

I clench my jaw. That was a rough way to talk about Gracie, but I can't let the Head Girl leave thinking I'm ungrateful. I want to keep getting invited to events like the Mixer by Scully Chapman.

"Thank you, Hayden," I say. "Really, this means a lot to me, and Gracie will be so happy." Wow. That sounds better than I expected. "Gracie's my best friend, and I didn't want to go alone. I know I'll be with Scully, but I'm nervous, you know? It'll be great to have her there. And she won't feel like a third wheel since she has an awesome date now, too."

Hayden's expression morphs into a blinding white smile.

Look, I made the two quiet girls open up to me! In her mind, she has just made World's Best Prefect.

Give her a prize.

"Oh, of course," Hayden says, beaming. "It's my job. You know the honor code: *We have no parents here, so we must parent each other.*" She pats me on the shoulder. "Just keep going to tennis and working on that waistline, and I promise—good things will happen to you."

Then Hayden floats out of the bathroom. Just when I'd finally forgotten about that night in the second-floor lounge, it comes back to find me again.

Needs Improvement. I'm still just a work in progress.

I look down at my hands and feel like they need a nice, long wash.

When I slip back into the room and tell Gracie about her match-up with Britt, she is not in raptures.

"Britt Walhausen?" She squeezes her eyes shut and rubs them with the palms of her hands. "That wasn't exactly who I'd had on my list. But he'll do, I guess?"

I've disappointed her, but what could I have done differently?

"Sorry," is all I can say.

"No, no." Gracie sighs. "It's fine. We'll have a good time together, no matter who our dates are."

Her upbeat attitude gives me hope. She'll bear it for me. It'll be fun.

The next morning, Gracie stops in front of Cath and points. "There he is. That's Britt." I follow the path of her finger toward the river of sleepy students heading to Morning Prayer.

Oh, no.

He's already balding, that much is clear. No hats are allowed during school hours, so the poor guy can't even cover his head with a baseball cap. But he tries anyway, gelling his thin, white-blond hair down all in one direction. He's not terrible-looking aside from that, a little dorky in a trim yellow polo shirt. I could have done better for Gracie—all those long legs and dark hair and luminous eyes of hers.

Out of my hands.

That's when Britt notices us looking at him. He gives Gracie a shy little wave, then hurries away like an elementary school kid.

Gracie tries not to let it show on her face, but it's obvious that she's not excited about her date.

I wouldn't be, either.

I suggest to Gracie that we go buy new dresses for the Mixer, and even though she resists the idea of getting something special, she can't deny the reality that neither of us owns anything close to appropriate.

It's a whole thing to get off campus to do something in the city like shopping, so we make a Sunday of it. We sign out at the main office, then head to the shuttle stop outside Hamilton.

I'm giddy about getting off campus, unchaperoned, for the first time. It feels like we're skipping school.

We don't chat on the shuttle ride. Gracie and I don't need to talk all the time to feel comfortable. I sketch cars and trees in my notebook and she gazes out the window. The silence is easy.

I wonder what Scully will wear. I want to get something the right color to match.

Gracie's obsessed with finding a dress at Nordstrom's that meets her ultra-specific criteria. "No colors, no frills, and especially no ruffles. Gray or black only."

"It's a dance," I say. "You can't wear gray."

She grins. "Black it is."

We spend most of our allotment of off-campus time looking for Gracie's perfect unfrittered black dress, and only ten minutes before we have to catch the shuttle do I find a dress for myself. It's a salmon-colored monstrosity.

"It looks amazing on you, though," Gracie says, tapping her chin. She spins me around in the mirror. "Perfectly complements all this." She makes a cupping gesture around her chest.

I pinch the dress. "But all these weird bows and fluffy bits—"

"It works with your hair. On anyone else it would look ridiculous, but on you I think it's perfect."

I guess with that kind of review I have to buy it.

On the way out of the store, we pass through the men's section to reach the exit. Three guys are trying on suits. I recognize one of them.

How does Scully Chapman keep appearing like magic? And he's trying on a salmon-colored tie.

"Nice pink," says one of his friends—a younger guy with slicked-back, dark hair. He plucks the tie off Scully's chest and smirks.

"What's wrong with pink, Cal?" Scully says.

"Uhh," the dark-haired guy grapples for something to say.

"You guys have something against men wearing pink?" Scully presses.

The two friends exchange a look.

"No," says the second one. "Guess not."

My affection for Scully increases a hundredfold. His masculinity is anything but fragile. I clutch the paper shopping bag closer that contains my beautiful salmon dress. *Thank you, Gracie.*

Scully adjusts his tie in the mirror. "I think pink is my color." He notices my reflection in the mirror and spins around.

"Scully's coming over," Gracie says under her breath, clasping my arm.

"I can see that."

Scully approaches us—me, really. He approaches me. He greets Gracie briefly, then says, "I know this is premature. Like seeing the bride before the wedding."

Oh my god, I think. *Like seeing the bride before the wedding.*

"But what good luck!" He flaps the tie. "I wanted to get a tie that would match your dress, but I had no idea what dress you'd be wearing, and how awkward it would be to call you up for that. Then, *poof*, you appeared!"

Magic, indeed.

"Y-y-yeah," I say, nodding. "Amazing coincidence. But you already read my mind with that tie." I lift the salmon-colored dress out of the bag.

A grin explodes across his face. "What's the chance?" he asks.

Gracie says, "I was the one who picked it out."

"Chances are low," I say, smiling back. I don't know how I'm managing to string words together. He's so hot that I need sunglasses. I hold it together long enough to say, "Must have been fate."

Gracie bumps my arm and points to the door. "We're gonna miss the shuttle."

Scully gives a little bow. "I'll be seeing you soon," he says, flicking the pink tie at us. "Don't miss your ride home."

He returns to his buddies, who stare at us with unreadable expressions. Disgust? Shock? Admiration?

Probably not that last one.

Gracie and I rush out just in time to catch the last shuttle. If those guys are missing it . . . Must be great to be friends with a Fourth Year like Scully, who passed his finals and gets to have his own car on campus.

"It's really happening," says Gracie, once we're on the bus. "We've got dresses and everything." She sighs. "I can't believe we're going to be at the dance with *that* guy."

The way she says it, her voice dreamy, kills the glittery feeling in my chest—and replaces it with dread. How is this going to go, with both of us drooling over Scully and only me being his date?

I study the graffiti on the back of the seat the whole drive back. I can't feel too down about the Gracie stuff while imagining Scully and me in our matching salmon, slow-dancing under the spiraling sparkles of an old, glittering disco ball.

———

http://privateschoolnewb.tumblr.com
Oct. 18, 2017

Boarding school looks like:
A sleepover every single night.

When we close our door at lights-out, it feels like a secret club that only me and my roommate are allowed into.

We turn off our big overhead light so it looks like we're asleep, then flick on the little ones beside our beds. We're both in Drawing Club now, which is great. We draw in our sketchbooks in the low light most nights, giggling at our renditions of Him. He models a lot for the Drawing Club, so we have tons of material to draw from (so to speak). Usually we sketch Him so His huge pecs stretch out His too-tight shirts.

We stay up late, talking about Him. He's like a magical beast that we see from time to time and admire from a distance—never acknowledging aloud that only one of us could have Him.

Afterwards, we put on Disney movies and split the earbuds between us, the laptop perched in front of us while we prop ourselves up on a bed with pillows and backpacks. The hours get so big that suddenly they start over small again, and we're so sleepy that we start to feel drunk, pushing each other off the bed and then trying to stifle our laughter so we don't wake anybody up.

Boarding school looks like:
Being alone, but maybe not so much.

———————————

Finally, it's Friday. The big day. Three hours before the Mixer's supposed to start, Gracie insists we take long, cleansing, luxurious showers. The bathroom is clogged with girls giggling and trying on their outfits.

In our room she blow-dries my hair and has me put on my dress.

"I dug out my kit," she says, sliding into my chair. I sit across from her on the bed in bundles of pink fabric as she unfolds a Costco-sized makeup bag. Normally she doesn't wear much makeup—some winged eyeliner, occasionally that maroon lipstick that looks best on an olive complexion like hers. So why have such a huge collection?

Everything in Gracie's kit is Sephora and MAC—higher-end stuff, even I can tell that. She has every color of eye shadow, ten tubes of lipstick, a sampling of foundation shades, and a half-dozen eyebrow colors with little wedge brushes to paint them on.

She plugs in the straightener and curling iron, then picks out all my colors and sets them on the desk. Once the straightener's hot, she gets to work. It takes almost twenty minutes to straighten my big, frizzy mess into something resembling . . . normal. When I spot myself in the mirror, I don't even recognize me. I look like a TV actress.

Next, Gracie picks up the curling iron. Why straighten my hair just to curl it again? But after she's covered my head in cute little ringlets that bounce around my shoulders, I can see her vision. A few spritzes of hairspray and it's locked in.

Gracie lets my hair settle while she does her own. She gives her black locks a '70s-style flat-iron job that makes the razor-straight ends of her hair hang low on her back. She finishes with her usual severe part down the middle, her long bangs ending just at the arch of her eyebrows.

I think I get the look she's going for now—like a goth Katy Perry. It works.

Gracie switches gears to doing my makeup.

She paints four different colors of foundation onto my face in big swabs, making me look like a science project. But once they're all smoothed out and blended together, I could swear I've been Photoshopped.

"Holy shit," I say into the mirror. Not a single freckle or blemish anywhere. It makes me look like I have higher cheekbones, a more delicate nose.

"You're good at this," I say.

"Just takes practice." Gracie stands in front of the mirror and performs the same makeup magic on herself, but in half the time. She has the ritual down.

Even if she doesn't act it most of the time, Gracie's still born and bred to be here.

Next, she plucks the edges of my eyebrows until my eyes prick with tears. She selects a small angle brush and dips it in brown clay, gradating my eyebrows from light and smoky near my nose, to dark and dramatic at the arch. She sucks in her bottom lip as she works, focusing hard on me. I've never been so fiercely the subject of someone's attention.

I feel like a spoiled princess.

Then she blends my eye shadow from gold at the tear duct, out to green, then blue across my eyelids, painting with such care and detail that I feel like one of Gentileschi's paintings. I eye the coral lip stain she chose, which looks atrocious in the tube—what if all this makeup turns me into a clown?

But when she paints the lip stain on me, I can see the image that Gracie had in her head.

She does smoky eyelids on herself and severe eyebrows that strangely suit her.

I had my doubts, but when we stand in front of the mirror in our dresses, we both look . . . exceptional. Even the salmon is majestic and almost royal with this epic makeup job. I grin at Gracie in the mirror in her tiny, slinky black dress. Night and day.

"We look sexy," she says.

I nod furiously. "Super sexy."

"Ready to go meet those guys?" she asks me, threading her arm through mine. I love this side of Gracie. Ready to go on an adventure.

"Let's get 'em."

CHAPTER SIX

As I walk into the anteroom of Hamilton Hall looking like this, I feel for the first time like a real Edwardian.

It's free seating for dinner. The giant whiteboard menu says meatloaf. Perfect. Meatloaf's hard to mess up, and the Hamilton kitchen is great at messing things up.

The whole school assembles in the cafeteria's anteroom in their finest evening wear, hair twirled and curled and stacked, gelled and spiked and combed.

Britt's the first to spot us in the crowd. He's wearing a soft, baby-blue tux. Gracie looks about to barf, but I think the '70s throwback powder blue suits his comb-over. It's a perfect contrast to Gracie's goth look. They're both so retro.

"Hello, ladies," Britt says, giving a little bow before taking Gracie's hand. He plants a polite kiss on the back of it, and she looks even bleaker. "How are you this evening?"

"Ready for that meatloaf!" I say brightly, and Gracie rolls her eyes.

Britt tries to strike up small talk with her while I search the crowd for my date. *My date.* A shiver runs down my arms. I know it's not supposed to "mean anything." I know it's not "a date." But I get to spend a whole evening getting to know this ridiculously handsome, cool guy who—for some inexplicable reason—has chosen me.

I am Boarding School Cinderella.

As if I've summoned him, he appears on the other side of the cafeteria. Scully's big, wide mouth gets even bigger when he smiles—like now, when he notices me.

We walk toward each other and meet somewhere in the middle of the chaos.

"Hey," he says.

"Hey," I say.

The ruckus around us fades, like we're standing inside a bubble. He slides a clear plastic box out of his jacket pocket.

Inside sits a crisp, salmon-pink corsage that matches my dress and his tie. We are the most adorable pair of salmon-colored people to grace Edwards Academy.

He opens the box and lifts the corsage out. "May I?" he asks.

"Of course." My voice comes out a whisper.

Scully slides the corsage over my hand. I am living, breathing magic. Every nerve ending in my body is firing as he settles the corsage around my wrist and tosses the plastic box in the trash.

His friends are off to one side—the two guys from Nordstrom's and their incredibly gorgeous dates. I hadn't even thought about this. His friends or mine? Combine them? I'd love to make friends with these four handsome people—

"Your friend is aggressively waving us down," Scully says, pointing behind me. When I turn around, Gracie gesticulates wildly at me to return to where she's standing with Britt.

Scully makes the decision to head toward them, and I follow. Gracie is frowning at us. Britt straightens to be as tall as he can and says, "Hey, Scully."

Scully nods. "What's up? You guys ready to eat?"

No small talk, no bullshit.

Thank. God.

We head into the main dining room and Scully scouts four open seats at the end of one of the long, wood tables. Special goblets are out, waiting to be filled with fresh sparkling apple juice from a bottle in a bucket of ice. The staff have dimmed the lights and hung colored streamers from the wrought iron chandeliers, creating just the right mixture of antique and cheesy.

Scully pours some juice for all four of us, ending with himself. What flawless manners.

"What's your favorite class?" Britt asks Gracie. Bottom of the barrel as far as icebreakers go.

"Crime and Punishment," she says. I didn't know Edwards offered a class like that, or that she's in it. I'm an abysmal friend.

Britt's eyebrows furrow. "That sounds cool. What are you discussing in it?"

"Crime," she says, smiling sweetly. "Oh, and punishment."

I stifle a laugh. So that's why I didn't know. Britt isn't fazed—he nods and smiles and says, "Like, famous crimes? I heard about this guy who escaped with a million bucks by jumping out of a plane right as the cops were about to nab him. Nobody's seen him since."

"He probably died," says Gracie.

"I know who you're talking about," Scully says. "D. B. Cooper, right? I heard he hijacked the plane. And it was only $200,000. Although I guess that was worth a lot more in the '70s."

"D. B. wasn't his real name," I say. It's one of my favorite pieces of trivia in my trivia lexicon. "Nobody knows his real name. D. B. was a miscommunication—his alias was actually Dan Cooper."

Scully sits back in his chair. "Wow, I didn't know that."

Gracie pours herself more sparkling juice. She already threw back her first glass like an alcoholic who was unaccustomed to social settings and trying to dull the edge. It's not even wine. Maybe she wants excuses to go to the bathroom.

"Do you talk about the school-to-prison pipeline in your class, Gracie?" asks Scully.

Oh man. He hasn't realized she was joking, either. Edwards kids are so genuine in their academic curiosities that it borders on cartoonish.

"Sure," Gracie says, downing her second glass. "We talk about the pipeline. The whole length, from Alberta to Texas."

Scully frowns, and I see it's dawned on him that Gracie's dealing out a heaping pile of bullshit. He glances sideways at Britt, probably wondering when the marshmallow is going to catch on.

"I'm really getting into my sculpture class," Britt says, to keep the conversation going. "We use every possible material. This week we had to build something out of found objects."

After a few minutes of laboriously discussing Britt's interpretive art projects, the meal is served. Who cares about meatloaf when Scully's sitting so close that I can feel the heat coming off his body and smell the spritz of cologne clinging to his lapels? It's strong, but I like it. From the corner of my eye, I watch him eat, and the tensing of his big, square jaw as he chews mesmerizes me.

Scully manages to make the rest of our awkward conversation not as awkward by asking questions and moving it along, just like a good socialite. Then, thankfully, it's time to depart from Hamilton Hall for the actual dance.

The Mixer's been set up in the Conservatory, which is built on a hill with walls of glass windows overlooking the campus. We join the parade of students traveling in their evening wear up the paved path, girls stopping along the way to take off their shoes and rub their heels or walk barefoot. Little lights along the path blink and glitter at us as we make our steady way up.

Inside the front doors, the Conservatory funnels us down a spiraling staircase that looks like a crystal nautilus. At the bottom we spill into a vast, high-ceilinged auditorium. Colorful paper lanterns strung overhead cast a dim, magical glow in the dark room.

Up on stage, a band dressed in sharp tuxedos plays soft rock.

Britt talks more as the room fills up, but it's easy to tune him out with the music going. Gracie looks bored as she picks up a drink that doesn't belong to her and starts in on it.

Then Scully turns to me and holds out one hand. "Would you care to dance?"

Oh, would I.

I drop my fingers into his and he leads me onto the dance floor. We're one of the first couples out here as the colored strobe lights blink and flicker.

He settles the other hand on my hip and slides it over the fabric of my dress, sending a little shiver of thrill into my neck. His cologne fills me up. The world swirls like I'm intoxicated.

We don't try to talk over the music. When I look up at him, Scully's eyes are the most perfect gray-green-hazel, like all the colors of a sunny day whirled up together.

I settle into his arms, which are warm and easy as they envelop me like a plush blanket. I spot baby-blue in my peripheral vision—it's Gracie and Britt dancing beside us, Gracie doing her best to avoid that same close-up move with Britt that Scully and I are doing. Poor Britt. He's here to have a good time, but Gracie is making it clear she'd rather be anywhere else.

I regret my fierce determination that she come along. Scully and I would have been fine alone. He's kind and accommodating, and I could've met his friends—maybe found a place among his posse of attractive, classy people.

But now I feel responsible for Gracie's enjoyment, and she seems resolved not to have a good time. What happened to Adventure Gracie? Why does she have to be like this so often?

After a few songs, Scully and I take a break and find our way to the food. We help ourselves to a sea of itty-bitty desserts arranged on white, tiered plates that remind me of a fancy garden party. As we're stuffing tiny brownies into our mouths, Scully's friend with the shiny dark hair interrupts us.

"Wanna join us out back?" he asks Scully, not acknowledging me.

"Hey, Cal," Scully says. "Have you met Sam?"

"Uh, no, I haven't." Not making eye contact with me, Cal extends a stiff hand. "I'm Calder. Nice to meet you."

"Nice to meet you, too."

"So," Cal says once again to Scully. "Out back?"

"Sure." Scully turns to me. "Sam, want to join?"

I don't know what "out back" means, but I'm obviously going.

"What about Gracie and Britt?" I ask.

He waves a hand. "They'll be fine for a few minutes."

Cal leads the way, sneaking through a black curtain that, in the low light, looks like a wall. We circle around the back of the stage and head down a short hall. Ahead of us, Cal pushes open a heavy metal door and holds it so Scully and I can pass under his arm. Then he takes off his shoe and plants it between the door and the frame so it doesn't close and, I assume, lock us out.

Outside, four guys and three girls stand under the glow of a dull orange light post. They nod at us, and the one smoking a cigarette offers it to Scully. He's about to take a drag when he turns to me.

"Do you mind if I . . . ?"

He's asking my permission? "Do whatever you like," I say. Ugh. I'd meant to sound cool and fun, not cold and dismissive.

Scully takes a long drag. To make up for my sass, I hold out my hand and ask, "May I?"

All eyes turn to me as Scully hands over the cigarette. I gently place it between my lipsticked lips. I've faked smoking before to impress my middle school friends, and I can fake it again.

I take the tiniest drag but pretend it's a lot longer, closing my eyes. I don't let the smoke into my lungs, as hot as my mouth gets, but flex my throat to make it look like I'm inhaling. I take out the cigarette and release smoke in a thin funnel.

I pass the cigarette back to Scully without coughing, and he takes it with wide eyes. Then his face transforms into a wicked grin, and I think I've impressed him.

The cigarette isn't the main affair, though. Soon one of the girls produces the real reason we're here: a silver flask with a shield-shaped symbol engraved on the front.

"Glad somebody brought the whiskey," Cal says, sighing. The flask goes around, and this time I don't fake taking a drink. It burns going down, and I make a face, which earns a laugh from the others.

"Sam, right?" says the girl who brought the whiskey.

"Yes," I say.

"Mallory," she says. "Are you a First Year? I haven't seen you around."

"Sure am," I say, my voice shaky. I'm a little woozy from the cigarette smoke, and the honest truth tumbles out of me. "And even though I'm a loser now, I'm gonna be Head Girl. And then a lawyer."

I cover my mouth. *What the hell, Sam?*

But everyone in the circle laughs.

"Can't be that much of a loser," Mallory says, nodding at Scully. "You got a date with him."

Scully shushes them. "Don't give me a big head, or I won't be able to get through the door."

"And Provost Portsmouth will definitely notice you creeping around to the front," says Cal. "Remember, *we vow to keep ourselves accountable*—or however that line goes."

But as the flask goes around—something the honor code certainly forbids—I wonder how much they really care about all that. Soon the whiskey's gone, and we all thank Mallory for bringing it.

"What's this symbol on the front?" I ask as I return the flask.

"Oh, just my family's coat of arms," Mallory says, shrugging. What sort of family has its own coat of arms? And then has it engraved on a flask for their underage daughter?

Cal pulls his shoe out of the doorjamb and everyone files back inside. It's much too warm in here with the hot whiskey floating around my belly, and I'm sweating. I hope I don't stink. Scully and I are the last to come down the hall and reach the black curtain that separates us from the dance floor.

"Mr. Chapman?"

We both freeze. Provost Portsmouth approaches us in the dark, eating a small cupcake.

"Oh, hey, Frank," Scully says, casually dropping his hands into his pockets. He gets to call the provost by his first name?

The provost stops in front of us, licking up the last crumbs of his dessert. Then he pauses and takes a long sniff.

"Scully Chapman." He arches an eyebrow. "Were you smoking just now?"

We are so dead. Deader than dead. And Provost Portsmouth will bury us out in old Morgan Edwards's creepy-ass graveyard next to all those bodies the old doctor autopsied.

"Only one," Scully says, shrugging. "We were just blowing off some steam. It's hot in here."

No way he just said that.

"It is pretty hot," the provost says, pulling his collar away from his neck. "But be more careful next time. I could smell you five feet away."

Scully nods. "Of course, Frank."

"Okay, no more smoking tonight, right?" Provost Portsmouth winks at me.

"Right," says Scully.

Then the provost waddles away and adrenaline is still racing through me at breakneck speed. Scully pulls me through the curtain, back into the dim, strobe-filled auditorium, and grins down at me.

"I wouldn't have guessed you smoke," he says, running a hand down my arm, like we weren't even caught just now.

"Only when the opportunity presents itself." I don't want him to think it's habitual.

Scully leans closer. "You looked good doing it."

For a second, I think he's going to kiss me. Then Gracie's angry voice cuts through the moment.

"Where have you been?"

I spin to find her standing behind us, wearing the deadliest glare I've ever seen in my life.

I abandoned her with Britt. Oops.

"Shit," I say. "I'm sorry. Scully and I stepped outside . . ."

"Outside?" she asks, stepping toward us. "Where? Why?"

I'm trying to formulate a response when she sniffs at me.

"You've been drinking? *And* smoking?"

They're phrased like questions, but she rains them down on me like bullets. I glance at Scully and say, "Can you give us a moment?" His presence is not helping.

"Of course," he says, and heads off to get a drink.

"How dare you," Gracie hisses at me when he's gone, getting close so no one else can hear. "I thought this *wasn't* a date, and now you're sneaking off together to do drugs?" *Cigarettes and whiskey aren't drugs*, I think—but I won't try to correct her. It'll only make her madder. "You know how I feel about Scully," she says.

Sure I do. She likes to lust after him in Drawing Club. Oh, and they apparently once went to a garden party together when they were kids.

But so what? She knows how I feel, too. And unlike her, I actually like him for *him*, not just for his pecs.

"I said I'm sorry," I repeat. "He invited me, and it was either go or get left behind. We didn't even do anything—"

"Then stay behind," she interrupts. "With your friend who you dragged along to this thing against her will because you were afraid of being alone."

"Look, I'm sorry," I say a third time, though my voice is getting angry now. "I thought you'd be okay on your own for, like, a couple minutes."

"Seriously?" Gracie asks. "You even thought of me? And you're going to make me sound like the big baby, when you're the one who took off with the guy you know I like?"

I knew she had a crush on him, but she's acting like this is a way bigger thing now.

"I don't see why it's such a big deal—" I start.

"It's a big deal because you're a shitty friend!" Gracie crosses her arms. "You ditched me with Donald Trump—"

"Britt's not that bad."

"—to go make out with Scully out back!"

The whiskey roils in my stomach. I look around for Scully and find him standing with Cal on the other side of the dance floor, sipping punch. Giving us distance. Watching me fight with my best friend at the dance like we're sixth graders.

"Oh my god," I say, throwing up my hands. "Can we please go outside if you're going to do this?"

"Do what?" Gracie's eyes get watery and her maroon lipstick clings just to the outsides of her lips, the middle all worn off. "Stand up for myself?"

"I regret getting you that date now. What a mistake."

"Don't act like that was some favor to me!" she snaps. "You hate being alone. You've been trying to suck up to every person who will give you the time of day since we got here."

It's a knuckle punch to my gut.

"But don't worry," she says. "None of these people care about you anyway, Sam. Trying to get with a guy like Scully will ruin you."

"You're such an asshole," I say, gritting my teeth so I won't cry. I always cry when I get mad. "At least I try. You just hole up in the room and act like you're better than everyone. You only do stuff when I do it first."

"Whatever. This whole place is a joke. And everyone just buys into it—especially you."

"If you don't like it, why don't you run back home, you big baby?"

The look on her face is like I've hit her. I can't believe I said that.

"You're a piece of shit, Samantha," Gracie says, tears rolling in fat droplets down her cheeks.

"Fine," I say. "If that's what you think, then I'm done."

I walk away, back toward Scully, my own eyes swimming. He looks more concerned than angry. I grab his hand in mine and hope Gracie sees. Then I say, "Let's dance again."

"Sure." He lets me lead him back out to the dance floor. I hear heavy footsteps and I imagine it's Gracie stomping out, but I won't gratify her by even looking.

Britt's been hanging around all night hoping Gracie will come back. When the dance ends, I go say goodbye and apologize for her.

He shrugs. "Gracie's responsible for herself. Don't worry about it."

Scully and I depart the Conservatory under the exposing glow of the lampposts that line the main path, and he walks me back to Isabel House. The buildings look like sleeping golems.

We are completely silent. The humiliation of the night envelops me. We stand together outside the front door of Isabel

House under some brown, skeletal trees that have lost their leaves early. Other girls arrive, eyeball us, and go in.

I ought to say something, but the whiskey gallops around in my veins, making it hard to find words.

"I . . . I enjoyed my night with you, Scully."

"Aw, thanks," he says. He looks so beautiful in the lamplight—I'm about to vomit out all my feelings and I can't stop it.

"I like you," I say. "A lot."

Scully is silent for a long moment. Too long. Then he says, "And I enjoyed your company, Sam."

That's not the reaction I'd hoped to get.

I feel tears starting to work their way up my neck, into my face. Hayden had tried to warn me about this.

"Thanks for inviting me," I say, trying to sound calm even though I am a collapsing skyscraper. "Even though Hayden was the one who technically invited me."

Scully's face clouds. "I hope you don't see it that way," he says. "When I saw your artwork, I thought to myself, *I want to know this artist. I want to show her what Edwards Academy has to offer.*"

So I'm a charity case. A tax write-off.

"That's why I asked to be matched up with you," he goes on. "I . . ."

"It's no biggie," I interrupt, wanting to hurry this along. I don't want to burst into tears in front of him—but if I don't leave soon, I will. "I totally get it. It was fun getting to know you."

I smile, offer my hand for a shake, and relief spreads across Scully's face. He goes in for the hug.

He lets me go, and before we can even say goodbye, I dart inside the front door. I check in fast and am only halfway up the stairs when the tears start. I hide my face inside my elbow and pretend like I'm coughing the rest of the way to my room.

Gracie's not here. I climb onto my bed, pulling the blankets up over my head.

You're a shitty friend!

I did everything possible to be a good friend. I got her a date. I pushed her to do activities. We wouldn't have even the possibility of a social life without me.

Everyone buys into it—especially you.

So what? Is it so bad that I wanted to have friends, or a boyfriend? That I wanted to have a place here and feel like I belong?

I fall asleep with my dress still on, my flawless makeup job seeping into the pillow.

CHAPTER SEVEN

It rains all night, pounding the roof and windows, waking me up every few hours. I have to drag myself out of bed for Saturday Session—and the polo game later.

If I'm still even going after last night.

As we tidy up for inspection that morning, Gracie doesn't say anything. She takes off for breakfast while I'm still getting my bag together.

She's never left without me before.

It's cloudy outside, and the walk to Hamilton is muddy. There's still a drizzle coming down, so I have to hold my backpack over my head to keep from getting soaked. Everyone walking into the cafeteria looks sleepy and washed out after last night.

At breakfast, Gracie doesn't even look up as I slide into our table with Bex, Eliza, and Lilian. She gossips and laughs with them like everything is normal as I eat my sausage and eggs across from her. Nothing she says requires a response from me.

My insides feel scooped out. First Scully, now this.

We've never had a serious fight before. I'm scared what it means. What about going to college together, being roommates, staying up late nights studying? Me going to Harvard, her going to art school, sharing an apartment somewhere in Boston? She was going to be my maid of honor.

On the way to Saturday Session, all the charming little dirt paths that snake between buildings have become mud pits that everyone avoids—and avoiding them only makes them wider. The mass of ivy seems to have grown closer to the doors of the building where I have Saturday Session, squeezing the brick like a choking hand.

Today it's my turn to meet with my advisor to discuss college plans.

"I want to do law," I tell Mr. Figueroa.

His gaze slides across my class schedule. "Keep taking classes from Mr. Jordan, then," he says. "He's got a law degree from Georgetown. He'll have plenty of advice for you."

Sure. Thanks. Very helpful. Except I already leafed through the course catalog on the second day of school and picked out which Third and Fourth Year classes would look best on my transcript.

I leave my ten-minute advising session with nothing.

Then we're herded into Cath for a mandatory "sports assembly"—I assume to prep us all for the water polo game tonight.

I don't even want to go anymore. I've had about enough of Scully, and Edwards itself, to last me all weekend.

"I want to stress good behavior at the game tonight," the provost says. "You are representatives of Edwards Academy. Remember: *We are all more than the shine on our shoes, or the pennies in our pockets. Our actions show who we are.*"

My actions have shown me to be a sixth grader who fights with her best friend at the school dance.

The provost steps back from the podium. "I'm going to hand it over for a moment to our captain of the water polo team," he says. "Scully Chapman!"

Scully jumps up from the front pew as the crowd breaks into applause, and he heads up to the podium. He has to raise the microphone because he's almost six inches taller than Provost Portsmouth.

"Thanks, Frank," he says. Everyone laughs. "I just wanted to say a few words. First—thank you for supporting us. Practice has been intense this past month, and everything you've done, from returning our dirty dishes for us in Hamilton, to bringing us snacks in the library . . . those little things are huge for us. They add up."

His friends take his dishes back? And bring him food? It must be nice to be the King.

"I want to tell you how much I appreciate every single one of you. Everyone who comes to our games and cheers . . ." Scully grips the sides of the podium. "You guys are the ones we do it for. Your support means the world to us. I hope I'll see you at the game tonight—we're not going to let that state championship get away this time!"

The audience erupts in applause. Someone shouts Scully's name as he heads back down into the pews, and Provost Portsmouth taps the mic a few times to regain control.

State championship? Sounds important—maybe I shouldn't miss this game after all. Even if Scully and I aren't, well, dating . . . I still met his friends. They know my face and my name now.

This could be my chance to get in.

Boarding school looks like:
The pool always being too small.

I wish I'd known she liked Him that much. You know—in that way. Not just amateur-hour lusting over His pecs, but a full-scale "Let's date and get married and have babies" kind of thing. I would never have accepted the "date" if I'd known.

Maybe I should get out of here.

Go home, swallow my pride, go to a normal school.

So much less homework. It was manageable for a while, but now that midterms are coming, I'm staying up late doing my reading every night and finishing my write-ups about it during lunch.

At a normal school I could chill out. Be myself. Have actual free time.

And the pool of eligible guys would be big enough that this shit wouldn't be a problem.

The dance was . . . I guess I'd call it humiliating. Definitely in my list of Top Ten Most Humiliating Life Events.

How can my roommate be so monstrously inconsiderate? It's like we're living on separate planets, shouting at each other across hundreds of miles of empty space.

I thought I had at least one real friend here, someone I could be myself with, besides those three tennis girls who sorta let us sit with them in the cafeteria.

Thinking that was a mistake. It's impossible to be yourself with anyone in this place. Like making a friend in prison—what you feel isn't real. It's just dependency. Survival.

At some point the school is bound to get between you. All the head games, all the conformity, all this mindless dedication to the rules. Ever since I heard this line of the honor code, it's been following me:

We vow to live by the rules set out for us, because those rules were created to keep us safe.

But what it doesn't mention is that living by the rules means living by *their* rules. It means moulding yourself into the thing they want you to be and then keeping yourself like that, posed and squashed and strangled, until you no longer remember what you once looked like, acted like, or thought like.

All I have left now is Him. I've decided for sure now: I *AM* going to that polo game after all. I'm going to root for Him, cheer with the best of them, and let Him know that I don't take to heart what happened.

That I'm still cool. Still in the game.

Still here.

———

I make a point of hanging out in our room after assembly, but Gracie never comes back. It's strange and quiet and boring without her. I'm almost never here alone.

Fine. It's time for the polo game anyway.

I've never been to the Edwards pool. The whole building smells of chlorine, and the walls swim with spidery water reflections. Through the chlorinated depths I can make out a massive black and red badger painted on the floor.

I search for Gracie in the bleachers. While I'm blocking the aisle, someone bumps into me.

"Jeez, get out of the way."

Music comes on over the PA to announce that the game's starting, so I rush to grab a seat.

The Edwards team comes out first. Scully looks fierce and sexy in his tight red speedo. There's something I never thought I'd say, but wow.

I went to the Mixer with that guy. Maybe I was a charity case, but I bet every girl in school looked at me with envy.

After the opening coin toss, the players dive in. There's a lot of splashing and yelling and boys in speedos hurling a yellow volleyball at each other's heads.

It's quite brutal.

I cruise the crowd every few minutes looking for Gracie. Of course she's not here—she loathes school activities. But if she were, she'd probably be making some snarky remark about the barbarism of it, or the tight, tiny speedos. I'd be laughing so hard I'd have to gasp for air.

In the pool, Scully leaps out of the water like a dolphin. One arm high up over his head with the ball cupped against his wrist, he hurls it directly into the goal net.

We're in the lead.

Someone starts a wave, and a row of people sitting nearby with painted red and black badger faces undulate like some kind of weird zebra.

The worship of Scully Chapman is a living, breathing thing.

They score again after halftime, and the crowd is in raptures.

And besides the few words I exchange with the girl next to me when she bumps my arm, I'm alone.

We win, of course.

We.

I consider this loaded word as everyone around me surges to their feet, roaring and clapping. The sound reverberates off the tin bleachers and the aluminum roof.

Scully's team does a lap around the pool, waving and soaking up the crowd's adoration.

Then the game's over and people get up to file out. I jump to one of the higher bleachers to look for Gracie, but it's a mess of bodies as people thunder down the stairs to get out first. A few people give me odd looks because I'm just standing there.

I sit down.

Why couldn't Gracie just be happy for me? But it was like if she couldn't have him, neither of us could. *And he doesn't even like me!* I want to scream at her. It shouldn't be up to me to apologize. She's the one who blew up at the dance.

I don't want to fight with the crowd, so I wait until almost everyone has gotten bored and filed out before I stand up to leave. Some teachers are standing around talking as I head down to the pool.

"Sam?"

My body lights on fire at the sound of his voice.

Scully stands at the door to the boys' locker room dressed in a tight white tee and equally tight jeans.

"Hey!" he says, walking over. "You came."

"Oh, uh, of course." I squeeze the straps of my backpack. Why did I bring a backpack? I look like such a nerd. "How could I miss it?"

"I hope you had fun, and about last night—"

That's when Provost Portsmouth steps out of the faculty office and throws up his arms.

"My man!" The provost approaches us and slings one arm around Scully's shoulders, squeezing him like a dad would do. "Have you decided on your plans for next year?"

"Come on, Frank," Scully says, sliding out from under his arm. "You and my dad both. I just got out of the water, and it's practically a year off. I don't want to think about college right now."

"Mike and I both care about you," Provost Portsmouth says. "And your future. After that game you played today, I want to make sure that whichever one of those California schools you pick offers a path in athletics."

I want to laugh at the way he says *those California schools*, like California is a less civilized foreign country.

"I know," says Scully, not hiding his impatience.

The provost turns a little to include me in the conversation. "You know I was a big tennis star when we went here? We've always had a great tennis program. If I'd been smart, I would have kept doing it in college. Everybody needs tennis players." Good thing I signed up. Maybe that's how I'll afford those four years at Harvard—tennis scholarship. "But I was nothing compared to Mike. Mike took the polo team to the state championship. And we'll be champs again this year. With you leading the team, Scully—"

"It will crash and burn." A leggy, red-headed kid wedges

between them and shows off how tall he is by draping his arm over Scully's shoulders. His face is a constellation of orange freckles.

"Waldo." The provost seems unfazed. "Glad you could join us half an hour after the game's over."

So *this* is the infamous Waldo Wilson.

"Sorry. Had to rehearse my lines for the musical. Singing is how you get the girls now."

The provost gives him a wry look. "Had no idea."

Scully slides Waldo's arm off his shoulder and drops it like he did Frank's. "I bet the musical will be a big hit."

"Why would I care?" asks Waldo, laughing with his huge mouth. "I learn my lines, and the cute girls come." Then, and only then, does he notice I'm there. "And who's this?"

"My friend," says Scully, "Sam."

His friend.

Waldo looks me over, like he's grading me in a beauty pageant. Then he shrugs and turns to the provost. "I need to talk to you about this car issue, Frank."

Just like that. Like I'm not even here.

"I told you, Waldo," the provost says, dropping the fun-loving principal act, "you didn't meet the grade requirement last year to earn your parking permit. Try again in a semester."

"But, Frank, I—"

"No *but Franks*." He crosses his arms. "You'll get your permit the same way Scully did."

"You should have actually studied for your finals last year, Wally," says Scully, not without pleasure. "Maybe then you could get a parking pass."

"At least I have access to you, who has a nice hunk of junk

with wheels." Waldo grins back at Scully and playfully punches him in the arm.

"That doesn't really make me want to drive you anywhere in it." I've never seen Scully like this—actually mad about something. "I think I should head home," he says, reaching for my hand. "I'm tutoring Sam, and we've both got a load of homework tonight."

Tutoring? His skin is blinding hot against mine. Suddenly my hand in his is all I can think about.

"But Ursula wanted to make you and the rest of the team dinner." The provost glances at Waldo. "All the usual guys are invited, too. I want to talk to you about your college plans, Waldo."

"But the good boy has homework," says Waldo, winking at Scully.

I sort of hate this guy, and I don't even know him.

"Please come," the provost says. "We're having empanadas."

"Come on, best friend!" Waldo says, elbowing Scully. "We haven't caught up in so long."

Scully looks at me, then lets out a sigh.

"Thanks again for coming tonight, Sam," he says. "I'll make up that tutoring offer to you later, okay?"

He picks up his gym bag and follows Frank and Waldo out, the provost resuming college talk like there'd been no interruption.

CHAPTER EIGHT

I give Gracie a day or two more to cool down. Anyway, I'm busy thinking about that tutoring offer. But the next time we're both in the room together, I start out with, "Gracie, I—"

She interrupts me. "Look, Sam, it's fine." Like she already knew what I was going to say. She opens the lid of her computer. "I'm over it."

"C'mon, talk to me." I sit down at my own desk, which faces hers. "We live together."

"There's not anything to talk about." She clicks her mouse and stares intently at her computer screen. "I'm not mad."

I lean forward over the desk and gently push the lid of her laptop down so I can see her. "Can we just move forward? Please?"

"We are moving forward." She gestures at her computer. "But my homework isn't."

It's just a desk between us, but it feels like a canyon, with a whole mighty river rushing beneath our feet.

I think I get it. To her, Scully was off limits. And I crossed her imaginary line.

But who cares about lines? Why does she even have to draw one?

Anyway, it's fine. I'm fine. She can just . . . sit over there and mope.

It's sort of a blessing, I guess, because midterms start this week and it feels like the world is on fire. Not shooting the shit all the time with Gracie means one less distraction. I don't remember how I used to do all my homework before dinner and still squeeze in a half-hour phone call with Mom every Friday.

And on top of the mountain of work I have, going to polo games takes up a ton of time. But every time there's a home game, I still head to the pool and cheer. I want Scully to see me there rooting for him. And I sort of enjoy watching now. He's magnificent, a pinnacle of human capability.

But trying to do everything is adding up. Even if we don't talk about our assignments anymore, Gracie and I still both stay up late working almost every night. I'm sipping an energy drink I bought at the commissary late on a Thursday when a knock comes at the door.

Prefects do rounds every night. If your light's on after eleven, you get a door knock. We're not in trouble—they just want to know what we're up to.

Gracie raises her face from her keyboard while I scramble to my feet. She's been sleeping there for a while and has red squares engraved in the side of her face. I tell her to get to bed, and answer the door. Instead, she lays her head back down on the computer. When I open the door, Hayden, Scully, and another prefect from Ernest House, who I think is named Francis, are standing outside. Scully's eyes twinkle and the hair stands up on my arms.

"What can I help you with tonight, officers?" I ask. Hayden narrows her eyes.

"Hey, Scully," Francis says. "It's your girl from the Mixer."

What's going on tonight, ladies?" Francis peers into our room and sees Gracie snoozing at her keyboard and chuckles. "Working too much?"

"I've got a big assignment due for Trig," I say. "I'm struggling when it comes to using the formulas."

"Formulas are the worst," says Scully. "Need some help?"

Hayden eyeballs him. "You're on prefect duty tonight," she says. "You can't just bounce out before finishing the rounds. That's the gig."

"Yeah, and?" he asks. "I'm Sam's tutor. It's my job."

"It's your *other* job. Doing rounds with me is your job right now."

Francis chuckles. "I think two of us can handle the rest of Isabel House, Supreme Ruler Hayden," he says, elbowing Scully. She gives both of them a look like this nickname isn't even remotely funny. "The Isabel girls are the tamest of the lot. We can handle it."

And he's right. When I peer into the hall, all the other doors are closed, no lights shining from underneath them.

"She's just a fucking Firstie," Hayden says, trying to be quiet, but still managing to sound shrill. She won't look at me, even though she's talking about me. Even though I'm standing right here. "Every Firstie has some long nights. That's how it goes! You can't swoop in like Superman every time."

Francis puts up his hands and backs away, like he wants nothing to do with this argument. But Scully isn't fazed.

"Hey," he says, putting a hand on Hayden's shoulder. She leans ever so slightly into his touch. "You two have got this. I'm just going to duck in here for a minute and help out. Remember how much it sucked back then, too? You got help as a Firstie, remember?"

Without waiting for an answer, Scully steps into my room, leaving the door open.

"You're gonna get in so much trouble," Hayden hisses at him.

Scully glances over at Gracie, who's emitting cute little snores on her laptop.

"Don't worry so much," he says with a grin, batting a hand at her. "We have a chaperone here to make sure nothing improper happens."

"Fine," Hayden says. "Don't blame me if you get caught." With one last searing scowl in my direction, she and Francis leave.

I wonder if Gracie's going to snap awake and freak out, but she hasn't budged. I let out a breath of relief.

"I get the basic concepts," I say to Scully, heading back to my chair. "But once the equations get complicated, I'm lost."

Scully plops down onto the bed behind me. This really is inappropriate. Our House Mom would flip out. It sends a sharp tingle of thrill up my neck.

Scully leans over the back of my chair and scans the textbook. His big polo arms stretch the sleeves of his shirt. "Oh, sine and cosine, my old frenemies." He takes the book without asking and sets it on his lap. "Let's start at the beginning. So sine is . . ."

I want to say again that I already understand the basic concepts—I'm just having trouble implementing them. But I don't want to interrupt.

"Does that make sense?" he asks after a while.

Yes, I understood all that two units ago. But I'm so grateful he's taking the time to help me. "I think I get it now," I say. "Thank you so much."

"No problem." He grins a wide grin. "So now, where this fits into the formula . . ."

"This is the formula I've been struggling with," I say, pointing to the one on my computer screen. "It's so complicated that I don't even know where to start with the order of operations."

"Well, actually," he says, still looking at the textbook and not at my screen, "if we start here on this old unit, I bet we can figure it out."

His hand moves across the back of my chair while he helps me. Fifteen minutes later, it rests on my shoulder. The point of contact between us is electrified, on pure fire.

I press the wrong key, and suddenly my computer makes a loud *bonk!* sound. Gracie shoots up from her chair. She stares at us like she's not sure if Scully Chapman sitting in her room at midnight is a dream or reality. I can't help the guilt that spreads across my face, but Scully says with complete nonchalance, "Welcome back, Sleeping Beauty."

"Uh, thanks," Gracie murmurs, rubbing the reddened side of her face. Or is she blushing?

"Guess I should move along," says Scully, getting up with a stretch. "The others should be done with rounds by now."

Gracie's eyes follow him like a wary animal as Scully makes his way to the open door, draping one hand across the doorknob.

"Thanks again for the help," I say, standing up, too. "I think it'll be ready to turn in tomorrow."

"Awesome. Glad I could help." I follow him to the door so I can close it behind him, but he takes my hand and pulls me into the dark hall. He shuts the door so we're out here alone.

I'm breathless as his hand returns to the same spot on

my shoulder as before. The live-wire connection is plugged in again.

"Hey," he says, voice husky. "Want to go on a date sometime?"

A date.

Not like the Mixer. But a real fucking date.

I feel like all of my nerves are firing at once. I manage to say, "Uh, yeah. Sure."

He grins.

"Sunday after Thanksgiving break? At the Roast?"

I nod. "Sounds great," I say, even though what I want to scream is, *Holy fucking awesome, Batman!*

"Great," he says, grinning, and releases my shoulder. "Can't wait, Sammy."

Sammy?

With that, he walks off down the hall, and I lean back against the door to my room.

I have a date with Scully Chapman, and I didn't even have to ask.

Gracie is staring at me as I come back inside and quietly close the door.

I don't know why I tell her.

"He asked me on a date," I say, getting back in my chair to finish up the assignment.

"Good for you," she says, but her voice has no color, no flavor. Neither of us speaks as she gets out of her chair and changes into pajamas, then goes to bed.

Fine. She can steam if she wants—she can't bring me down. People like Francis are starting to know who I am. And now I have a date with the hottest guy in the universe.

I'm finally "getting it."

He was in my room last night.

Right here, where I sleep. Where I get undressed, where I strip down to being completely naked . . .

I can't stop thinking about that. I wish my roommate didn't have to be there—she's killing my buzz.

Well, not just her. Midterms are kicking my ass so hard I've had to track down a few study groups. She's in one of them, too. We can't seem to escape each other.

Want to know a dirty truth about private school?

Everyone's faking it. Faking holding it together, faking how easy the work is, faking how much time they spend studying and writing. People have bags under their eyes at study sessions and try to cover it up with makeup.

I brought it up one time when my physics group had secured a private room in the library.

"How do you guys find time?"

Everyone looked at me like I'd asked about the frequency of their sexual activity. There were some awkward coughs and everyone brushed it off like it was no big deal.

Fakers. I know I'm not the only one staying up all night, falling asleep in class, turning in half-assed assignments.

But then, after one group yesterday, a girl came up to me in the library and asked if I was doing okay.

"Hanging in there, I guess," I said, hoping that would get her off my back.

But she was relentless. She told me about a tutoring center behind the Conservatory, where you just put your name down at a time that works and someone will help you.

That was pretty nice, her telling me that privately. And I remember He tutors. Maybe there is hope for this place.

I decided to check it out. And there, on the corkboard of sign-up sheets, was His name.

If I sign up and He sees me there . . . what will He think? I don't want to look desperate to spend time with Him. And I don't want Him to know how badly I'm doing in school.

I'm not ready to be that transparent.

Boarding school looks like:

A girl crying in the library. It's not over a breakup. She clutches her textbook and some crumpled paper in her arms as she sobs in one of the big, comfy chairs, her river of tears filling the creases in the fabric.

Midterms finally end in a flurry of falling red-gold leaves, and it's like a marvelous show that Edwards puts on just for us.

The Saturday before we all get to go home for Thanksgiving break, it's cloudy and cold out, so one of the Isabel House prefects starts a fire in the fireplace in the first-floor lounge. We all cuddle up around it with our favorite throw blankets, while our House Mom makes hot cocoa with tiny marshmallows.

I know a few of the other Isabel House girls now through tennis, so I'm not always alone without Gracie. We giggle together while we go over our assignments for break.

I finally have a place. And it's here, with these girls, in front of the fire, getting marshmallows stuck between our front teeth.

I'm leaving home when I leave Edwards for break.

Getting in the station wagon is like moving from one planet in a space shuttle and arriving on a completely different one at our house.

The whole week I can't wait to get back to Edwards for my date with Scully.

Which is fine, because by the time Thanksgiving break's over, my parents and I have gone through all the stages of excitement and joy at having "quality family time" and have returned to mutual annoyance.

This is good, I think. Healthy-normal.

But it's impossible to focus on my homework when I get back, because all I can think about is going out with Scully tonight. I check my email, agonize over what I'm going to wear, meet the girls in Hamilton Hall for dinner.

Should I even tell them about my date? It would be so humiliating if Scully put me in the friend zone again.

But I can't contain it, even with Gracie sitting at the table.

"Don't look," I say during a lull in conversation, "but Scully Chapman asked me to go to that coffee shop on campus with him tonight."

Of course they all immediately turn their heads toward where he's sitting.

"I said don't look!"

"Sorry," Lilian says, shriveling a little. "I'm so jealous! First the Mixer, now an actual date to the Roast?"

Gracie just keeps on eating her food. The tennis girls have noticed we don't talk much anymore, but they're not big into prying.

"Our little Firstie is on fire," Bex says, putting an arm around my shoulders and squeezing me. "Soon you're gonna be boyfriend and girlfriend, and then we won't get to hang out with you at all!"

I laugh along with them as if something like that would never happen. But this could be the first of many times Scully and I go together to the Roast.

And after that, prom. In blue, this time, maybe. By then, everyone at school will know my name. Scully will call out to me at sports assemblies: "I dedicate this next game to my awesome girlfriend," he'll say into the mic, while everyone cheers.

I'm trekking up a very tall mountain, and I've just stopped at base camp.

But I will reach the peak, I know it.

———————————

I run home from dinner, get changed into my second-favorite outfit: a cream shirt with a swooping, lacy collar and a pair of new jeans. I'm saving my favorite one for our second date—I hope I'm not jinxing it. Then I slap on a coat of lipstick, and I'm off.

I'm buzzing like a hummingbird as I check out and find Scully waiting in the courtyard, glazed in white lamplight. The perfect scoop of his nose, the way his flannel sweater hugs his big chest, how his gray slacks hang off his hips . . . is he even real?

"H-hi," I say.

"Good evening." Scully takes my hand and gently presses his lips to the back. "Shall we?"

Nobody has ever kissed my hand before.

I nod shakily, give him my most radiant smile, and we head off together toward the Roast. Other people are out on evening walks, coming home from activities, or going to their friends' dorms to socialize. I feel like every single person stares at us as we go by together, not holding hands but definitely walking close enough that our arms touch. My blood is pumping so fast that I don't even feel the autumn chill.

"Did Gracie get her project done?" Scully asks. I assume he's referring to how she was passed out on her keyboard last week.

"Don't know," I say, shrugging. "She doesn't tell me stuff anymore."

"Not at all?"

"Not really."

"Aw," Scully says, reaching out to squeeze my hand. "I'm sorry you two fought."

He's so perfect it makes me want to die.

"It's okay," I say. "She'll get over it."

But that's a lie. The elephant in the room will only get bigger, louder, uglier. Especially after tonight. What should I have done? Turned down this amazing opportunity for myself just because Gracie is jealous?

The green and white striped awning of the Roast appears. During the day it's a regular coffee shop, but in the evenings they serve non-alcoholic drinks like daiquiris, margaritas, you name it—all minus the booze.

I order an iced chocolate martini with extra whipped cream, and Scully gets a piña colada.

When the barista asks, "Together?" Scully pulls out his card. I think he's going to pay for both of us when he says, "Separate, please."

Separate? He was the one who asked me to go out with him. His dad works on Wall Street and I only have so much money on my meal card. That's why I never come to the Roast normally—because a single drink costs as much as a meal.

But Scully must be a feminist—of course—since he believes in each of us paying for ourselves. He's always full of wonderful surprises. Even if this one's a hit to my credit balance.

While we wait for our drinks, Scully says, "How's tennis going?"

I didn't know he paid that much attention to me or my activities.

"It's good. I'm not that great a player, but they still let me onto the JV team, which was nice of them."

"I saw you made friends with Rebecca and crew," he says. "They're great. I bet you'll be on the varsity team by Third Year."

"Hope so," I say. "Then maybe I can qualify for a scholarship. Only way I can afford Harvard."

As soon as it comes out, I want to stuff it back in. I've never told anyone but Gracie that I'm a scholarship student.

"You know, Sammy," Scully says, the scholarship remark disappearing as quickly as it was spoken, "I see great things for you at Edwards." I cringe slightly at this nickname, but I know he means it to be cute. "This semester has been tough, but the first one always is. You just have to—"

The door to the Roast flies open, sending the overhead bells into a cacophony. Waldo Wilson strolls in.

Scully lifts his drink menu to hide his face. I do the same. We peer at each other around the other side.

"What's the deal with you and that guy?" I ask.

Scully's face screws up. "Ugh. Our dads were, like, best friends in high school." He shakes his head. "Waldo and I were best friends, too. Back in middle school."

Waldo walks to the counter and starts loudly placing—no, demanding—an order.

"What happened?" I ask. I know it's rude to pry, but Waldo is the only person I've ever seen who can ruffle Scully's iron feathers. What gives him that kind of power?

Scully looks pensive for a moment. "You know our dads own a hedge fund together?"

I do, because Gracie told me. But it seems like a rather personal thing to know about someone, and I don't want him to think I'm weird, so I shake my head.

"My dad, Mike, and Waldo's dad, Ron, started their company, Blue Crescent, together when we were little. Our families used to be real close—we even lived down the block from each other in Long Island. But then it was like . . . Ron snapped. Like maybe the money got to him. He started throwing huge parties, rolling around in limos, picking up pretty women—I'm pretty sure there were drugs involved. Definitely lots of drinking." He shrugs. "I felt bad for Wally, having this going on around him. But then he became a jerk, too, as soon as middle school was over. We haven't actually hung out since we were Firsties."

Waldo has seen us but is pretending that he hasn't. He waits for his espresso drink by the counter. When it arrives, he takes it and strides out the door.

We put down our menus.

"My dad's worried that Ron is destroying the firm." Scully turns his head away, like he's ashamed of even saying it. "He makes bad decisions, doesn't call people back, loses his temper. We're trying to buy him out before he runs it into the ground, and that has really pissed off Waldo."

We both go silent. He's shared so much with me that I don't know how to respond. This is so much more intimate than I expected. I'm flattered, but surprised, too.

"Sorry about all that," I finally say.

"It's okay. But that's why we both act weird."

Used to be best friends. I know what that's like.

We talk more about other stuff—water polo, school, Mr. Jordan. He apparently has a super-hot Icelandic wife, and I'm not surprised by this at all.

"I should get you home," Scully says after a while, as if I live at a house with my parents and a dog, and not the dorm next to his. "We've both got class tomorrow."

He's so responsible. It's kind of . . . sexy.

As we exit the Roast, Scully takes my hand.

Third time, I note to myself. Not counting the Mixer. But I don't count that in the story of Scully and Sam.

The sun has set, but now the moon is out and full, suspended in the sky like an enormous silver coin. The edges of the maple trees are coated and shimmering, and the face of the clock tower is a perfect reflection of the moon.

A few hundred yards from the front door of Isabel House, Scully stops. We stand under a tree that vines and moss have completely taken over.

"Thanks for going out," Scully says.

"It was my complete pleasure."

He still hasn't let go of my hand. "Can I kiss you?" he asks.

No one has ever asked me before. I was kissed one time. Okay, a few times, but we were nine and it was stupid.

"Yes?" I say.

And he kisses me.

This is definitely not kissing in a plastic playhouse. It doesn't last long, but it feels like cool droplets of glittering magic on my lips that burn all the way to my ankles.

I want a hundred more.

"Wow," I say, once we pull apart. I feel unsteady on my feet. "Thanks."

He laughs, and the crinkles around his eyes are adorable. "No one has ever said 'thanks' before. You're welcome?"

I laugh, too, but it cracks. "I had a great time," I manage to say.

"Me, too," he says.

This was definitely a *date*-date.

CHAPTER NINE

My elation over the date dies a quick death the next day when Mr. Jordan hands out prep packets for finals, which we'll take as soon as we get back from winter break. And the packets are twenty pages thick.

"Read it over now so you can ask questions before break," Mr. Jordan says, "because you'll be on your own for three weeks during Christmas break, and then it's test time." Even though he says it in his usual mild, kind way, it sounds like a threat.

The prep sheets give me a small heart attack. The amount of material our teachers expect us to know from memory is . . . astonishing. Pages of definitions. Dates and names. Formulas I thought we'd be provided, but now realize I'll have to memorize.

No calculators.

It doesn't help that I'm in mostly Second Year classes, so my classmates have already been through the wringer once, and have very little sympathy for me. Though one girl in my government class did recognize me as "the girl who was with Scully the other night at the Roast."

"Ohmigod! You must be pretty smart if you're a First Year in this class. And if Scully is interested in you." What's unspoken: *You must be smart if Scully's dating you, because you're certainly nothing to look at.* "You just have to come to our study group. We need more smart people."

I could kiss her shoes.

The group meets on Wednesday evenings. And while it's incredibly helpful—since I only need to do a fraction of the work to pull together everything we need for the test—getting all the work done and turning things in on time is still a game of *time, time, time.*

Scully and I haven't gone out again since our date, but a lot of people saw us at the Roast together. People I don't know have suddenly started speaking to me in the buffet line, or asking my opinion on whether the cubed ham in the salad bar is a health hazard. Scully's friend, Cal, and his girlfriend, Sloane, even sit next to me at a polo game.

So school is killing me, and my roommate is floating off in space, but at least I have a life. If I can survive exams.

---

http://privateschoolnewb.tumblr.com
Dec. 6, 2017

I don't know how to keep this up. I'm turning things in late, trying to keep on top of school, Drawing Club, polo games, while not dropping out of tennis. Sometimes I don't eat because I'm too busy finishing my reading. I get half my food in my mouth before lunch is over and I have to dump the rest out.

Even though we have the whole break to study, study time won't make up for missed assignments. It will be a miracle if I pass.

Thank you to my two readers who sent me notes on my last post. I think you're the only people in the whole world who read this, so I appreciate that you keep coming back. I've read your notes over and over. Especially the one that said, "Definitely get tutoring from the hot dude."

Okay. I'll do it. I'll put myself in His hands.

I'm going to make an appointment tomorrow and see what He can do for me, if anything. Or maybe I'm too far gone to help? At the very least, it'll give me a chance to see Him again.

Hold my hand, dear readers. Digitally, of course.

———————————

"Come to my room tomorrow at eight p.m. sharp," Scully's email says. "I'll meet you downstairs at check-in. Clearly you need an emergency tutoring session."

I'm glad I sent that email slightly exaggerating how badly I'm doing in Trig. An emergency tutoring session to help me pass a test? I have never felt more important.

Inside Thomas House I find Scully perched on the check-in desk, waiting for me.

"Hey hey hey!" he says, climbing down. His House Dad, Barry, a white-haired guy in his mid-fifties who I was assigned to for a Family Dinner a few weeks back, pulls out a clipboard.

"This your tutoring student?" he asks.

"Big test coming up, Barry. Probably needs an hour-long session, but the tutoring building is closed this late."

"Okay," the House Dad says easily. He turns to me. "Sign in here, please. You have to leave before nine."

I sign in and we head upstairs. Just like in Isabel House, the Head Prefect's room lies at the very end of the hall. As soon as we're inside, Scully turns and closes the door behind us—with a surprisingly enthusiastic *slam!*

A stone sinks in my gut. We're not supposed to have the door closed. Surely his House Dad will walk by and we'll both be in big trouble.

But Scully seems unconcerned as he flips on a small lamp instead of the overhead light. I think he means it not to blind me, but it makes the rest of the room outside the reach of the lamplight look dark.

We're going to be alone in his room together. At night. For a whole hour.

The door really should be open.

"Take a seat," Scully says, gesturing to the couch against the wall. I can't believe he has a couch in his room. I guess that's the benefit of being a prefect—you get a double room all to yourself to do with as you please.

"Tea?" he asks.

"Oh, sure." How do you make tea in a dorm room?

I sink into the soft cushions and take off my coat while he plugs in a silver kettle. Flipping the switch and leaving it to heat up, Scully plops down next to me.

"I'm glad you came to me when you needed help," he says. "It makes me feel . . . good, I guess. That you trust me."

"I didn't know what else to do."

"It's okay." His hand lands on my thigh. "It happens to everyone. No shame in asking for help."

There it is again—that electricity between us. But the closed door stares accusingly at me.

He's right. Everyone needs to lean on something sometimes.

"In fact, I'm proud of you for admitting it," he goes on. "And I'm flattered I'm the person you thought of."

"You help everyone," I say.

He smiles. "You always see the good in people. I like that about you."

He likes me? It's as if my veins are filled with light, silver bubbles. Then he leans forward . . . and kisses me.

Keep calm. Don't get too excited. Don't freak out and freak him out. But oh my god, we're kissing again.

His tongue teases my lips, so I let them open. He slips it into my mouth and I respond with mine and it fills me with lava. I've never kissed like this before—full-scale making out. His hand squeezes my thigh and I tangle my hand in his hair as the kiss deepens. It's like math: this goes here, then there, in this order.

Then his hand grasps my right breast. My eyes fly open, but his are still closed. He kneads my chest through the fabric of my shirt the way a cat might knead you through a blanket. I think it's supposed to feel good, but the flesh of my breast gets trapped by the underwire of my bra.

Scully's other hand travels up my thigh, under my skirt, to the waistband of my leggings. My body goes stiff, and reflexively, I pull my leg back. He loses his grip.

I'm about to say, *Shit, I'm sorry*, when the kettle chirps. Why did I pull back like that? Scully gets up to turn it off and I feel . . . relieved.

I think about saying something—but what, I don't know. Something to get him to cool off on feeling me up.

Scully and I, kissing, alone, in a room with a closed door should be my dream moment. Except I feel like I could vomit.

He takes out two mugs, pours the hot water into them, and

drops a tea bag into each mug. He carries them to a dresser next to the couch, spilling a little boiling water. The droplets steam as they hit the wood.

He sits back down on the love seat and says, "Now, where were we?"

"Tutoring," I say, my voice coming out weak and high-pitched.

He arches one eyebrow. "We're still using code words?"

Of course I had hoped to spend time alone with him. But I didn't think . . . We got so far so fast.

"Your House Dad said one hour, right?" I ask. Even though it has, according to the clock, only been fifteen minutes. My chest hurts where the underwire pinched me.

"It's fine even if we go a little over," he says with a laugh. "Barry trusts me."

Before I can reply, he presses his mouth against mine. His tongue darts between my lips, prying them apart while his hand grabs my upper thigh again. It snakes up to the hem of my leggings.

Kissing is about the farthest my imagination ever got in my fantasies. I haven't freshened up down there. I haven't put on any of that vanilla-scented lotion the girls in my study group use when they know they're headed to Cath to hook up. I haven't shaved or trimmed or anything.

I gently push his hand away, imagining how repulsed he'd be when he found all that hair and weird, fishy vagina smell people joke about—but the hand goes right back again, while the other one returns to kneading my chest.

A rush of cold runs down my arms. I pull away, pressing myself into the squishy arm of the couch.

"I'm sorry," I say, trying to keep my voice low in case

anyone in the next room can hear. "I'm not really prepared—"

"What?" Scully says. "Didn't you want to make out?" He smiles, lips peeled back over perfect, white teeth. "So here we are. Making out."

"I know, but—"

He kisses me again, hard, silencing me. *But I'm not ready for this*, I want to say. He presses me against the sofa and his hands are all over me, hot and scratchy. One peels down the waistband of my leggings, then wedges itself between my hip and the elastic band of my underwear. The other pinches my nipple through my bra. A dog bite.

"Ouch!" I pull my arm away to cover myself, to put it between my sensitive body and his hand. But he is immobile. Steel. "Scully—" My blood is so hot, I feel like I'm suffocating. I want to worm out of my own body, leave it there for him to squeeze and scratch while the rest of me walks away.

His hand on my hip won't let go. "Hold on," I say, my voice cracking and breaking, "I'm not—"

"You're not what, Sammy?" That name again, like nails on a chalkboard. "Come on. We both know this is what you've wanted since you drew that picture of me."

My head buzzes. I'm not ready. This isn't what—

He grunts. Yanks down my leggings and underwear at once. I cross my legs to keep them on, but I'm revealed. Exposed. The fabric tears, staying bunched around my thighs.

"But I—"

"Shh," he says into my hair. "It's no problem."

Everything smells sour and sharp, like bleach.

He buries his hand in my leggings again. Pulls. Tugs. My legs pinwheel trying to keep them on. I get one elbow into his chest and push. Nothing.

A scream builds inside me—but if I let it out, Barry finds us with my underwear around my thighs. We're suspended, maybe expelled.

The leggings and skirt stop at my knees. A voice in the back of my head is shouting, *Run, run, RUN!* But he's so heavy.

"Please," I gasp. It's as if I haven't spoken. I am a doll being undressed, posed, flexed. Everything that is me is also fear.

Somewhere up above me floats his invisible face. He shoves me down with one arm, unzips himself with the other. *Zzzzzt.*

He yanks his pants down just to the thigh, exposing his hairy skin. Tears rushing down my cheeks, I shove him again. But he is stone. Then he grabs some of my flesh and some of my shirt like it's all the same slab of meat.

"Isn't this what you wanted?" He leans down so his face hovers over my shoulder, his lips just behind my ear. "Isn't this what you wanted all along?"

---

http://privateschoolnewb.tumblr.com
Dec. 8, 2017

No.

That was never what I wanted, not like that. Who would want that?

I knew what was coming next. Doesn't change what it felt like.

I could've screamed. And then every boy in his dorm would have come running to see that their Head Prefect brought up some lucky Firstie girl, pretending to tutor her. Some making out became feeling up became something else, and now she's screaming.

I'm only halfway through my first year.

I stayed quiet and still, thinking that would help. He moaned. It was the most disgusting sound I've ever heard.

I thought if I didn't fight, it would hurt less. I was wrong.

He walked through me. He took off my skin and wore it, back and forth, a seesaw with no face.

The second he let me go, I grabbed everything and ran. Put back on what I could in a bathroom stall. Someone checked me in at my dorm, but I can't remember who—just long hair and long nails. Could have been any prefect. My roommate wasn't there when I got back, thank fuck.

I crawled into my bed and curled up as small and tight as possible. Because every part of me ached and stung and when you curl up real, real tight, when you press your knees to your chest and wrap your arms around them, somehow this compression dulls the pain just a little. Just enough.

I didn't cry. I couldn't, really—there wasn't anything left in me that could.

I was still in my clothes. They hurt. My shirt was torn where he had pressed me down and a seam caught on the love seat.

Treat your fellow students as you would want to be treated.

So much for the honor code.

Expect the best, and your compatriots will deliver.

No, they wouldn't. Because it's all a lie. Everybody obeys the honor code—until they don't want to anymore. Until they're after a cigarette or whiskey or sex.

I couldn't sleep, but I pretended when my roommate eventually got back.

I could hear his zipper coming down, over and over again.

Zzzzzt.

Zzzzzt.

Zzzzzzzzzzzzt.

CHAPTER TEN

I lie scattered in a hundred thousand pieces under my blanket the whole night. My face is covered in cracks, splitting, breaking, like an old porcelain doll. You could have seen me from across a football field and known, that girl has gone rotten. That girl has had her insides scooped out. That girl is no more a girl than a bucket of metal scraps bound together with flesh tape.

Give me one million years on this Earth and I will never, ever be whole again.

Gracie looks at me funny the next morning while we wait for Jean to stop by for inspection. There are bags under her eyes, too. She must have been at the library with a study group late last night.

Does she know where I was?

I can't tell her. She said it herself: *Trying to get with a guy like Scully will ruin you.*

She knew this would happen. She was always saying it—how Edwards was fake, how it would betray you as soon as it got the chance—and I never listened. She knew how high the price was.

But I am an Edwards student. I should be happy that the hottest, smartest, coolest guy possible picked me. I could tell anyone we did it last night, and I'd suddenly be Scully's Girlfriend.

I'd be in the club.

My insides churn as we wait for Jean to come and inspect our room. It feels like some of my organs have switched places.

I want my entrance fee back.

Maybe Gracie's right that I was in the wrong at the Mixer. And maybe wrong follows you around.

---

http://privateschoolnewb.tumblr.com
Dec. 9, 2017

Boarding school looks like:

Knowing there are a lot of fucked-up things hiding under the surface of your school. But not realizing just how fucked up exactly until it's too late.

To everyone who sent me a message after my post yesterday, all three of you:

If I did tell someone that he raped me, the first thing they'd do is tell me to go to the police. (Police don't care. Police don't want to help.)

Tell your parents. (They'd freak once they learned who it was.)

Tattle to House Mom. (Great, then the whole school finds out, and my life here is basically over.)

But I'm the one who was too stupid to notice the monster underneath his skin. I was the one who walked up there late at night and let him close the door. I was the one who wanted him to kiss me so bad.

I was the one who threw away the only relationship here that meant anything to me—for him.

I did this, and now it's up to me to clean it up.

The sun is out, but everything is cold. I spaced checking the temperature like I always do before leaving the room, and now I'm totally underdressed. My legs are icicles by the time I get to Morning Prayer, but the sting of it feels good. Distracting. A different kind of pain.

I pass under bare, skeletal trees on my way to Cath. Their limbs hang out over the main walkway like warped, arthritic bones.

I slide into my seat right as the doors close. Thank god the First Years are relegated to the far back pews so I don't have to worry about seeing . . . him. I don't try to talk to Gracie.

I am made out of playing cards. Even a light breeze could send me scattering.

Later, Gracie and I end up standing next to each other by accident in the long breakfast line, and it takes forever to get our meal cards swiped. I wonder if she'll ask about how bad I look this morning, but she says nothing. Once I'm inside, I scan the whole cafeteria, searching for him.

There. By the buffet exit, walking off with his buddy Cal, carrying a tray stacked full of yellow eggs and shining-greasy bacon.

It's a stab through my abdomen.

They're joking about something. Laughing.

My vision pulses with black and red, watching them enjoy themselves. How dare he! How can he act like everything is normal?

All the places he touched me ache. I can feel every single one of them as if they are glowing red hot, right through my clothes. I turn away to pick a carton of milk off the rack, in case he looks over. But he won't.

Because I was disposable to him. I was a stinky little burger wrapper that went in the trash once it was done being a napkin. I don't know why I bothered buying a meal today—I'm not hungry. Anything that goes down will surely come back up.

I stick to the wall with my tray to put as much space between me and Scully as I can, keeping my eyes on the floor. Even my toes feel not quite attached to my body, out of my control, just like the rest of the world.

Only one more week until we get to go home for break. I just have to make it one week.

It feels like the rest of my life.

Lilian and Eliza are already sitting at our usual table, chatting about something asinine. Gracie sets down her tray across from them and gets out her homework. She scribbles out her assignment for math later, mumbling some curse words to herself as she erases a problem and starts over for the second time.

None of the other girls talk to me, as if I'm emitting waves of *fuck off*. I force myself to toss down as much buttered toast as I can. Hayden can pinch my fat as much as she wants next year, and it won't make a difference to me.

In Art History, it seems like people sit an extra six inches away—as if I'm contagious. Or maybe I'm the one doing it.

I don't want anyone to touch me, even by accident.

Paying attention in class is impossible. One of my teachers is saying something interesting about conspiracy theories, but not five minutes deep, and my own personal video starts again in the background. A scene-by-scene, slow-mo instant replay of last night.

My own brain has betrayed me.

I grit my teeth together and press the graphite tip of my pencil into my notebook. *I'm going to take notes.* But the lecture doesn't keep me for more than a few minutes before the memory worms forward again.

Zzzzzt.

The sound travels through me whenever the replay starts over, reverberating in my elbows, knees, anywhere my joints connect.

I skip lunch. I'm still not hungry, and I can't sit through another meal, pretending to smile, trying to act like everything is fine as Bex, Gracie, and the others go on as usual. I have this irrational feeling that anyone who gets too close to me will know. They'll smell it on me. Whatever it is, this disease—I'll pass it on to everyone within my vicinity.

As I trudge across brown, crispy, dead grass back to Isabel House, a bitter winter gust blows past, buffeting a flag on the flagpole so it makes a wretched snapping sound. I thought I knew this place, but now, I feel like I'm walking across the surface of Mars. I keep scanning the horizon to make sure I don't run into him, since our dorms are right next to each other.

The first thing I do in our room is yank open my wardrobe. Clothes avalanche out from when I shoved them all in there to pass inspection this morning. Buried under my stinky tennis shorts are the blue shirt, the black skirt, the torn leggings.

What was once my favorite outfit. The blue shoes are smeared with mud.

I look at them for a long time, and my throat and stomach lurch as if I might throw up.

I shove the clothes in the plastic Nordstrom's bag that my dress came in and seal it up. Then I walk downstairs to the dumpster out back, lift the heavy metal lid, and throw the bag in.

Gone. Forever. The lid clangs closed. But somehow my head is still pounding, and my body is still stinging.

I go tell Jean that I'm sick and I need to skip class.

"Do you want to see the nurse?" she asks.

"No. Cramps are just worse than usual."

She takes one look at me and clears me for a sick day.

I clean up as many of my things around the room as I can, until my half sparkles. I make a trip to the basement and wash all my clothes on HEAVY SOIL. When they're clean and dried, I fold them and put them away and head into the bathroom with a towel.

I turn on the hot water and just stand under it. Starting at my hairline, I take a bar of soap and start scrubbing. It's one of those fancy soap bars with coffee grounds in it, something my mom gave me because it would be good for my skin. "Exfoliating," as she calls it.

I've always hated it because it's so scratchy. Right now it's perfect.

I work the soap down the sides of my face, across my mouth, where his mouth was. Where his tongue lapped up mine. On the underside of my breasts I find scattered red stars where blood vessels burst, from when he grabbed and twisted my flesh through my bra.

I reach the crux of my legs and for a long moment, I can't touch there. My own body has become foreign to me, an alien body.

Outside the bathroom stall, somebody complains about there being no hot water. "Someone's been in here showering for a long time," a girl says. "So freaking rude!"

There's still some warm water, I want to screech at her. *Anyway, cold water is good for you. Maybe your skin won't break out all the time if you stop inflaming all your pores.* She's probably one of those girls who watched gleefully as Hayden poked and prodded me that first night of school. I hope she gets athlete's foot.

I squash my tongue between my teeth until it hurts, then reach for the spot between my legs with my melting bar of scratchy coffee soap. There, I scrape hardest. I punish and punish. I think about what these parts were made for and I feel sick again.

I scrape and scrape. The water turns lukewarm. Girls in stalls on both sides let out groans.

"Where'd all the hot water go?"

"Take shorter showers, you vain people."

But I don't care about any of them. I finish up at the crux and work my way down my legs. The water goes from lukewarm to cold. Everybody's bitching and moaning. I put the soap back in my soap box, turn off the cold water, and towel off. I exit the stall like nothing is wrong.

From across a football field, anyone could tell: this girl is rotten.

I had to go back to classes today unless I was willing to visit the nurse and obtain a note (spoiler alert: I'm not). So instead I excuse myself a lot to go to the bathroom, just to escape being close to other people.

Boarding school looks like:
Living inside an ever-shrinking metal box.

I can't escape him anywhere. I hear him laugh in the dining hall, even though he avoids looking at me. The sound of his voice makes bile come up my throat. He hasn't spoken to me once, and I work hard to keep it that way. Every time I see him I fill up with something sour and sharp. But I can't help passing him on my way to class.

I always duck into the crowd, evaporate, disappear.

I hate them—all these vapid, boring creatures happily living out their pointless little lives. I am a satellite revolving around the planet that all the other normal, insipid people inhabit. Going about their useless daily business, unaware of all of the chains holding them down, the fake world they swim inside like feeder fish in an aquarium.

———————————

We have Chemistry in the computer lab this week, because we're making renderings of molecules out of 3D atoms. Thank god. Lectures are the worst—my mind floats away and the memory worms its way forward. The sound of my own strug-gle, his voice saying *Isn't this what you wanted?* clobbers any-thing that might be happening in real life, in front of me.

Hands-on classes, at least, hold my interest longer, despite how little I've been sleeping. I've learned Scully's schedule, so I spend hours awake, obsessing over the best route to class that will avoid even having to see him.

It's harder than you'd think at a boarding school to avoid someone. Everyone is everywhere all the time.

I sit down next to two girls looking at the internet, while the teacher sets up for class in the front of the room. They're giggling about something, scrolling down. It's rude to snoop, but I've got no self-control anymore. I look over at their screen.

For a second I don't believe what I'm seeing. One of the girls covers her mouth as she reads.

We draw in our sketchbooks in the low light most nights, giggling at our renditions of Him. He models a lot for the Drawing Club, so we have tons of material to draw from (so to speak). Usually we sketch Him so His huge pecs stretch out His too-tight shirts.

This can't be real.

I reach over, grab the mouse out of the girl's hand, and close the window. She gasps and spins in her chair toward me.

"What the hell?"

"What? You know how Mrs. Romero is. If she catches you goofing off, we all get a shit grade for today."

They whisper some rude things about me, but keep the window closed and switch over to the assignment. The rest of the lecture, my heart is thundering.

Has that blog gone all around the school by now? It would be so easy to figure out who wrote it.

My hands are shaking when Mrs. Romero gives us the go-ahead to start building our molecule. I shuffle my chair closer to the two girls from before, and they glare at me.

"What were you looking at?" I whisper.

"Aren't we gonna get in trouble?" the first girl says in a mocking voice.

"Did you not hear me?" I ask. "What the fuck were you looking at?"

They both stare at me. I guess that unexpected aggression has bewildered them out of a snarky reply.

"Just some stupid thing we found reblogged on the private school tag," the second girl says defensively. "Chill out. I don't even remember what it was called."

So they didn't get to . . . well, anything else. That's one small good, at least.

Back in my room, I look up the tag the girls mentioned and try to get an idea of how far it's spread.

Only a few notes. Good.

But it should come down before anyone else finds it.

The next day is the last day of school before we're released for winter break. It's been raining nonstop, and the paths and streets run black with mud. I think Gracie wants to get out of here as badly as I do. She doesn't hustle at all at tennis, and she barely responds when I ask her questions about our homework.

People feel farther away than ever before, like Edwards itself is trying to eject me. *You were never welcome here,* it says, covering my pant legs in mud. *Now have you learned your lesson?*

That afternoon, when I get up to close the blinds, I see Gracie staring intently at something on her computer screen. Out of curiosity I peek over to see what she's looking at.

Gray background. White, script-like text.

The blog.

Goosebumps creep down my arms. I can't pretend like it doesn't exist anymore. We have to talk about this.

I sit back down on my side of the desk, my throat tight and tingly.

"Gracie?" I ask.

Her head snaps up from the screen, and she hastily closes the computer.

"Yeah, what's up?" That's probably the friendliest tone she's used since the Mixer.

"Last week . . ." I force down the bile crawling up my throat. "I went to Scully's room. For tutoring."

At the mention of Scully's name, her face changes. Her lips are flat, her eyes staring intently at me.

"He . . ." I want to reach into my own throat and pull the words out, since they won't come on their own. "He made us tea. And then he . . . he pushed me down on the couch and . . ."

"Sam." Her voice is strained. "This happened to you?"

I nod, slowly, and I can't keep my composure any longer. The tears wrench themselves free. Within a few seconds the steady stream becomes a river. My chest is seizing, heaving, as Gracie comes around the desk. I slide out of my chair, onto the floor, and she falls down to her knees next to me. Her arms wrap around me as each sob comes in a lurching gasp. It's as if my body is an exploding star, slowly sucking itself in, until all that's left is a black hole.

All the secrets between us spill out in a flood—every last one. Ugly and wretched, knotted in themselves like steel wool. I still have the bruises, but she doesn't need to see them to know. My sobs are all it takes.

"He's . . . he's . . ." I press my wet eyes against Gracie's shoulder. "He's a fucking monster."

She rubs a circle on my back, not speaking.

"How . . . how did I not . . . know?" I cry. There are so many things I could have done differently. This is all my fault. None of this would have happened if I had just—

"People like him—they're good at hiding it," she says, pulling away from me. Her eyes shimmer with tears, but her face is hard and cool, like stone. "This is Edwards Academy, Sam. You aren't supposed to know. And everyone lets him get away with it."

I wipe my face with my hands. She's right. Scully's House Dad cleared me, no problem. Surely he saw that the door was closed and just didn't care. Maybe he knew exactly what was going to happen that night.

Maybe he let it happen.

I remember how Scully's name was missing from the *Naughty* and *Nice* lists. How I never mentioned it to Gracie.

Maybe Hayden just let it happen, too.

When I look at Gracie now, it's as if the whole shape and color of her has changed. Like the thin screen of glittery, nostalgic sepia tone that covered everything has finally been lifted, and the ugliness underneath is all there is.

Who else has seen the real Edwards Academy? How many other people simply watch, and don't say a word?

Coming clean with Gracie doesn't change things between us as much as I'd hoped. We try to talk, to be friends like before, but our old pattern continues on: pretending like nothing is wrong; pretending like Scully doesn't fill up the air, leaving no space for words. My guilt has consumed whatever we were.

Edwards has gotten inside us. Acting like everything is okay, when really we're stretched like taffy so far that we're about to split in the middle.

Scully's presence hovers, a shadow creature that has sunk its curled claws into us—and holds on.

Gracie can't seem to look at me. I feel angry. Not at her, not even at Scully. Just . . . angry. In a way I've never felt before. Like an ember of coal, just hot enough to stay lit.

I can't believe how unfair it is—that Scully still walks around school, laughing with his friends like everything is fine, and only we suffer. Only we carry this burden on our chests. Only we drown under it.

Thankfully, it's time to go home for Christmas break. Getting away from this place for a while will be good for me. I hope it will be good for Gracie, too, not to have me around her as a reminder of what happened.

When I go to meet my parents at pick-up, I stop in front of the white clock tower, covered in grime from last night's rain. At least, for a few weeks, I won't have to hear that obnoxious thing ringing out on the hour, every hour.

I could hug my parents' station wagon when I see it at the curb and climb in the back.

CHAPTER ELEVEN

http://privateschoolnewb.tumblr.com
Dec. 25, 2017

It's Christmas Day. There's snow on the ground outside. And it's the first Christmas morning of my life that I haven't woken up excited to go downstairs and open my presents.

I hate being awake in general, because then the replay goes on again, nothing to stop it. Even when I watch a movie with my family, I can only absorb it for four or five minutes before it starts up again.

Zzzzzt.

I wonder if my family notices that I'm different. I don't go downstairs much. I have a lot less to say to them. I worry that if I am around them too long, they'll know.

The one thing I am grateful for is that I got my period. Who knows if that slimy meathead gave me something. At least I know this: I am **for sure** not pregnant.

This lets me believe that eventually, everything will be okay again.

Someday.

Winter break is long and dull. I expected to relish having all the hours in the world to study and prepare for finals, but I just obsess over everything. The Mixer. Scully. Gracie. How I could have stopped it all from happening in the first place.

I try to call Gracie, just to see if we can clear the air. Restart again in the new semester.

I need her.

But she doesn't answer. I leave a voicemail. Surely she'll hear it and change her mind by the time we see each other at school again. We will reunite back in our room and throw our arms around each other, now that she's realized how terrible it was being apart for so long without speaking at all.

We'll get through these next three years, because we're doing it together. If I have Gracie, I can hang on, I know it. And we'll get accepted to our dream schools and live in a big college house together. Maids of honor.

Best friends forever. Despite all this. Maybe even because of it. Unbidden, I think of a line from the honor code:

> *Everything worthwhile takes time, work, and sacrifice.*
> *The sacrifices asked of us are often greater than we*
> *expect, but they are what make us true Edwardians.*

Fuck that. Gracie never wanted to be an Edwardian. She never wanted sacrifices. She just wanted to be . . . herself.

The first day back after winter break comes too quickly. I haven't studied nearly as much as I'd meant to. I don't want to go back.

When my parents drop me off on campus, the lawn is cloaked in a thin layer of snow. Everything else—the parking lots, the paths—are slushy and muddy. Everyone walks with hands stuffed in pockets, shoulders hunched over, just trying to stay warm until they get to their rooms.

At the wagon wheel at the center of campus, the statue of Dr. Edwards has icicles hanging from his chin, making him look like an old billy goat. It's like he's looking right at me, saying, *What are you doing back here again, girl?*

I'm the first one to our dorm room.

Except that Gracie's wall is bare. All her sketches, movie artwork, and reprints of Dalí paintings have vanished. The mattress is wrapped in a thin white fitted sheet. No pressed pillows, no shiny laptop.

That's when I notice the note on her desk.

> *I give up.*
> *Everything here . . . It's too much for me.*
> *I can't help you. I'm sorry.*
> *See you sometime.*
> *—Gracie*

I read it four times before crumpling it in my hand.

Gracie was right. It's a game. A rigged game. And it's not without casualties.

I have to do something.

I imagine sitting down at the table with Bex, Lilian, and Eliza. Telling them what Scully did to me. They believe me, just like Gracie did. They have stories of their own, even, about the creepy guys they've encountered here. We share tears and we all hug, together.

What if someone had told me that Scully Chapman was a rapist, before I knew the truth?

"There's no way he would do something like that," I'd have

said. And I would have been absolutely sure of it.

No way will I tell them. With Gracie gone, they're all I've got left at this school.

There must be someone—someone who'd believe me. Someone who doesn't think Scully Chapman is God's gift to Edwards Academy.

Oh.

Waldo doesn't eat in Hamilton Hall—too many peasants. So at lunch I find him in the Juice Bar on the other side of campus, half sitting on a bar stool and half standing up, because his legs are so long that one touches the floor. He's sipping some slushy green stuff when I go up and order a drink.

I walk to the bar and stand behind him. Waldo looks up, and he recognizes me right away. But he shrugs and looks back at his book without speaking. Not even a nod.

I am detritus to him.

"Waldo, right?" I say it like I sort of remember, but maybe wasn't paying attention when it was said. That's his brand of cool kid—aloof, pretending like you don't exist. I can emulate.

His eyes dart up from his book. He nods, then goes back to reading.

My voice drops low so the guy working behind the counter won't hear me. "Do you also make a habit of sexually assaulting women?"

His gaze leaves his book.

"Pardon me?" He puts both feet on the floor so he's actually standing now. He's a foot taller than I am, even while still slouching. I have to tip my head up to keep eye contact.

"Or is it just Chapman?" I say, taking a step closer. I don't know when I became this aggressive, but now it's boiling up inside me, pushing against the limits of my skin. All that silence, all the unfairness, has swelled up into something mean.

"Not this again." Waldo looks me up and down, then lets out an exasperated sigh like it's only reaffirmed his original judgment: I am not particularly noteworthy. "That guy, I swear. And really? With *you?*"

It's a smooth, sharp dart in the chest. I am the size of a child's toy. I have been played with until my little wooden appendages broke off. I know that I'm bedraggled and frizzy-haired and *I Need Improvement*, but I do not deserve this.

"*To* me," I hiss at him. "He did this *to me.*"

Waldo winces.

"Scully—" he starts. "You're not the only one, if that makes you feel better. Scully's been at this game since junior high. I tried to talk him out of it, but . . ." He shrugs. "You know how that ended. Let's just say that he doesn't invite me over anymore."

"You knew?" I am overwhelmed by a hurricane of fury. "You *knew*, and you didn't tell anyone?"

"Like they would believe me?" He snorts. "The Chapmans take from everyone, however they can—even from us. Scully's just like his dad. Does whatever he wants, at anyone's expense. Fuck the maid. Screw the secretary. Mike's trying to push my dad out of the business he helped start, and has everyone convinced *he's* the good guy."

Just like Scully. Everyone thinks he's a saint, but he's a monster wearing a costume.

Waldo lowers his voice so the other people standing around can't hear us. "But it's not you, and it's not me. It's

Scully who's the snake charmer. You don't notice he's singing a song 'til it's too late."

Waldo takes a long, slow sip of his drink, tilting his head as he observes me. My face must make a hundred expressions simultaneously.

"Aw, it's sad," he says. "I'm surprised he did it to you. I thought he liked you. You know, considering . . ." He looks me up and down. "It's you."

I want to take out all my simmering rage on him. Hurl my fist right into his smug face. I could look like a frog and I wouldn't have deserved this.

But now I know there are others. Probably many, many others. Who have been pawns, toys, used and thrown away.

The anger flares, a spark into a bonfire. My whole body is ignited.

Waldo gets up and strides over to the garbage. Then he dumps his cup, half-full, into it and heads to the door. As the bells clang, he calls over his shoulder to me, "Toodles. I hope you have a better second semester than your first."

As I watch him go, I think, *I'm going to fix this.*

Somehow I'm going to get all the wrong off me and make this right.

ACT TWO

CHAPTER TWELVE

SAM

The coffee shop is so normal and adult-looking that I stop short of opening the door. Big windows overlook the busy downtown street, with the café's clever name, Java Jitters, splashed across them in espresso-colored, curlicue lettering. I'm so out of place.

Bells jangle overhead as I finally open the door.

I got Mom to call in permission to the office for me to leave campus today to study downtown. I told her I needed a change of pace to get my head straight for finals.

Java Jitters was the safest place I could think of. Nobody from school would be here. And there was no way I could make up an excuse to go to New York.

One sweep of the coffee shop is all it takes to spot Harper Brooks: a willowy woman with deep brown skin, natural hair pulled back in a blue floral band, wearing a crisp gray pantsuit. She looks just like her picture on *The New York Inspector's* website. She's sitting at a lone table in the very back of the shop, just behind a low wall.

Perfect. Just where I wanted us to sit.

I clutch a rolled-up newspaper, funneling all my anxiety into the crumpled sheets, and approach the table.

"Harper?" I ask.

The woman looks up from her phone and smiles. It's a good smile, comforting and disarming. She's younger than I expected—mid-twenties, as far as I can tell.

"That's me," Harper says, rising and stretching out a hand to me. "You must be Sam. Thanks for being able to meet with me."

I'd rehearsed over and over last night what I was going to say, but now, in the moment, I flub around for a single word.

After a few seconds of silence Harper says, "I'm glad you reached out, you know. I'm interested in your story."

Right. I'm here to tell a story.

To roll the ball toward justice.

I sit down across the table and flatten the newspaper. The headline says:

REPORTED SEXUAL ASSAULTS SOAR ON COLLEGE CAMPUSES

"You found me through my article?" Harper asks, sliding the paper toward herself to get a better look at it.

"Yeah."

She slides it back. "What school do you go to?"

"Edwards Academy," I say. That's when I spot the black recorder in Harper's hand. "Is that on?"

"Not yet." Harper sets the recorder on the table and takes out a notebook. "I won't put anything on the record without your permission."

"Thank you."

"That's my job." She waits for me to say something, but I don't know where to start. So she adds, "It was brave of you to send me that email. If you're ready to start, may I start recording?"

I nod. The recorder switch goes from OFF to ON, and a rock drifts to the bottom of my stomach.

"Can you tell me what happened?" Harper asks, pen poised over her notebook. I guess she takes notes while she's recording.

I take a deep breath. Anything I say now is immortalized. Every last word, in exactly the order that I choose to say it.

I try to remember what I rehearsed.

"I first saw him early in the morning, on the second day of school," I begin. "Doing tai chi in the Morgan Edwards Memorial Graveyard."

HARPER

"The Fourth Year girls do this thing every year to the new kids," Sam says. "They make us strip down. Then they grade us on how we look."

It's been more than an hour now, and Harper's hand is cramping. Not even the email subject line, "I was raped at my private boarding school," could have prepared her for this. The paper gets lots of emails—rarely does one come specifically to Harper's address.

Her first instinct had been to drag it to the trash. Rich white kids assaulting each other at their fancy private boarding school? You don't want to get in the middle of that kind of thing. Slippery and murky as a city river—and way too easy to get stung.

Harper hadn't wanted to take this interview, but she had written that campus rape story last year. And Sam had read it.

So now here she sits, dishing everything Harper had never wanted to know about a private school, like Edwards Saturday Session, House Mom, Cath. It sounds like Hogwarts.

Sam's now talking about some "body survey." She shrinks into herself as she talks about being pinched, poked, prodded, like a science experiment. High school girls can be so cruel where a little belly fat is concerned.

That alone is a story Mark would drool over. Private schools have been fighting to stop degrading hazing rituals for years—a few kids have even died. Harper could leave now with plenty to write about.

"I knew going in I was never gonna fit in," Sam says. "Being a scholarship student."

Harper's pencil stops moving. So she's an outsider. A rich boy victimizing a girl on scholarship—the class angle is easier for her to work with. There are fewer land mines to navigate.

Sam goes back to talking about Scully. From her descriptions, he could very well be the perfect man. A romance novel hero. But Sam is timid, almost ashamed as she talks about him. As if she is saying, *I should have known. I should have known.* She mumbles, like she's not completely sure that what she's saying even deserves to be said—like when she fought with her roommate over Scully at the Mixer.

"The provost didn't mind that he caught you smoking?" Harper asks. What is going on at that school?

"Scully can do whatever he wants," Sam says. She sinks even lower in her chair as she talks about going on a date with him. This girl is so fragile, she's going to crumble. Is there anyone sitting close enough who could hear if Sam started crying? Harper doesn't want to guess at what that would look like.

As Sam describes walking up to Scully's room, the door closing, the tea kettle chirping, her voice trails off. She gets as far as her clothes ripping before she folds in on herself like a star that's given all it's got, just before collapsing into a black hole.

"It's okay," Harper says. "You're doing great."

"Yeah, sure." Sam sits up and tries to go on, to describe exactly what Scully did to her, but she stalls out.

Shoot. As painful and ugly as it must be for Sam to relive this, the story has to have these details. It's what'll get readers right in the chest.

"What made you decide to come to me?" Harper asks, hoping to calm Sam down and come back to it later. "Why not your parents? Or the police?"

Sam's face falls. "Going to the cops would be breaking the Edwards honor code in a huge way."

"You mentioned the honor code earlier. What is it, exactly?"

"It's just like . . . It's a prescription. For how you should act. For how to be a good Edwardian."

"Why would telling the police not make you a 'good Edwardian'?"

"*Keep this community sacred.* The most important line of the honor code. If you have a problem with another student, you're supposed to confront them directly. Work it out, because what's ours is ours. Like 'what happens in Vegas stays in Vegas,' you know?"

"Right," Harper says. "But that line's for adults engaging in consensual, legal debauchery. Not for minors at a boarding school."

Sam shrugs. "If anyone found out I'd gone to the cops . . . it would be social suicide." Sam squeezes her eyes shut, as if the thought of it makes her want to hide.

"If it's supposed to be all within the school, then what about reporting him to the school? There are federal laws in place that require them to take reports like that seriously."

"You mean, report him to the exact same provost who caught him smoking and just let him go?"

She has a point there.

"But that's why you came to me, isn't it?" Harper asks. "If you report it and the school tries to silence you—that would be a big story."

"A big story that I'm at the center of," Sam says. "This isn't about me. I just want people to know about Scully. That's the only way I can protect other girls from him. And if I reported him to the school, it would be all about me."

"Don't you want justice for what he did to you?" Harper asks.

"That would be enough justice for me," Sam says. "If everyone knew."

"Without revealing yourself."

Sam sets her jaw, and her wet eyes turn icy. "You agreed to that in our email," she says.

Oof. That's how she'd read it? All Harper had said was she'd give Sam a pseudonym—anonymity is standard where crimes against minors are concerned.

But Sam's face is stony. She has set out her terms and seems intent on sticking to them.

"What about your parents?" Harper asks. "Have you told them?"

"No. I don't need to drag them through that."

"But what about real justice?" Harper persists. "Somebody like Scully should be in jail. Where he can't hurt anyone anymore."

"I just want people to know the truth."

Harper squeezes the handle of her bag . . . then sighs, and releases it. She won't win this fight right now, not with Sam dead set.

"I'm so sorry this happened to you, Sam," Harper says. "Thank you for sharing this with me. I'll do my best to get your story to the light of day, but I can't guarantee anything."

"Sure," Sam says, but it doesn't look like she's happy about it.

"It'll take me a while to interview witnesses and corroborate your story," Harper says. "So—"

"What? You're going to interview people?" Sam's voice grows panicked. "As soon as you talk to anyone, they're going to know it was me."

"Try not to worry," Harper says. "I'll make up a cover story. I'm good at this, you know. It's my job."

Sam is breathing hard.

"And Waldo already knows, right? Do you think he'll talk to me?"

Sam thinks a moment. "I'm sure he will. He loves attention."

Harper offers her a reassuring smile. "Perfect. Then I'll be in touch to check your quotes with you when I'm done. Okay?"

"Okay," Sam says. They get up, and Harper holds out her hand. Sam takes it and shakes. Her skin is hot. "Whatever it takes."

Harper was able to keep her cool in the coffee shop. But as soon as she leaves, Sam's story hits her square in the face.

Public college campuses, where her last rape story took her, are one thing. But this place—Edwards Academy—is different. That cultish honor code has created a self-regulating community. A lot of wealthy, white people could get very pissed off if it were exposed. There's a big sign on this private school reading TREAD WITH CAUTION.

Once inside her apartment, Harper collapses into one of the two small chairs.

What is she getting into?

Ever since she got that internship at *The Inspector*'s news desk, fetching everyone coffee, she's fantasized about getting a job at a real paper. It kept her waking up at five a.m. after bartending all night, to sit in the junior reporter's chair and monitor the police scanner.

Then she saw a nugget in a university newspaper about an alleged rape on campus, one of many. That was the first time the idea of moving up had rushed hot in her chest and said, *Honey, you're onto something.*

The university had ignored the government's Title IX regulations on how schools should handle sexual assault—and simply buried it instead. Harper saw corruption.

Silencing.

But nobody read the article, so she stayed a junior reporter on the beat nobody else wanted, and her editor still treated her like she spent her nights listening to the scanner.

Someday she'd find her breakthrough story. She just hadn't thought it would be this messy.

Sam hasn't pressed charges. Didn't save evidence. And her rapist's dad works on Wall Street.

Untangling all the little complexities takes Harper the whole drive home, and it only gets bigger and uglier.

First complication: Sam has to tell someone.

Harper can already hear her boss Mark's voice saying, *There's gotta be a court case. People want to see justice.*

She can work on that part. Cities aren't built in a night.

But for now, one foot in front of the other. Transcribe the interview. Make calls, verify details. Write a draft.

Transcribing the interview takes hours. Sam's voice is quiet and restrained, so Harper has to replay some parts two or three times to get it all.

The transcription fills dozens of pages. She stops around three because she needs a change of pace, and she starts searching online for Waldo Wilson. He's her first target for verifying Sam's story—and Scully's history of abuse.

Surprisingly, Waldo doesn't have any profiles anywhere. Weren't teenagers heavy social media users now? Having a prominent parent must make someone keep pretty private.

When words on the screen start to blur, Harper stops searching. After writing up a short pitch for Mark, she sets aside her computer, recorder, and notebook and crawls into bed.

If only Sam had been able to give her a bit more, describe the rape in the same detail as she described her school, or the Mixer, or Scully. The article needs that gruesome detail to hit home, as much as that hurts.

The phone gives a little *ding!* A new email at three in the morning?

TO: Harper Brooks (hbrooks@nyinspector.com)
FROM: Sam Barker (sbterrier@shmail.com)
SUBJECT: Additional materials

I debated a long time about whether to show this to you. But after meeting you, I think you should see.

I started an anonymous Tumblr the day I started at Edwards. I was going to document private school life for people outside. Maybe write some funny, pithy things that would get shared around.

Harper leans forward in bed, bringing her phone screen close to her face. It's as if Sam has been reading her mind.

It was the only place I could get personal and real. No one found it except a few strangers.

Here's the link:

http://privateschoolnewb.tumblr.com.

After a while it became the only place I could really write what I was feeling.

This can't go public. It would be easy to trace back to me. I'm only sending it hoping that it'll make your work easier—so you can publish the story without revealing my identity.

There were some things in here I didn't know how to say to you. I hope this gives you what you need.

Harper clicks through the link.

Page after page of posts, from newest to oldest. The first one drops her in at the worst part—Sam trying to get through life at school after Scully raped her.

Harper goes backward. She reads one where Scully asks Sam, "Isn't this what you wanted?"

Harper's whole body contracts, drawing away from the glowing screen. She feels a phantom ache in her stomach as she reads.

It's almost dawn when Harper reaches the old Sam, way back at the beginning, who was so eager to start at her new school. Who was bright, shining, optimistic.

Harper swallows back a lump in her throat. She makes a few notes to herself of new details. There's so much Sam never said out loud in the interview—how she and her roommate were both artists. The girls who got caught smoking pot, but no one outside Isabel House found out.

That's how the honor code demands their silence. *What happens in Vegas stays in Vegas.*

This is one of those stories you have to carry out perfectly, with exacting precision. If only she was covering college basketball instead.

CHAPTER THIRTEEN

HARPER

Harper's not surprised when she gets into the office and finds a note on her desk from her editor, Mark.

"Sit down, sit down," he says in his usual too-loud way when she enters his office. He gestures four times at the open chair.

"Good morning to you, too," says Harper, dropping into the chair.

"I read your pitch."

"I figured—"

"Michael Chapman's son, huh." Mark doesn't say it like a question, though it is. He spins halfway around so he's facing his computer.

"Do you know that Mike Chapman is worth $4.5 billion?" Mark asks. Before Harper can answer, he says, "I do. Because I looked him up. Did you look him up?"

Mark's a good editor: He catches her mistakes; he pushes her to push her sources; he backed her up when the university story got some blowback. But it's like pressing tiny wood stakes under her fingernails when he starts to talk to her like she's a small, unintelligent child.

"No," says Harper. "I thought the article was about Scully, not Mike."

"Of course it's about Mike. If you write this, the way you're framing it—'Rich Private School Boys Take Whatever They Want, No Apologies' is what this headline should read—it will definitely be about Mike. It'll be about every rich daddy who sends his kid to Edwards Academy, and they'll come out for our blood."

"So, do you want me to drop it?" she asks, almost hoping he'll say yes. She could do a hot think piece about her three days using Tinder in Brooklyn instead.

"You have other sources to confirm the girl's story?" Mark says.

"Working on it."

"If you can corroborate the big stuff," he says, "then I think it could be a bombshell story. But."

The word *but* stands between them like a brick wall.

"She has to press charges and try justice before we run this," he says.

Duh. "I know," Harper starts. "But she doesn't—"

"I'm just as inclined as any editor to want to jump on a good story," he says. "But this isn't just rape; it's statutory. The DA might press charges. The school will have something to say about this whole hazing allegation." He waggles a finger at her. "We'll be right at the center of the crossfire if we push out this story too soon, before the wheels of justice can start moving. You know, CYA."

Yes, she knows. *Cover Your Ass.*

Harper simmers while she thinks of what to say next. It's not that simple. Except Mark doesn't leave her room even to speak. "Talk to this girl and get her to come forward—to the

156

school or the DA. That trial is the story."

Harper can see what he's thinking already—the court theater, a school in uproar. A scandal that they can run with for weeks. It's a thin shot considering how rarely the DA takes on rape cases, but covering a controversial court case is the kind of thing that wins Pulitzers.

"Court or not, it still revolves around Scully Chapman," Harper says. "A story doesn't exist without outing him as the rapist."

"Is he eighteen?" Mark asks. Before she can reply, he says, "Find out. If you do this the smart way, the negative publicity could help put this guy away. Like you want." She never said that was what she wanted, but he's not wrong.

Mark points to the door, effectively dismissing her. Harper knows her way out.

"One more thing," he calls after her. Harper leans back into the office. "Don't be afraid to walk away if you need to, if something feels off. You're on the hook if anything goes wrong."

As if she'd stick around in this viper pit—but she says nothing. Then he waves her off, and Harper hurries back to her desk, eager to escape from the weight of Mark's condescension.

Harper pulls up her transcription, looking for some way she can convince Sam that it's in her best interest to reach out to the police. To tell her parents.

"Yeah," Harper mutters to herself, thinking of Sam's blog, where the last few entries read like broken glass held together with Scotch tape. "Like that'll happen."

SAM

I'm holed up in the library, breathing the same recycled air as the dozen other kids sitting at our huge table. I'm covered in sweat. I have never been so nervous about anything in my life.

Not my upcoming exam. That interview. Telling that reporter everything yesterday . . . I still can't believe I sent her the blog link. I couldn't hit the button until three or four in the morning, when I was so tired that it didn't mean anything anymore. Now every one of my nerves is pulled tight as a guitar string, ready for whatever happens next.

The other kids go over discussion questions and quiz each other on dates, but it flows over me like white noise.

When will this explode? I got scared when Harper said she'd call people from school. The blog was risky enough, but a reporter asking around about what I said, even if she doesn't mention my name . . . if she asks the wrong questions, someone will connect the dots.

What then? Will people who saw me at the Mixer with Scully, or spotted us together at the Roast, believe me? They might say they're my friends, but we're all Edwardians first. And Scully is our King.

But if this goes public in a newspaper, the school will have to act. If they want to preserve their image, they'll have to kick Scully out, won't they? Edwards can't afford the bad publicity. And without Scully hanging between us anymore, Gracie will definitely come back to school. It might be hard for me here for a few months, but Scully's reputation will be destroyed. The public schools will deny him, and his daddy will have to hire a private tutor.

Hot, silvery vengeance shoots through me, coating me in a protective layer of Kevlar. I can take on anyone, endure anything, while I wear this.

Maybe I *should* bring an official complaint—whatever Harper called it. But then it might just stay inside Edwards, and Scully would just go on to college to find other victims.

Harper's got to back down from this "going to the cops" thing. Maybe it'll be enough that she talks to a couple people, verifies the details, feels confident that I'm telling the truth. She believes in justice, too. I can tell.

We could be a pair of avenging angels.

My computer, where I've been taking notes and writing essay answers, lets out a bonk. A new email.

It's from Harper.

I go to the bathroom and open it on my phone so no one can read it over my shoulder.

TO: Sam Barker (sbterrier@shmail.com)
FROM: Harper Brooks (hbrooks@nyinspector.com)
SUBJECT: Moving forward with your story

Sam,

Hope you're doing well. Thank you for sharing your story with me, and your very personal blog. I know how hard it was for you to share it, but it will help me flesh out the details and sell this story to my editor.

I need your help contacting a few individuals you mentioned in our interview to corroborate some details, such as Waldo Wilson. Can you provide me with his school email address, or a phone number?

Also, was S.C. under eighteen, or over eighteen, when it happened?

I know you want this to run in order to protect other women—I share this goal with you. But what would really inspire so many girls is if you came forward. Of course I'll keep you anonymous, and the police will protect your identity as a victim.

I have to let you know that the paper can't run the piece unless you've taken this step. I know you have reservations, but this is our best and only way forward to justice.

I'll be safeguarding all the information you gave me like my life depends on it.

Best,
Harper Brooks

When I've finished reading the email, my breath comes fast. I push down the fury working its way up to the top like lava.

She never mentioned all this stuff about the police in her first email. I've watched plenty of *Law & Order* with Mom—regular girl versus wealthy Wall Street mogul? The court case will be drawn-out and painful.

No. It can't go like this. I need to get my hands back on the wheel of this car.

I leave the bathroom and ponder Harper's email for a good hour. Back in my dorm room, I start typing up a reply.

TO: Harper Brooks (hbrooks@nyinspector.com)
FROM: Sam Barker (sbterrier@shmail.com)
SUBJECT: RE: Moving forward with your story

I've thought long and hard about this answer. I promise, I really have.

Even if I did go to the cops, the case won't go anywhere— you know that. They never do. It's my word against his. Words, words, words. I can't do that to my family.

And by the way, Scully is eighteen. That's why going to the cops is such a terrible idea. It'll blow up in my face if they can try him as an adult.

I don't want to bring someone like Mike Chapman down on me and my family because I ruined his son's life.

HARPER

Harper's on her way to meet some friends at the corner bar when her phone dings. She yanks it out and sucks in a breath when she sees who sent the new email.

Its contents are pretty much what she expected.

... *ruined his son's life.*

What about the way *his son* ruined *Sam's* life?

Chapman can keep people quiet before they even open their mouths.

Harper growls to herself and shoves the phone back in her pocket. That silencing tactic should be enough reason for Mark to publish this story.

Isn't that the point of journalism? To dig up the illegal stuff that people are trying to hide?

SAM

I jolt upright out of reflex, and it startles me awake. I straighten my shoulders and rub my eyes with one fist.

I've been doing this all night—falling asleep without realizing it, then all the caffeine kicks in again and I jump awake. The text on the printed study packet bleeds like someone spilled water on it. I shake my head and start reading the paragraph over from the beginning. It's so hard to pay attention in this quiet, empty room that used to belong to me and Gracie: where she'd sit and eat Twizzlers while reading in her textbook; where we'd watch stupid TV shows on her computer when we were done with our homework, bundled up in all our blankets.

Now I'm a stranger in this room with its whitewashed brick walls and brown, Scotchgard-sprayed carpet.

The day we all got back to school, Jean came to tell me that Gracie wasn't returning. I hid her note.

"The whole room is yours until summer," Jean had said.

When I asked her why Gracie wasn't coming back, Jean confessed that she didn't know. But she didn't seem too concerned.

How come I'm the only one who's worried about Gracie?

I've called a dozen times, but she never answers. I also write her emails.

> Please come back. I miss you.
> I'm sorry. I'm sorry about everything.
> I can't be here alone.
> Please answer me. I don't want to do this by myself.
> Gracie?
>
> Gracie, please write back.

What if something bad has happened? Maybe someone is watching her, keeping tabs on her, and that's why she doesn't return my calls or emails. What if Scully is intentionally trying to keep us apart? To keep me vulnerable? I know it sounds paranoid, but I can't help it. The only remnant of her I have left is an old sketchbook of hers that must have fallen under her bed when she moved out.

My phone rings, and I almost fall backward in my chair. When I check the screen, the number has a New York City area code. Harper.

"Hello?" I say.

"How are you?" Harper asks, sounding upbeat and friendly.

I don't respond, because the answer right now would be too long.

"I wanted to talk to you about your email yesterday," Harper continues, despite my silence. "I want you to know that I hear your concerns about coming forward."

I bite my lip. I know what's coming.

"But I absolutely can't write the story without you telling some authority figure," Harper says. "Try the school grievance system first. Under Title IX sexual assault laws, they're not allowed to retaliate."

"I don't give a shit about Title Whatever," I whisper into the phone. No—she needs to think that the article is the only way forward. "Mike Chapman is Edwards Academy's biggest donor. They wouldn't punish his son, no matter what."

"Then go to the police," says Harper.

"Who has more money for lawyers?" I ask. "Scully, or me?"

"You don't need a lawyer," Harper says. "The district attorney would take the case. That's their job."

"I'm still sure he has better lawyers."

"Sam." I hear her take a deep breath. "Scully can't buy his innocence. He thinks he can—that's why he keeps doing this. Because people let him get away with it."

"That's why I contacted you in the first place," I say, frustrated that she can't see the obvious. "So he won't keep getting away with it."

"We have to give the justice system a chance to work before we can call it out for not working."

"No." My voice is hard and unyielding, as I'd hoped. I'm not letting Harper think she can change my mind about this. "You said all you needed to publish my story was to corroborate some details," I say. "So call Waldo. Get what you need. And write it like you promised."

"I'm really sorry you read my email as a promise," Harper says. "I didn't mean to get your hopes up."

Right. Whatever.

"I wish I could change it," Harper says to my resolute silence. "But my editor won't back this story unless—"

"Fine," I say between my teeth. "Throw me under the bus. Forget about me."

Just like everyone else will. Like Scully already has.

"I don't want to do that. Of course I have reservations, but I'm only suggesting you do this because people need to know. I believe Scully should be held accountable."

"No, you don't." She doesn't want it as much as I do. She just wants me to parade around in front of a judge or a jury because it will make a good story for her.

"Yes," snaps Harper, "I do."

"If it means so much to you, you should be willing to go to bat for it!" I could break this phone in my hand. Smash it against the desk. That'd get my message across.

"I *have* gone to bat for it!" Harper's voice roars in my ear. "I drove out to interview you, read your blog, advocated to my editor for you. Because I want *The Inspector* to stand up to that guy."

"Then all you need to do is write the article."

"I have limitations, Sam. And you know what, I do want him put away. That's what's right."

Harper breathes hard on the other end of the line. But it doesn't matter how much she argues. I need this to happen my way.

"I can't do it," I tell her. "But I'll get you Waldo's phone number."

I press the END button on my phone, my heart going wild inside my chest. I've never talked to an adult like that before. But something inside me started speaking that I've never heard speak before—something that wasn't going to accept the bullshit any longer.

CHAPTER FOURTEEN

HARPER

Harper puts her phone down on her kitchen table, only barely managing not to slam it.

Fine. No point waiting for Sam to come around. The sooner this is done, the sooner Harper can get back to writing less stressful stories, like that profile of the old ladies in Jersey who have played bingo together for twenty years.

It's easy to find Sam's father on LinkedIn. Darryl Barker's a banker, and balding, from the looks of his picture. Forty-five—maybe fifty. Sam has his nose and stubborn, petulant pout.

Harper takes down the name of his company and looks up the office number.

When she gets to work the next morning, Harper calls.

"Castlewood Mortgage," answers a man who sounds like he's probably writing an email while he talks. "This is Darryl Barker."

"Hello, Mr. Barker?"

"Can I help you?" he asks in an easygoing tone, like he's not too concerned about his fading hairline. "If it's about our new low-APR refinancing program . . ."

"No, no. My name is Harper Brooks, with *The New York Inspector.*"

"*The . . . Inspector?*" he asks, dropping the salesman act. "What can I help you with, Ms. Brooks?"

"I'm calling about your daughter, Samantha. Do you have a moment?"

Harper hears him suck in a breath.

"Sam?" he asks. "Why? What's going on?"

"Sam asked me to meet with her a few days ago about something that happened at Edwards."

His voice takes a sharp edge. "What's happened to my daughter? If this is some kind of prank, lady—" His voice rises.

"It's not, I promise you. If you don't believe me, look me up. You can find most of my bylines online."

"What's your name again?"

"Brooks. Harper Brooks."

She hears a mouse click, then some typing. A scroll wheel whirs.

"You do a lot of student stories," he says, not as a question. Like he hopes that's what this is about.

"Yes," she says. "I'm working to shed light on the rise in reported campus sexual assaults."

"Sam," he whispers. Then his tone turns businesslike. "Tell me what this is about."

"Mr. Barker," Harper says, "it was an incredibly difficult decision for me to breach Sam's confidence like this. But she's only fifteen, and—"

"Tell me what happened!" His voice ratchets up, making the line crackle.

Harper takes a deep breath. "Sam alleges that she was raped. By a boy at her school."

On the other end, she hears labored breathing.

"How do you know this?" he says, his voice a growl. "And why didn't I know first?"

"She wanted to tell you, I know she did. She's just terrified of the consequences if the person in question seeks retaliation. He's a big shot at her school. That's why she came to me—"

"Who?" he demands. "Who did this?"

"Let me explain something first," says Harper. "Sam has no physical evidence. Her word against his. And this boy's dad is incredibly well connected. She was afraid of—"

"Who. Was. It."

"She alleges that it was a Fourth Year boy named Scully Chapman."

"A senior." His voice is the voice of the Grim Reaper. "That's who did this to her? You're sure?"

"That's what she told me in the interview."

"Interview?"

"Sam reached out to me because she wants me to write a story for *The Inspector*," Harper says slowly. "She wants to get her story out there without having to come forward herself and risk . . . well, everything."

There's a huffing on the other end of the line, like he's starting to cry. A middle-aged man is crying over her phone. This is just getting messier with each passing minute.

"What did I do to make her think she couldn't tell me?" Mr. Barker says between breaths. "W-where did I go wrong?"

"You didn't do anything wrong, Mr. Barker. She didn't want to involve you and she doesn't want to violate that school's ridiculous honor code by coming forward. She's scared to tell anyone about it."

"That thing? I remember thinking what a good idea that was when we read the brochures—like just the sort of education I wanted my daughter to get. Honor, respect, integrity . . ."

He dissolves on the other end. Harper stays quiet while he puts himself back together.

"Thank you for calling me," Mr. Barker says suddenly, his voice clipped and ragged but trying to sound firm. "You're running a story on this? On a fifteen-year-old girl without asking her parents' consent?"

"Mr. Barker," Harper says, "I'm calling you. Right now. And I think it's a good time to get the police involved, or the school, at least. I don't want to tell you what to do, Mr. Barker, but a criminal charge would force Edwards to act."

"Sam . . ." His voice collapses. "My baby . . . How could anyone . . . ?"

"I'm sorry."

He clears his throat. "Sam's mother and I have a lot to talk about before I can give you any kind of answer," he says, his tone suddenly hard.

"Mr. Barker—"

"We'll be in touch," he says, and the line goes dead.

Harper's hands are shaking as she hangs up. She knew she'd gone against Sam's wishes. Broken confidence. But if she'd done nothing, the silence would have lingered forever.

SAM

I'm trying to cram as much American Government into my brain as I can when Jean's three-tap signature knock comes at my door. My heart flings itself into my throat. She never comes to talk to me unless she has a reason.

What could she want?

"Sam?" Jean says when I open it. "Your dad is here to pick you up. Why didn't you tell me you were leaving campus?"

My throat closes up. "My dad?" I squeak out.

"He signed you out for the weekend and is waiting downstairs. Something going on? Normally we don't let students just go whenever they want, but he made it sound like there was some family emergency . . ."

"I don't know why he's here," I say. "Sorry."

"Not your fault. Pack up, and I'll tell him you're coming down."

———————————

Dad shoots up from his chair in the lounge the moment I appear, duffel bag over my shoulder. His eyes are red, his face even more. He rushes to my side and takes the bag, only then pausing to wrap his arms around me.

Gently, I push him away.

"Hi, Dad."

"Hi, baby."

Oh, no. He never calls me that anymore.

He leads me by the hand the whole way out of the building and to the car. I don't even take it back because I don't want to upset the balance. I'm eight years old again, and I've just gotten in trouble in class.

Dad tosses my bag in the back seat as I climb in the passenger side, my hands trembling.

Once we're inside the car, Dad suddenly begins to . . . sob.

"Dad?" I ask, hearing the horror in my own voice. He's only cried in front of me one other time, when Grandma passed away. "Dad, what is it?"

"I'm sorry," he says, rubbing his eyes with his closed fists. "I'm so sorry, Sam, that I let this happen to you."

Happen to me. So he knows. Harper must have told him.

He reaches across the center console and wraps his arms around me, tugging me awkwardly over the emergency brake. It digs into my hip bone.

He didn't do anything. Why would he think he caused this? What exactly did Harper say?

"Dad . . ." I awkwardly pat the back of his head and he lets me go, wiping his eyes. "It wasn't your fault—"

"I pushed you to go to Edwards," he says. "I'm the one who made it so important that you seize the opportunity, get a free pass into a great college. I didn't think about—"

"*I* chose to go," I say. He's sure taking a lot of responsibility for choices that were purely mine. "*I'm* the one who went with Scully up to—"

"Sam!" He grips the steering wheel. "I'm concerned by how calm you are."

Of course I'm calm. I've had weeks—almost a whole month now—to stop freaking out about it.

"Dad," I say, exhaustion settling over me, "it's been a long semester. And I'm kind of right in the middle of finals, by the way."

"I'm taking you home."

"What? Why?"

"I'm not letting you within five hundred yards of that guy again until he's behind bars."

This is not at all how this was supposed to go.

171

"Dad, you can't. Finals are—"

"Yes, I can!" My dad is not the kind of guy to have a temper—that's Mom's forte. But he's angrier now than I have ever seen him.

We are spinning out of orbit, and I'm hanging on by one finger. "But then what was the point of it all?" I ask, pushing tears down. "I've worked so hard. I busted my ass all semester to get good grades. And you're just going to force me to quit?"

His shoulders hunch toward the steering wheel.

"Sam," he starts, "do you really want to stay at Edwards after what happened?"

"I've worked so much," I say. "How can I throw it all away? There goes my chance of getting into Harvard, of getting that lawyer job I've always wanted."

Dad stares at me, the whites of his eyes spidered with red. Finally, he says, "I'm going to tell your mom that I think we should press charges."

I bring my knees up onto the seat. "I wish you wouldn't."

"Sorry."

"It's going to make my life at school even harder."

"Then don't go back."

We're going in a circle. But I need him to understand what finishing at Edwards means to me.

Dad beats me to it. "It's brave of you, but Mom won't like it."

"Have you told her?"

"No. I wanted her to hear it from you first. But I know your mom will agree with me."

Once Mom has set her mind on something, there's no changing it.

I nod. "Do I really have to come home for the next few days? I have this group project due, and study groups for finals."

Dad tilts his head, studying me. Then he turns back to the windshield.

"We're going home for tonight," he says. "We'll have a talk with your mom and decide together. Then we'll see."

The clock on the wall of the police station reads eight thirty. Long past dinner. Mom had made a roast for my unexpected return home, but as soon as I told her about Scully Chapman, she turned the oven off and left the roast in it while she hurried us all to the police station.

Now my empty guts are grinding and growling. I am stretched so tight and thin, any small thing could break me.

"Mom, can't we get some Wendy's while we wait?" I ask her. "I'm starved."

Mom shoots me a demon look. I had anticipated some waterworks, *sorrys*, hugs. Instead, Mom is pure fury. And it has not melted off at all in the last hour and a half.

"Why didn't you tell us?" she'd demanded. "I can't believe this!"

No crying, just anger. Within seconds Mom had gotten up out of her chair, grabbed her purse, and said, "We're going to the police station. Now."

I didn't understand why it had to be *now*. It had happened a month ago, and it's not like I'm pregnant or something, so why couldn't it wait until tomorrow?

But Mom's in action mode.

A young cop talks with an older one behind the desk as the three of us wait in the precinct office. I made it clear to them when we first arrived that I didn't want to be here, but Mom quickly shut me up.

Soon the cop comes for us—but not me. Only my parents. The three of them disappear into a back room.

Because I wouldn't cooperate, they're cutting me out.

I fiddle with my phone, ignoring the small pile of text messages that have accumulated since I left school, asking me why I'm missing this or that.

My chest burns the longer I think about how people at school will react when this all comes out—that is, if Mom and Dad let me go back. The place where my panic lives is aching and raw, as if someone has drilled a hole through me and the open wound drips out.

Eventually Mom, Dad, and the cop return.

"It'll be up to the DA's assistant to press charges, but we'll present the case to her," the cop says to my parents. He crouches down in front of me like I'm a little kid and looks right in my eyes. "It'll be a lot easier with your help, Samantha."

"It's Sam," I snap.

"Sam," the cop amends. "Will you talk to us? We have an expert coming to interview to you. She handles a lot of cases like yours."

I don't bother saying no, because it's clear I don't have a choice. Just adults doing adult things. Refusing to listen. Going over my head.

Thanks, Harper.

The "expert" arrives a half hour later, and I still haven't eaten. She appears at the reception desk in a green cowl-neck tucked into black pants, cinched by a big black belt, her blonde hair pulled to one side with a tiny barrette. Her name tag reads MELISSA. She meets with my parents in another room, leaving me alone, again. Then she returns with a muted, soothing smile.

She introduces herself to me, saying, "I'm a victim advocate for Castlewood PD." She looks me over. "You look hungry. Are you hungry? Should I order something for us?"

"Order what?" Mom asks before I can answer.

Melissa doesn't even look at her as she asks me, "Do you like Chinese food?" Then she takes out her phone.

"Uh, I guess so." I haven't had takeout in weeks, maybe months.

"I'll place an order."

She makes a quick call, orders some chicken, noodles, beef, and rice, and then leads me into a separate room. The walls are cinder block and gray. It feels like an interrogation room, with a giant mirror on one wall that's obviously two-way. She notices me staring at it.

"Are my parents over there?" I ask.

"No," she says. "Just a detective." She takes out a notebook and sets up a recorder. "I want to hear it all, Sam," she says. "From the beginning."

I clench my lips and slide deeper into my chair, as if I could just spill right into the drain tile in the floor and disappear.

"I heard you didn't support this move to press charges," Melissa says. "And I respect that. It's incredibly difficult to confront the idea that someone has done something so wrong to us that the police need to get involved. But they do. What this boy did to you is not only morally reprehensible, it's illegal."

This all feels like a nightmare, the kind where you try to run and your legs are gelatin, where you speak but your words come out muddled and wrong, and no one listens or cares about what you want. But I know that my only way out of this room is to talk.

"He's just a guy I go to school with," I begin.

———————

The food arrives right before I get to the really bad stuff, and we take a breather long enough for me to inhale an entire order of orange chicken. Melissa's all right. Even though her barrette's super-dorky, she seems like the kind of person who took this job because she cares.

As I talk, I can feel his hands again, squeezing my flesh the same way Hayden did that first day of school. The *sshhht* as fragile underwear tear.

I can't stop before I get to the gruesome part the way I did in my interview with Harper. I have to go where the blog goes. And as I talk about how he said *Isn't this what you wanted?*, I can feel the claustrophobic fear surge inside me again.

I force myself to describe how he penetrated. I can almost feel the scathing fire spidering across my body. The faceless creature over it, pumping like a robot, the foul sound of its monstrous grunts.

By the time the story is all out, I am empty. It must be midnight by now. My eyes and face ache. I want to go to bed and never have to wake up.

"Can we be done?" I ask. "I need to be done."

"Sure," says Melissa. She stands up and goes to the door, where Mom and Dad are waiting, and invites them back in. Their eyes are rimmed with red as they sit down next to me. Seeing my tired face, Dad wraps me up in a hug.

"Before we call it a night, I just need to know if you still have anything from that night." Melissa says. "Like what you were wearing when you went out?"

Mom gasps. "What do Sam's clothes have to do with this?"

Melissa shakes her head. "That's not what I mean to imply. I'm asking if there's any physical evidence Sam can provide—something that Scully might have touched on the night it happened. There's not much for us to go on besides your testimony."

"You mean, it's all circumstantial," Mom says, using whatever she's acquired from binge-watching *Law & Order.* She always acts like a know-it-all when she has no clue.

"Um, sure," says Melissa. "It's Sam's word against his."

"Right." Mom glances at me. "So what were you wearing, Sam?"

"A shirt, skirt, and leggings," I say. The blue shirt and black, high-waisted skirt, my favorite black leggings, and matching blue shoes.

"Where are they?" asks Melissa.

"I threw them away."

It hangs there for a second. *Threw them away.*

"Why?" asks Melissa.

"Because they were all ripped up."

Mom goes stiff. She turns wide, disbelieving eyes on me, as if this is the first time she's understood that I was raped.

"Ripped?" she repeats, her voice hoarse.

"I didn't want anyone to ask questions, and I was never going to wear them again, so I threw them away." I also never, ever wanted to see them again and have to remember what happened.

Mom's eyes are glossy. She blinks them rapidly, turning her head away, then back. Suddenly she flings her arms around me.

"Oh, Samantha!"

She starts to cry.

It comes in slow, gentle waves at first, just her hands gripping my arms, but then it grows into a storm. She's sobbing, repeating, "Samantha. Oh, Samantha. My Samantha."

I wrap my arms around the woman who has suddenly become small, the same size as me. Or have we been the same size for a while now and Mom just always seemed bigger before?

"I'm sorry," she says between gasping breaths. "I'm so sorry."

After a time Mom sits up, wiping her eyes with her sleeve. I have wet splotches on my shirt in the shape of her face. I don't want to let her go.

"The next thing you should do, Sam," says Melissa, leaning forward over the table, "is report this to the school. Take it through the Title IX complaint procedure. The government requires every school to have one for students in your position. I can walk you through it. It's important that Edwards investigate how this could happen on their watch. It's a boarding school—they're tasked with protecting you 24/7. Whatever they find will be critical to our investigation."

Melissa looks at me expectantly, waiting for an answer. If she wants an agreement, she should have asked Mom. I don't need this right in the middle of finals.

"And I want to get you in to see our assault counselor," Melissa adds. "Then we're going to set up a call between you and Scully, and see if we can get him to admit anything. This is a routine tactic we use to try to coax him into an admission."

What? Like . . . a setup? As if anyone would be stupid enough to admit guilt over the phone. Dread fills my ears like water.

"He'd be suspicious right away," I say. "I haven't tried to contact him since—"

"Don't worry." Melissa gives me a reassuring smile. I am not reassured. "I'll help you prepare. We'll come up with a good reason why you've called. There are people here on staff who do this for a living."

"Fine," I say. I'm done with all this. All I want is to climb into my bed and pass out forever. "Now can I go home?"

Melissa glances at my mom. "I think you all could use some rest. We'll be in touch with you to organize the call."

As we leave the precinct, Mom slips on my jacket for me, as if I'm a toddler again. Then, like I'm a tiny baby bird she's rescued and has to feed every two hours, she even opens the car door for me.

On the drive back home, I am almost asleep in the back seat when I hear Mom talking about how she's going to have to enroll me in the public high school.

"She really wants to go back to Edwards," Dad says quietly. "She doesn't want this to get in the way of her Harvard Law dream."

"She's not safe there, Darryl."

"Melissa says if we file that complaint with the school, they'll issue a No Contact order. She won't have to see him."

"Yeah, sure, if they do what they're supposed to," Mom says bitterly.

"We have to trust Sam. If she thinks she can handle going back, let her try. And she can come home if she can't handle it anymore. We don't want it to seem like we're punishing her."

I open one eye and catch Mom slowly nodding her head.

"Fine. But I get to pull her out if things get too bad. Okay?"

"All right."

CHAPTER FIFTEEN

HARPER

Sam could react a million different ways, and none of them good.

She probably felt betrayed. Definitely pissed. Maybe she won't even talk to Harper again.

No use obsessing. For now it's expedient to act like everything is moving forward.

Harper digs up the phone number for Sam's House Mother, Jean DuBois, on a school webpage. Jean should have something useful to say. After four rings, a woman answers the phone breathlessly.

"Hello? Who's this?"

"Hello. Harper Brooks, from *The New York Inspector*. How are you this evening?"

"Busy," Jean says in a clipped voice. "Trying to get fifty girls sorted for the night."

"I'll make it fast, then. I'm researching an article about Edwards Academy—'a scholarship student finding her place in private school.' My subject is Sam Barker, who I believe is one of your students? A glowing quote from you would cast Edwards in a good light."

"I'll have to run it past the provost first." Suddenly the speaker is muffled and Harper hears Jean yelling, "Molly! Why are you running in the hall?"

"I only need to confirm a few details," Harper says when Jean comes back on the line. "We can do it right now over the phone so you don't have to spend any more time on me."

"All right. Real quick."

"Sam and I have talked at length about how difficult Edwards is academically," Harper says. "She's expressed to me that she struggles a lot in school, and I just want to confirm this with a faculty member before it goes in the article."

Jean clams up.

"I can't share anything like that," she finally says. "Sam is absolutely a great student. Her teachers have no complaints. And that's all I'll say to you."

The phone bleeps. Harper blinks down at the screen. Jean hung up.

A great student? That doesn't jive with what Harper has gathered from the Tumblr blog—she'd seemed to be really struggling. Worried about her grades.

Not a big deal. Who hasn't misrepresented themselves a little in a diary to make their drama even more . . . dramatic? Especially for an online audience.

Harper searches for contact information for everyone else she'll need to interview—Hayden, Bex, Scully's House Dad. Waldo Wilson. Most of them are high school students, so finding phone numbers for them online will be difficult without Sam's help.

And if the honor code is as pervasive as Sam says, will they be willing to share anything?

So Harper tackles her ever-evolving draft of the article

instead. It's nearly one in the morning when an email pops up.

TO: Harper Brooks (hbrooks@nyinspector.com)
FROM: Sam Barker (sbterrier@shmail.com)
SUBJECT: No Subject

I spent my whole night at the precinct. And by the way, my parents okayed your story.

That's all it says.

She doesn't sound as mad as Harper had expected. Not even on the same spectrum as mad.

So Sam isn't going to cut her off from the story. Not at all, actually.

Harper writes back immediately so Sam doesn't have time to change her mind.

I'm really sorry. I just wanted to protect you.
Can I make it up to you? A coffee at Java Jitters? Maybe I could meet your mom, make sure we're all on the same page?

The reply comes in less than a minute:

Mom doesn't need to know. This is between us. You'll have to come to school, and we'll meet at the Juice Bar.
Your treat.

Harper reads the message twice and lets out a breath. She got off the hook easy. Maybe after meeting with the police, Sam understood Harper's reasons?

She calls up Mark's office number and leaves a voicemail explaining that she won't be in tomorrow because she has to follow up on her story in person.

SAM

The drive back to campus makes me late to class, but it doesn't matter anyway. Mom's already excused me so we can go to Provost Portsmouth's office together.

The entire walk there I'm sweating, even though it's below freezing. People stare at me as I go by with my mom holding my hand. Why are my parents suddenly so into hand-holding? But I feel too guilty about everything to take it back.

Melissa thinks it will help for Edwards to conduct an independent investigation. They may learn things the police can't.

Yeah, right. As if Provost Portsmouth will help them. I've seen fliers for the big annual auction all over school—the one where I've heard Mike Chapman donates a few hundred thousand dollars every year. Edwards Academy needs him.

We reach the administrative office and Mom asks the receptionist for the Title IX paperwork. It's tedious to fill out. I have to write everything that happened, and then we deliver it the provost's office.

Mom doesn't even check in with his receptionist. She walks right in the door.

"Let me do the talking," she says.

Provost Portsmouth glances up from his computer when we enter. He looks like he vaguely remembers me. Maybe from that day at the polo game, when Scully grabbed my hand.

Mom hands him the forms we've filled out.

"Mr. Portsmouth," she says, "we pay a lot for Sam to go here. We trusted your school's reputation. And then your faculty let this happen?"

"Pardon me?" he says, eyebrows drawing in confusion. He skims the document. As he reads, his face grows paler and paler.

"This . . ." He stutters for a second. "But, Scully is a good student—"

"That's what you've got to say?" Mom snaps instantly, like a cobra. "You're going to defend him?"

"N-no, I mean . . ." The provost has to stop and close his eyes for a moment before he can respond. "I wish I'd been told about this before you went to the police."

"Why, so you could stop us?" Mom asks.

The provost seems so pathetic over there, sweating in his chair. Trying to please an angry parent and not incriminate the school at the same time. I wish I could laugh at him.

"We would have addressed it internally," he says, with patience, "then sought a resolution that suited everyone—without all the publicity."

"Sam's House Mom left an entire dorm of students alone together for this 'body survey,'" Mom says, crossing her arms. "You and your faculty have completely failed to keep my child safe. Why should I trust you to handle anything?"

"Mrs. Barker, I know this is easy to say in hindsight, but perhaps if your daughter had *told* us about this . . ." He swallows. ". . . this body survey months ago, when it happened, we could have—"

Mom looks like she is about to explode. I push past her before she can burst, and put my hand on the provost's desk.

"So, what?" I say. "It's my job to report my own House

Mother hanging me out to dry? The person who can give me a demerit for talking back?"

Provost Portsmouth's mouth flaps, but Mom interrupts him. "Maybe this 'publicity' you're so afraid of is what it will take to make a change around here," she says, giving me an approving nod. "We expect to see you fully cooperate."

The provost's face slackens. Control over this situation is slipping through his fingers like water.

"Of course we'll cooperate," he says, sinking back into his chair.

I was certain that Provost Portsmouth would try to derail us, to protect his old friend's son. But he's spineless. I wonder where his vertebrae have walked off to without him.

"And you'll turn over anything you find to the police, right?" Mom asks, insistent.

His voice is defeated. "We'll contact you as soon as we schedule a hearing."

"Good." Mom turns to me. "Let's go, honey. You have studying to do."

"Yeah," I say, just to say something. "I do."

This time when we leave the building, it's me holding Mom's hand because, holy shit, my mom is a badass.

HARPER

Harper parks in the lot located behind Thomas House—the dorm closest to the Juice Bar.

It's lunchtime, so Edwards is awash with people running from one place to another. Good. While it's still the most overwhelmingly white crowd she's seen since her time at Columbia, it's chaotic enough that nobody will notice her.

She beats Sam to the little shop with the tiki sign that says JUICE BAR over the top, and orders a coffee and an apple turnover.

When Sam arrives, she gets in line to order and waves Harper over. Sam picks out a sandwich, a smoothie, and a brownie, and steps aside to make it clear who's supposed to pay.

"How are you doing?" Harper asks, once they're seated at a small table they were lucky to get.

"Finals," Sam says. She calmly sips her smoothie.

"You surviving?"

"I'm here, aren't I?" Her gaze bores into Harper. "Not that you made it any easier for me, talking to my dad. That was smart, going for the protective dad."

She's so casual about it. She didn't seem like the type during their interview to let something like this slide quite so . . . easily.

It's a relief. Harper did what needed to be done. At least Sam's parents can support her, no matter how the legal system treats her.

"What are the police going to do?" Harper asks to divert the conversation.

"I have to make a recorded call to Scully." Sam clenches her plastic smoothie cup. "Try to get him to admit to what he did on the phone, if we can."

"If you can't?"

"They told us the DA will decide if they want to press charges. The Chapmans might accept a plea bargain, just to kill publicity. But if they don't, we go to court."

Harper nods. Sam is so calm. It's weird.

"I hope he takes it," Harper says. "And the school investigation?"

"They're starting today. Mom and I filed an official complaint with the school this morning."

Harper raises both eyebrows. "How'd it go?"

"Mom kicked ass. It was amazing. You should have seen the way she talked to Frank Portsmouth. Complete KO."

Good. Sam's parents remind Harper of her own—fierce and loving. Sam will need them if they go to court.

"I called your House Mother, Jean, last night," Harper says. "But I can't get a hold of anyone else."

"Here's everything." Sam pulls a piece of paper out of her bag and shoves it across the table. "Names, phone numbers, whatever."

Wow. She's prepared. It's almost as if she made the list weeks ago.

SAM

That reporter is persistent, I'll give her that. I knew she was the right person for this.

She'll get it done.

I gave her everything she needs: Bex's phone number. Hayden's phone number. The Second Year prefect who I'm pretty sure checked me in and back out again on the night I went to Scully's dorm room. Barry, the House Dad of Thomas House. Waldo.

"What about your roommate?" Harper asks, scanning over the list of names. "I'd like to talk to her, too—since she interacted with you daily. It would be really helpful to interview her."

Great. I tried to leave Gracie out of the interview as much as possible, because I knew this would happen. If Harper thinks we were close, it will bother her that Gracie is totally unresponsive now. And it's too complicated to explain.

"I didn't tell her anything about what happened. Anyway, she hasn't answered a single call from me since we left for Christmas break," I say. "Trust me, I've tried. But it's not like we were that close, so I just gave up when she blocked me."

That hurt the most. Like the guillotine falling, permanently severing our relationship at the neck.

Gracie's not about to answer a call from some reporter. Especially if she knows it's about me.

But I give Harper the number anyway, and Gracie's personal email address for good measure. I don't mention that Gracie will avoid her, the same way she avoids me.

Harper will figure it out. The story will just have to survive without her.

HARPER

Sam said Waldo would probably appear at the Juice Bar sometime before dinner. "He's here all the time."

So Harper waits. And waits.

"Just a regular banana-strawberry," somebody says with a strangely deep voice. "None of that protein powder crap you put in everything."

Harper keeps her phone in front of her face as she peers

up at the counter. He's six feet, two inches at least, with shaggy orange hair, a pimpled face, and legs like scraggly aspen trees. Based on Sam's description, this is him.

While he's waiting for his order, Harper sidles up to the counter. "Waldo Wilson?"

The barista serves up his drink. He doesn't look at her as he pops a straw into the lid and says, "Yup, that's me."

"I have a question for you about Scully Chapman."

"Again?" He sucks on his drink. "Who are you?"

"Harper. Harper Brooks." She holds out her hand and gives Waldo her most winning smile. He tilts his head, evaluating her, and doesn't take her hand. "With *The New York Inspector.*"

The look of surprise barely has time to register before Waldo squirrels it away again, shifting back to impassive.

"Cool, *The Inspector.* What're you doing at Edwards?" He points to her chest. "You don't have a visitor's pass."

"I'm not a visitor," says Harper coolly. "You and Chapman grew up together, right? Your dads are friends?"

"Yeah," says Waldo, his voice betraying some of the suspicion that his face won't.

"You told someone that Scully has a habit of forcing himself on women," says Harper. "Can we talk about that?"

"Are you asking me to incriminate Scully Chapman to a reporter from *The New York Inspector?*"

Hmm, she hasn't given Waldo enough credit. Maybe another tack would work better, approach it less aggressively—

"If I tell you," he says, "are you going to print it in the newspaper?"

What Sam had told her about Waldo hadn't really prepared her for this.

"Maybe," Harper says. "If it's good."

"Cool." Waldo takes a sip of his drink. "What do you want to know?"

———————

Harper decides to drive straight home, because it'll be impossible to locate any of the other students she needs with after-school activities going on—and she'll be less conspicuous if she calls.

Posting up at her kitchen table with a frozen pizza and her laptop, she rereads her notes.

Waldo gave her everything.

"Scully preys on the Firsties every year," he'd said. "He goes through their pictures on Instagram and picks the best ones, then coordinates with his prefect buddies. That's why I was surprised when I saw him with Sam at the polo game." He had sunk back into his chair then, sucking the straw of his drink thoughtfully. "Grabbing her hand in front of Frank and everything, even though she's so frumpy, I thought he liked her. Guess not."

"She's a person, not a thing," Harper had said, trying not to sound as irritated as she felt. "And she didn't deserve to be assaulted in a senior's room."

"Yeah, that part's weird. He usually doesn't take them to his room." Waldo had looked pensive. "Usually he picks some other spot around campus where he can get away fast, like Cath."

"How do you know this?" asked Harper. "If you aren't friends anymore?"

"We *were* friends. I like to think we still are, in our own way. But Scully's been at this for a long time. Since eighth grade, probably."

"Why did you never do anything?"

"I did. I stopped hanging out with him. That's doing something. But sometimes Scully just tells me about it straight up because he knows it pisses me off."

Waldo had taken a big bite of his lemon bar. Then he looked at her and said, "Personally, I like to make a girl fall in love with me before I fuck her. I'd rather she enjoy taking off her panties than me having to rip them off of her. There's no fun in a girl who doesn't want to be there."

Adolescent boys can be so gross. And yet Waldo still grasped basic ethics better than Scully Chapman.

"It's not like I enjoy going to Edwards," he'd then said. "But I have to graduate from here if I have any hope of taking over my dad's spot at Blue Crescent someday. And that's all I want. As much as I loathe the idea of sharing my dad's company with a rapist piece of shit like Scully Chapman, the Crescent is still my responsibility. It belongs to my family."

Then he'd decided he was done talking.

"Look forward to reading it," he'd said, scribbling his phone number on a piece of paper and handing it to Harper. "Call me if there's anything else you need." Then he waltzed out. "Toodles!"

CHAPTER SIXTEEN

HARPER

If only she could spend her evening doing anything else. Harper had gotten a message on OKCupid from a cute guy wanting to meet up for a drink—but she has more phone calls to make.

Bex answers after three tries. Harper introduces herself as a reporter writing a story about Edwards Academy. A student had recommended Bex as an interview subject—someone who regularly reached out to younger students and helped get them involved.

"You must mean those Firstie girls," Bex says. "Sam and Gracie. Yeah, they're good kids. A little weird, though."

Under the pretext of writing about "Edwards's culture of scholarship and excellence," Harper asks her more about the Firsties she's mentored. Eventually, Bex mentions that Sam and Scully went to the Mixer together—and later, she heard, they went on a date.

"Never found out how it went, but I assume good," Bex says with a giggle. "I like to see that. Someone who struggled at first figuring it out—getting it, you know?"

But Harper can't get through to Hayden as easily. And the girl who Sam said was running check-out that night refuses to help her at all with confirming Sam's check-out and check-in times. "That's confidential," is all she says, before referring Harper to the administrative office.

Barry, Scully's House Dad, picks up on the first ring. Same story: an article about "Edwards Academy and the culture of mentorship at private schools."

"Scully Chapman," Harper says. "I hear he tutors a lot of younger students?"

"Often," the House Dad says proudly. "He's my best student. Always helping others succeed. Takes a lot of pride in it."

"I spoke with one student, Sam Barker, who says he's the only reason she's passing her math class. Do you know anything about that?"

"Let me look at my check-in forms. Sounds familiar." She hears some papers rustling. "Yep, Sam came in pretty late just before winter break. I was surprised by that one. Chapman really put his own work on the back burner to help her out." He rustles some more paper. "And another girl, the night after. A lot of last-minute folks needing help, and he's always happy to help."

Another girl? Harper's chest constricts, imagining Scully doing the same thing he did to Sam to another girl one night later.

"Who was it?" Harper asks.

"I can't give you her name, but it should suffice that there was more than one student who came for last-minute help, and Chapman is just the kind of student who gives it."

He's clearly done talking to her after that, so Harper thanks him for his time and hangs up.

Then it's time for the last one: Gracie. Sam's roommate when it all happened.

Gracie's phone goes immediately to an automated voice-mail message, so Harper writes her an email.

This story's so close, she can feel it. Just a few more loose ends to wrap up.

It can wait. She needs a good night's sleep for once.

SAM

I wake up the next morning in my bed at Edwards to my alarm beeping urgently. My eyes feel like they have sand in them. I obsessed about the call with Scully all day and night yesterday, going again and again over the script that Melissa had written for me.

They gave me a counselor to talk me through the assault and manage my "emotional fallout." We walked through the call together. I'll ask about math—something familiar, and find out whether he has tutoring hours available.

"Bring up your last 'session' and we'll try to get him reminiscing about it," Melissa had said.

It's Sunday, and tomorrow is the first day of finals. I should be studying, but instead I'm making my way down to the pick-up area to wait for Dad.

At the station, Melissa's wearing a pair of headphones so she can hear what Scully says. They've rigged up my phone to a speaker, and I'm supposed to wear another pair of headphones with a built-in microphone so I can talk while their machine records me. Melissa sits across from me with cue cards, prepared to scribble out assurances to help me when I get Scully talking.

"We've got your back," she says as we sit down with two officers. We go over the script and what kinds of things Scully might say. Then she taps the top of my hand. "Ready?"

As I possibly can be. I put on my headphones and read through the script one last time.

"Ready."

Scully's number is still saved in my phone. It just takes tapping his name to dial him. For a second it feels like a mistake, and my whole chest lights on fire.

It rings. Four rings, then Melissa hangs up before it goes to voicemail.

"Shit," I mutter. Luckily my parents aren't in the room.

Now what?

The table buzzes.

It's my phone ringing. The name SCULLY CHAPMAN pops up on the screen.

It feels like the temperature has dropped twenty degrees. Melissa holds up one finger, gesturing for me to wait.

We let the phone buzz again to let the setup connect, then she nods and I tap the green phone icon to accept the call.

Fuzz swells in the headphones.

"Hello?" I say. It sounds like a squeak to me.

"Hey."

Scully's voice fills up my ears, my head, my body, and I want nothing more than to vomit it out all over the floor. The red hang-up button's right there on the screen. I could reach out and touch it, give up this ridiculous thing, and not exchange even one more word with him.

"H-how are you?" I say, choking a little.

"Fine," says Scully. It's clear he doesn't want to waste time talking to me right now—during finals. Why did he call back? After a moment he says, "And you?"

It feels like Spanish class. ¿Cómo estás? Bien, ¿y tú?

"I'm not so great," I say, remembering the script is there. I glance over it. "I'm actually really screwed in Trig."

"Kind of late to be calling for help, isn't it?" says Scully, his voice taking on a note of good-spirited ribbing.

"Yeah." I emphasize the pause with a deep breath, for feeling. "It's pretty late. But I'm fucked if I don't get some help."

"Is it the same stuff we covered before?" Scully asks. Now he sounds more neutral than ever. Does he know he's being recorded?

I'm being paranoid.

"Yeah," I say. "Still having trouble with sine and cosine."

The line goes silent for so long that I check the phone to make sure the call is still connected.

"I don't know what I can do for you," says Scully, his tone careful. "Finals start soon. I'm busy myself. I don't have any more tutoring slots available until next semester."

"Oh." I let that one word hang, filling it with as much disappointment as I can, inflating it to hot-air-balloon size. He has to say something damning on the phone or we've got nothing, and the DA won't pick up my case.

"Still," I venture, "I think you should free up some time to work with me. That's almost a fair trade for what you did."

Melissa's head shoots up. I was supposed to stroke him, play into his belief that I wanted it—not fire accusations. But I have to get him to say something fast, before he has too much time to think about it. I'll take anything. I figure I've got less than a minute before he stops being interested.

Scully doesn't speak for a few seconds. "Yeah," Scully says finally, sounding almost . . . sympathetic? Regretful? No, that's not it.

I lean into the phone.

"You could at least apologize."

I don't know what to expect when I say it. Melissa has written a cue card that says BACK OFF. She wants me to play nice.

I won't.

"Sam," Scully says, voice dropping so low I can only hear him because the headphones amplify him directly into my eardrums. "I don't know what you think I should apologize for." Then he continues, "But I'll still help you with your Trig if you really need it. You're my friend."

Melissa is waving at me. I know I'm letting this conversation spin off the tracks, but I can't seem to straighten the wheel or take my foot off the gas.

"I have never had a friend who'd do what you did to me."

Melissa scribbles on another cue card.

"I've never done anything that wasn't asked for," snaps Scully, his voice rising. The creature finally emerges. "I've never touched anyone who didn't want it."

"Really?" I ask. Melissa holds up a card that says STOP, DON'T ANTAGONIZE HIM and shakes it. I ignore her. "Never? You would never make someone tea and—"

Melissa is angry and waving another cue card. It just says STOP.

STOP.

STOP.

"What is this call about?" asks Scully. He is pulling away. He reverts back to sarcastic, distant, cold. "Getting revenge?"

"No." I try to sound sincere. "I called because I am ruined if

I don't pass this class." My voice breaks and I hope it sounds like tears. "I'm terrified that I'll get kicked out of Edwards, and you're the only person I could think to call, because I am hopeless."

Melissa lowers the cue card. She pulls out another one and starts writing.

The other end of the line is silent again.

"What grade do you have?" Scully asks. He sounds almost interested. Like he wants to know how far I've fallen from grace so he can help dig me back out.

He'd relish that.

"A C-plus," I say. That's a big stretch. I'd have to bomb this final to get that grade.

"That's bad," he says. "A C-plus will look bad on your transcript."

"I know. It's been a hard quarter."

"You can do this," he says.

Then it hits me. He'll never admit to anything, because he doesn't believe he's done anything wrong.

Melissa's writing another suggestion on a cue card, but there's no point to this. Only a judge and jury will ever wring a confession from Scully Chapman, and even then, he might still be too convinced of his own innocence.

"Fine," I spit, glaring at his name on the phone screen. "You're right. I can do this on my own. See you in hell, Scully."

Melissa is waving a cue card, but I don't care what it says. I press the red button and the line goes dead.

On the other side of the table, Melissa drops the cue card. She shakes her head.

"He was never going to give me anything," I say. "No matter what I said."

Not while he thinks he's blameless.

"Yeah," Melissa says, sighing. I think she's finally grasped the same thing. "I know."

HARPER

Sunday night. Harper's butt's glued to her chair, a steaming cup of tea beside her computer. All weekend she waited to get an email from Gracie, but nothing. She called again yesterday— and it rang twice before going to voicemail.

Gracie had deliberately ignored the call.

Sure, Gracie's account would be great for fleshing out the degrading "body survey." But this story needs someone who shared space with Sam, who could describe her withdrawing, shutting down, after the rape. No matter what Sam says about her not telling Gracie, there's no knowing what Gracie might have suspected.

That's good journalism. That's what will sell this to the public, before the trial starts and the public turns on Sam instead.

Harper calls once more. This time it rings once before the computerized voice says, *"This caller is unavailable."*

Blocked.

Oh, high school. Where arguments at dances about boys could feel like the end of the world. You could hold a grudge for eons.

Minutes later, an email appears.

> I know why you're calling, and I don't want to talk
> to you. I have nothing to say. Sam and I were friends

once, but not anymore. We lived together and that was
it. I know nothing about her life after we stopped talking.
I dropped out of Edwards because I hated it. I hated all
the drama, the hero worship, that idiotic honor code.

So please, for the love of god, leave me alone.

Sam was right. Gracie doesn't have the stomach for it.
Everyone has people like that, who bounce out of your life as
soon as things get messy because they can't deal.

Fine. The story will happen anyway. Bex and Waldo have
given her plenty to work with. On a second call to Hayden, the
bubbly Head Girl picks up.

Hayden willingly dishes about all her success with First
Year mentees, like Sam Barker. "I single-handedly helped her
out of social obscurity" is just one of many quotes.

It's perfect. Now Harper can write.

The article starts off with Sam's mom, just to set the mood.

"It's the most horrific thing a parent can imagine happening to a child who's away at boarding school," Mrs. Barker had
told Harper. "You trust these schools. You believe they'll keep
your children safe. But what you don't realize is the enemy
might not be on the outside, but inside the school itself."

An honor code that hovers over everyone.

Hazing rituals. The body survey, designed to annihilate
the new girls' self-esteem.

Rich boy, polo captain, King—who gets whatever he wants.
Whom the administration protects.

A victimized girl too scared to tell.

A call for justice.

When she's finished, Harper addresses it to Mark and hits
the SEND button.

CHAPTER SEVENTEEN

SAM

"There's no need to be nervous," Melissa says as Mom, Dad, and I follow her down a long hallway. We're running late for our appointment with the Assistant District Attorney. Melissa pushes open a door at the end of the windowless hall.

Inside, an older, wiry woman with a mountain of snow-white hair piled on top of her head sits at a long conference table. Her nose is hawklike and her bone structure severe.

The woman gazes only at me as we all take our seats. What have I gotten myself into? The room is large, silent, lighted with fluorescents, and smelling faintly like cleaning solution.

"Anastasia Weber, assistant to the District Attorney," the woman says, standing up and offering her hand. My heart roars as I shake it. "Call me Tasia. I'm glad you've come around and decided to work with us. I heard it was a tough choice for you."

I came around, huh? How far could they have gotten without me?

"Yeah," I say.

"Rape is severely underreported," says Anastasia. "We need people like you to come forward in order to encourage others to do the same."

Same line I get from everyone. I'm the leader, the inspiration, whatever. But I don't want to be an *inspiration*. I just want Scully punished.

"Philosophically," Tasia says, sitting back in her high-backed office chair, "my job is to ensure the safety of the public."

I'm one of the public.

"We're not representing you specifically, Sam. The DA doesn't press charges on behalf of a victim, but on behalf of everyone. The point is to keep dangerous people off the street—to ensure that someone who presents a clear and present danger to the public is properly prosecuted, punished, and rehabilitated."

Rehabilitated. As if.

"It's hard to win rape cases, so my office doesn't often take them. But the police department has interviewed a number of witnesses at Edwards Academy, and everything you've said holds water." Tasia narrows her eyes. "If there's a serial rapist walking around that high school, it's within both the purview and duty of my job title to do something about it. So I'm launching an investigation into Mr. Chapman."

They're taking it. My case will move forward. I glance at Melissa, and she gives me a tiny thumbs-up.

Tasia leans forward. "But right now, it's just your word against his. Is there anything else you have that could help us?"

"Yes," I say slowly. "There is."

Melissa is watching me, her eyes saying, *You could have told me.*

I gesture for Tasia's notepad and pen, and she slides it across. I scribble down the address of the Tumblr blog.

"It's the address of a blog I was keeping," I say, handing back the notepad. "Each post is time stamped. I couldn't fake it. It has details in it about what happened."

Tasia reaches into the briefcase on the floor by her chair, takes out a tablet, and enters in the address. She scans the page.

"Yes," she says, lowering her glasses to look at me. Her blue eyes are peeling me, exposing me. "We'll check the email address linked to this account to verify it's yours."

"I used an anonymous email address to register the blog," I say. "I deleted it after."

She *hmms*. "Still, this is very helpful. Thank you." Tasia bookmarks the page. "A timeline helps. I can ask Scully about specific events, and his answers will give me—and the judge—clues about how much he's willing to lie." She offers the smallest of smiles. "I'll have my secretary make a copy for us and the opposing counsel, and then you'll have to take the blog down."

"Take it down?" I'm genuinely not sure if I can do that.

"Once this story is out there, that blog will be discovered in a second, if it hasn't been already. I don't want this leaking to the public during an ongoing investigation."

Next to me, Mom and Dad are both nodding.

"What can we expect will happen?" asks Mom. "We've never . . . we've never gone to court before."

"Your daughter will only be called as a witness," Tasia says. "Not a plaintiff. Though I'm hoping we don't even have to get to that stage and the Chapmans' lawyers will take a plea bargain to keep him out of the papers."

I almost laugh out loud. After my call with Scully, I wouldn't bet a penny on him admitting guilt.

Tasia looks right at me, as if she can read my mind. "But I won't depend on that. Mike Chapman has access to a lot of good lawyers, and they'll come up with some ridiculous stuff to use against us. Against you." Her gaze turns to steel. "I want you to know, Sam, that you don't have to come to the courtroom if you don't want, unless it's your turn to testify. This is about me and Chapman now."

I don't know what to say. I just hope she can bury him.

"Thank you."

"I should be the one saying thank you," Tasia says. "Thank you for telling us. And for helping other girls stay safe."

I'm doing this.

And there will be a reckoning.

═══════════════

HARPER

Mark should have read the piece by now. Harper's about to slide into his office and make sure he got it when someone taps her.

"Hey, look," her co-worker Josh says. "It's your girl's school on TV."

He points to one of the giant televisions hanging on *The Inspector* walls playing a silent, closed-captioned broadcast. The camera sweeps the gorgeous Edwards Academy campus. The closed captioning starts scrolling across the screen.

A FRESHMAN STUDENT AT THE PRESTIGIOUS
PENNSYLVANIA PRIVATE SCHOOL, EDWARDS
ACADEMY, HAS ALLEGED SEXUAL ASSAULT BY
A SENIOR STUDENT.

THE SENIOR DENIES IT, ACCUSING THE
PROSECUTION OF TRYING TO SABOTAGE HIS
WELL-KNOWN NEW ENGLAND FAMILY. HE IS
THE SON OF A PROMINENT WALL STREET
HEDGE FUND MANAGER.

The text is replaced by some smartphone footage. The wobbly, vertical screen shows what looks like the front door of a dorm. Police lights flash.

Harper runs over to the filing cabinet where the remote is sitting and un-mutes the TV. The anchor's voice fills up the space.

"The footage was taken by a student and put on social media last night. Police arrived at the school and arrested Scully Chapman, the school's star water polo player and captain of the team. He was gearing up for a state championship. Now his acceptance to Berkeley might be in jeopardy."

The fuzzy footage shows two cops leading a boy with wavy blond hair away. Other boys are clamoring behind him. He looks defiant as the cops open the back door of the squad car.

Harper turns to Josh, who's watching next to her.

"'Berkeley might be in jeopardy'?" she asks with air quotes. "Good Lord. Poor boy, being a rapist got in the way of his college education."

"What do you want from TV news journalism?" Josh asks.

The news throws an image of Scully, grinning, up on the screen. It's his senior photo. So that's what people see in him. Not quite tan, with a chiseled jaw. Playful, sandy hair, and a wide mouth. A young Channing Tatum.

"They never use the mug shots," Harper growls. "Bet he looks like shit in his mug shot."

She is about to head into Mark's office, when she turns around and finds him standing right behind her.

"Let's talk," Mark says. He's glowing.

She's treaded some wobbly lines to get here, but now that she stands on the precipice . . . they both have a right to glow a little. This story's going to put Scully Chapman up to the light for everyone to see—and reporter Harper Brooks will be the one standing with the spotlight on him.

SAM

I barely slept after the commotion over at Thomas House last night. I didn't leave to go see the arrest, like most of the Isabel House girls did—just watched from my window.

People are shouting in the hall the next morning before I'm even out of bed.

"He could never do something like this," a girl says.

"Whoever this person is, she's a lying sack of trash."

What are they even complaining about? Scully posted bail immediately. I could sock them.

This fury I feel is getting familiar. I like it. It's better than the guilt, the bitterness.

I wish Gracie were here. She'd love to make fun of them all, tittering over this new scandal. I write her an email on my way to Morning Prayer.

I did it. The police know now, about everything. He was arrested last night. The blog has to come down. There's probably going to be a trial.

The arraignment is happening in one hour.

In Cath, I sit down in the back pews, with the rest of the lowly First Years. Reminded of our place as Jesus watches us from the stained glass window—as he stares down at me accusingly, the way everyone else will soon.

Gracie's seat is empty. That's okay for now. Once Scully's gone, once Edwards is safe for her again, she'll be in that seat again. Maybe she doesn't support what I'm doing; maybe she wants me to bury the whole thing. But when it's all over, she'll see why I did it.

As the heavy doors of the cathedral close behind us, Hughes isn't playing his organ intro like he usually does. Provost Portsmouth goes up to the podium and clears his throat.

"I want to address what happened at Thomas House last night," he begins. "Rest assured, the administrative staff and I are managing it. This is a good time to reiterate that any time we receive information about an incident or a complaint, we have a process in place to handle it. Trained investigators look into these situations carefully. I will not go into details, but if you would like to know more about this process—" he leans into the microphone and casts a meaningful look around the assembled student body—"please contact me or the dean."

He sighs so quietly it's almost imperceptible to the microphone. This must be his obligatory response. Provost Portsmouth then gestures to Hughes.

"Take us into it, would you please, Mr. Hughes?"

The organ starts. As the music takes over, the provost steps down from the podium. I don't want to make eye contact with him. Instead, I keep my gaze on the old organist's fried-egg head so no one will have any reason to guess that it was me.

HARPER

Sam's actually upbeat when she answers the call. "Finals are over soon!"

"That's great!" Harper says. "Then you get a little break, right?"

"Yep. Philly Weekend. They take us into the city for a few days for a vacation." Sam sighs into the phone. "I could use it."

"I hope that's not a bad idea," Harper says. "With the article coming out."

"Whatever," says Sam. "If they find out, they find out."

That's a switch. What about *Keep this community sacred?*

But it's good that Sam's gotten her sea legs.

"I'm sorry this has been so hard," Harper says.

"Thanks."

"Just so you know," Harper says, "I finished the piece. My editor really likes it. We're set to publish tomorrow."

"Will anyone care now, though?" Sam asks. "Now that Scully's been arrested?"

"This article's not about that. It's about *your* side of the story, Sam. This is what Scully doesn't want people to hear. Everyone who saw that clip on the news, or read about it in the paper, wants to know the whole story. Why would someone accuse that hot guy of this? This story humanizes you, speaks your truth. Now we control this narrative." She's using that word again—*we*. As if they're a team. A team dedicated to spreading truth. "Your struggle and your pain will be the first thing that people hear about, instead of crybaby rich boy losing his state championship. You'll get better access to the public's sympathy if you can get there first."

She'll need it. Everyone will have a hot take once this goes wide—and the court of public opinion is cruel.

"This story will let *you* control the mood out there," Harper says. "It'll go live with the article online tomorrow right after the paper edition."

"I can't wait," Sam says. She sounds like fire. "We did it."

We did it.

Harper likes Sam's new enthusiasm. But *it* has only just begun.

SAM

I get a text message on the way to my first exam. Melissa's supposed to let me know what happened at the arraignment—if the Chapmans will take the plea bargain or fight. But I'm running late, and I get into my desk just as the exam is about to start. I can't check it for another three hours.

The contents of that message are all I can think about as I turn over my paper, open the blue test booklet, and start to read. The questions blur together.

I wonder what Scully thinks. Does he imagine crushing me the way I imagine crushing him?

See you in hell.

If Scully decides to fight this fight, I'll take him there.

No. Focus. I need to get through this government test. Three hours to write out all the names and dates I've been cramming into my skull the last few weeks.

Half of my answers are bullshit, but bullshit I can do. Somehow I finish and hand in my test early.

Mr. Jordan nods and says, "Nice work this term. Really good work. I've enjoyed having you as a student, Miss Barker."

I don't even have the energy to be excited that beautiful Mr. Jordan decided to pay me a compliment. I tell him thank you and hurry out of the building. Once I'm standing outside, I rip the phone from my pocket and check the text message from Melissa.

It's done. His plea is in.

Not guilty.

So he's going to fight.

For a moment, I doubt myself. Did I do something really catastrophically stupid by taking this on?

I decided this battle was mine. I called Harper. I started this.

And now the tidal wave I've made is bearing down.

ACT THREE

CHAPTER EIGHTEEN

SAM

It's not my alarm that wakes me up the next morning. It's the girls screeching out in the hallway.

Is there a fire?

I scramble out of bed and throw open the door. My neighbor runs by in her pajamas, waving a newspaper over her head. "Katie! You have to see this!"

Rubbing the sleep from my eyes with the heel of my palm, I blink a few times and peer the other way down the hall. Half-dressed girls have crowded around the bulletin board.

The article.

I am instantly awake. Everything in my body is pumping at maximum speed, all the tubes and pistons spitting out steam.

Shaking, I walk up behind the cluster of girls and hope no one can hear my heartbeat. Like that Edgar Allen Poe poem, right? The telltale heart that gives your guilt away?

But nobody even looks at me as I wiggle in close enough to get a look. Someone has posted the front page of *The New York Inspector*, dated today. At the top it reads:

FRESHMAN STUDENT AT PRESTIGIOUS PRIVATE SCHOOL ALLEGES RAPE BY SENIOR CLASSMATE

Stretched across the top of the article is a grimy, black-and-white photo of the Edwards Academy clock tower. It's supposed to look beautiful and epic, but the trees all look like skeletal zombie arms coming out of the ground. The arrangement of the hands on the clock makes the face seem angry.

Down below, embedded in the text, is a photo of him.

The TV news had played that stupid senior photo a bunch of times—the one where he's got that big charming grin that everyone around here loves. I hate that photo. The word *rape* looks like a joke next to it.

But *The Inspector* uses a photo I haven't seen before. Scully's hair is mussed from sleep. His lips are parted, mouth tipped up on one side as if he's trying to smile, but doesn't have it in him.

He looks like the word: *rapist*. It must be his mug shot.

"I just cannot believe this," says one of the girls from the room next to mine.

"Me neither. Who would do this to Scully?"

"Someone with an axe to grind," Manda says. "Probably got turned down and couldn't take the rejection." She raises a copy of the paper high up in front of her, then attempts to symbolically rip it in half. But the paper is fifty pages thick and she ends up just struggling with it.

Someone has set out extra copies of the paper in the lounge, so I nick one for myself and head back to my room before anybody notices. Best stay as inconspicuous as possible while I still can.

In the dining hall, I skim the article through again as I scarf down my breakfast. Harper has chosen to refer to me as "Jen."

It's disembodying to read someone else's account of me. It's like watching those horrible moments unfolding again, but through a periscope, and from a safe distance.

The article's long—half of the front page and a quarter of page 3A.

Eliza, Bex, and Lilian are uncharacteristically quiet during breakfast. They're absorbed in reading, too.

Every minute or two, Bex raises her eyes and looks right at me. And each time, a shiver runs from my ear, through my jaw, into my neck, and down to my feet. I feel my entire face turn red, and it stays that way until the bell. But she doesn't do anything more than stare.

I gaze back down at the article. Harper did a good job. She captured everything I'd hoped she would, played up what I wanted, completely avoided the things I didn't—like my argument with Gracie.

I thought seeing this in print would salvage me. That the guilt and regret that sleeps on the edge of my dreams, that hounds me every moment I'm awake, would finally make themselves scarce.

But they don't. The wrong is still like a stain that won't come off, especially now that this is out there. I want that anger again—that hot, life-sustaining stuff I felt when I thought about bringing Scully down.

But reading about it again, all I feel is guilt and disgust. I keep coming back to the mug shot of Scully, sleepy and pissed off. What is he thinking about me right now? Does he want to hurt me, again, even worse? He and his dad are probably sitting over a fancy breakfast in their fancy house, made by their fancy chef. They're talking about the pre-trial hearing. Laughing as they discuss how they threw away the plea bargain because they know they can crush me in court.

Harper calls right as I'm leaving the dining hall to make sure I've seen the article. I duck into the dark corner of a nearby building.

"Do you like it?" she asks, and I think it's the first time she's ever sounded insecure.

Like is not really the word I would use to describe it. Evocative, maybe. Powerful.

"I do," I end up saying. "It's fantastic, Harper."

"Wonderful. I'm so glad. We're getting a big response on the website. Let's go out to lunch soon, okay? And I'll take you to dinner when I win the Pulitzer."

When the evening news comes on that night, every girl in Isabel House crowds into the second-floor lounge to watch the segment we've all heard is going to be about Edwards and Scully.

The story opens with a wide, panoramic shot of the campus. Then a face appears: Scully Chapman with that big, vapid, water polo captain grin. The TV blares at maximum volume.

"The prestigious Edwards Academy is under fire after a senior student, Scully Chapman, was accused of sexual assault of a freshman student," says the anchor.

They replay the phone video of Scully being led out of Thomas House in handcuffs.

"Chapman was arrested Thursday night. The case might have remained under the radar, but The New York Inspector *then published an exposé of hazing at the school and the alleged rape."*

The news flashes quotes from the article published in *The Inspector*.

> The first night of school, they take off fresh-
> man girls' clothes to evaluate them for imper-
> fections. Then they tell us how to improve.

"Edwards Academy's strict code of conduct kept the anonymous victim from coming forward about her alleged assault for more than a month," the anchor goes on. *"The claim could have far-reaching effects for the prestigious private boarding school."*

> I pushed him away repeatedly. I didn't scream
> because I didn't want everyone else on the hall to
> hear, but I wanted him to stop, and he knew it.

> . . . upperclassman students like Chapman
> have the authority to do whatever they want.

As the girls start to chitter among themselves, I keep my face blank. A few people throw candy wrappers at the TV screen.

"That girl is such a coward," a Third Year says from where she sits on the couch arm.

"Seriously, hiding like that behind a pseudonym to talk to some reporter," Hayden says. She turns her head, and like Bex, her eyes focus right on me. The police must have talked to her, too. "That's definitely a violation of the honor code. If she had a problem, she should have let us resolve it before she aired her dirty laundry to the whole world."

I don't return the eye contact. I suddenly feel so light-headed that I might pass out.

Then she turns away, back to the TV.

I return to my room before the segment is over, saying I have to study, and fall face-first onto my bed.

I am perched on the edge of a cliff. Bex and Hayden stand right behind me, ready to push me over. But they aren't touching me yet. They aren't pushing.

They could at any moment, though, and I would fall right off the side.

I get on the computer and reflexively check for an email from Gracie, like I always do. Nothing, of course. The same nothing it's been ever since Scully took her from me.

On Facebook, I find *The Inspector* article pasted all over my feed. Everyone, Edwards student or not, has an opinion about "Jen."

"How could anyone say this bullshit?" someone says.

"Scully would never do this," a girl from my study group says. "She's just dragging him because she got turned down."

"Selfish. She's totally unaware of the consequences of her actions."

"I bet somebody's paying her."

I knew some Edwards kids would be loyal to Scully. That's not news to me. But I didn't expect all of them to fall so neatly in line.

I climb into bed. Even though I have two finals tomorrow, there's nothing left in me.

I start a countdown to someone discovering that Jen is me.

But nothing happens as finals creak on. Word travels around that the body survey exposé got Hayden suspended for a few days, and outrage spikes again on campus. But she hasn't told on me.

Heavy snow falls one night while everyone is asleep, and the next morning we wake up to mounds of white heaped up in front of the doors. It makes the slog to my last final long, cold, and wet, even though crews are out already clearing the snow from the walkways.

Everything said, my tests aren't terrible. I've had to study in the worst conditions possible, but at least I have so much to say in my essay for Women in Art History that I go right up to the finish time.

As I turn in my blue book, Dr. Winegard touches my hand. "Can we talk for a second after class?" she asks.

"Uh, sure."

I sit at my desk until everyone who's still left has turned in their finals and filed out. I have a lot of good teachers at Edwards, but Julie Winegard is the one I'd want as my friend. If she lectures me about going to the police first the way the provost did . . .

After the last student leaves, Dr. Winegard closes the door and slides into the seat next to mine.

"I shouldn't be speaking to you about this," she says, "but when do I ever do what I'm told? You know what they say: *Obedient women rarely make history.*"

I have to smile at that.

"I'm one of the faculty members on the committee that oversees Title IX complaints," she starts. Here it comes. I brace myself. "I'm not really supposed to say anything, but I just want to tell you that . . . you're not alone. I know how hard it is to come forward. I know that it feels like everything is stacked against you. You're so brave."

Brave. Is that what this was? Because I've been feeling lately like the word is actually *stupid.*

"If you ever need a safe place to eat your lunch," she says, "or a shoulder to cry on—I'm here. Okay, Sam?"

I almost do start crying, but I pull myself together.

"Thanks, Dr. Winegard." I mean it.

And then, finals are over. It's like the entire school exhales a breath we've all been holding for days.

Provost Portsmouth called my mom last night about the upcoming Philly Weekend—a three-day trip the school takes to Philadelphia, where we do all sorts of fun touristy things around the city.

"I don't think Sam should go," he'd told Mom. "We have a No Contact order in place, so all the faculty are instructed to keep Sam and Scully apart. But that will be difficult to maintain on a field trip."

She left it up to me to decide. But why shouldn't I go? Why does he get to enjoy himself and I don't?

I'm going.

There's really no way we can stay completely apart. As if it matters what the faculty have been asked to do when every single Edwards student gathers on the curb with our backpacks, duffel bags, and roller bags, waiting to get onto buses.

I wish Gracie were here. We could lock elbows just like we did that first day of school. Even if the whole school turned against us, we'd still have each other.

A flash of blond hair. A familiar laugh. Somebody tall is pushing their way through the crowd of students.

Every muscle in my body tenses, ready to run if I need to run. I yank my bag along as I duck behind some students.

Scully. He hasn't come to Hamilton Hall once since his arrest—probably since he can afford to eat at the Encore Grill every day. But now he's here with an Edwards Academy duffel bag, waiting to board a bus like everyone else.

Eliza finds me in the crowd. "Come on, Sammy! Be on our bus!"

Scully started that stupid nickname, and now everyone has adopted it. *Sammy* is a toddler's name. I have never loathed anything more.

"Coming," I say to them. I pass Dr. Winegard as I lug my bag up the steps of the last bus. We exchange nods.

Once I take my seat in the back with Bex, Eliza, and Lilian, I hear a commotion outside.

Scully's trying to get on my bus, but Dr. Winegard has turned him away. Everyone on the bus is peering out the windows, trying to figure out what's going on.

It feels like a gerbil is running around the inside of my ribcage. Scully throws up his hands in annoyance, but Dr. Winegard just points to the next bus, and eventually, Scully and his friend Cal move on.

As the bus pulls away from the curb, the news travels down the seats. *The girl who accused Scully must be on this bus.* "Jen" is right here, among them.

Bex gives me that look again, but then turns to gaze out the window and doesn't speak the rest of the trip. The sleazy "Jen" is the only thing people talk about the entire ride. I wish I hadn't come, but it's too late now.

Once we arrive at the hotel in Philadelphia, it's the same thing: Everybody off. Everybody wait in a huge cluster on the sidewalk. It's dark and stinky, and the edges of the buildings jut out like teeth. Then it's everybody find your roommates and head up to your hotel room.

There are two beds in my room. This must have all been reserved when Gracie was still in school.

Suddenly my phone lets out a *ding*. A Facebook message.

It's from a girl named Jackie—I think she's in my study group. My whole body clenches, but it's probably nothing.

I open it.

> It was you, wasn't it?

I almost choke on my own spit.

> I saw you and Scully at the Roast. And you went to the Mixer with him, too, right?

I read it twice, then want to barf all over the perfect, crisp hotel bedspread.

> I had a feeling. Loser Firstie with no friends. He told me once—he just wanted to help the meaty lizard move up the social ladder. He pitied you and how you had no friends.

Jackie's messages keep coming. I have a hard time reading them through the thick, wet film in my eyes.

> Don't worry. I won't tell. Whoever outs you will get in a lot of trouble. I don't need you to sic the police on me, too. But it was easy to figure out. We aren't stupid.

Jackie includes some happy, smiling emojis that look grossly ominous.

> I hope you liked your ride while it lasted. Maybe take the hint and transfer out. We don't need people like you.

And then, finally, Jackie stops. The three flashing dots that meant she was typing on her phone don't appear again.

I switch off my phone, place it on the other bed, under the comforter. Then I lock the door and climb under the blankets and cover my head with a pillow.

I don't leave my room the rest of the night, not even when someone comes and knocks on my door. Multiple someones.

I turn off the light and pretend I'm not there.

I think I understand what people mean when they say *The world is falling apart*. This unusually small hotel room is now ground zero of the apocalypse, and all that will be left of me at the end is an irradiated skeleton.

The next morning, I delay the inevitable as long as possible. I take a long shower, dress myself in the best outfit I brought, and put on the shoes I got over break just for walking all over the city.

I have to face them sometime.

As I walk down the three flights of stairs to the lobby, where the pamphlet said the continental breakfast would be, it feels like my body is covered in a colony of ants.

I enter the low-ceilinged, fluorescent-lit room. As people glance over at me, their conversations stop. Even the boy using the waffle maker is staring while the machine beeps, letting him know his waffle is done.

I'm not hungry at all now, but the only thing I can think to do is pretend like everything is normal. I load a small plate with miniature blueberry muffins, bacon, dry scrambled eggs.

The whispers start in corners, at tables in the back of the dining room. It's like a nightmare I used to have in middle school, where I'd walk into a room naked and everyone would stare, chuckle, whisper behind their hands.

Except this time I can't wake up.

Pretending is pointless. I leave my food on the Formica bar as I rush out of the room and dash up the stairs. Once I'm back in my room, I yank out my phone and call Mom.

"I need you to come get me," I tell her, my voice overcome by tears. "Please. I need to come home right now."

———

The plan is that I'll spend the weekend at home until the school figures out how to deal with my identity getting out. I get to sleep in my own bed, use my own bathroom, and eat real, homemade dinners, without anyone watching me.

It's an okay substitute for the trip I'm missing, but I know it's just the calm before the storm.

"I want to know who told!" Mom says over dinner that night, her voice rising. "They should be punished."

"Nobody told, Mom. They figured it out. It wasn't that hard." All the arrows pointed at me.

"You could withdraw," Dad says. "Transfer to Castlewood High. You'd get to see all your old friends."

Give up and walk away after everything I've done to stay at Edwards?

"Screw that," I say, surprising Dad. "You paid a lot of money to send me there. I'm not gonna let him drive me away."

"Sam, nobody will think less of you if you decide—"

"No. If I transfer out, Scully wins."

Mom sighs. "Fine."

"Remember to call Melissa if anything seems wrong," Dad says.

Yeah, right. Melissa can't help me with kids going quiet whenever I enter rooms. Staring at me. Whispering about me.

Anyway, she sent me a weird text right after the story in *The Inspector* came out. I haven't wanted to talk to her since.

> Think carefully before you talk to the press. Remember that anything they print about you is a factual admission in court.

Is she right, that it's foolish of me to be talking to Harper? Was the article a bad idea?

No. My identity was going to get out anyway, and it was stupid of all of us to think it wouldn't. At least now, Harper is right—I seized the narrative. We've put Scully on the defensive.

And nobody thinks straight when they're backed into a corner.

When I get on my computer after dinner, my message inboxes are all flooded.

I heard it was you, you meaty lizard.

Who the fuck do you think you are?

I crouch low in my desk chair, covering my mouth to block the mewling sound that comes out. There are so many of them. Almost a dozen just in the few hours since Dad picked me up in Philadelphia.

I looked at your pics and you're basically ugly and gross. Scully would never touch you, lol. Bet that made you mad so you picked the nicest guy in school to wreck. Bitch.

Feeling heat working its way from my chest into my throat and head, I close my browser window. It feels like my face is going to explode.

How could people do this to me? How could they think these things about me? Thank god I took my town and personal email off my Facebook profile.

My school email has blown up, too, with senders I don't know.

what an attention-seeking whore.

You're lucky a guy like that wanted to fuck you. what's your damn problem. sandy vagina?

Every nerve in me is pulled taut, ready to snap in half as I read, read, read. The letters imprint themselves on my eyeballs. Finally, I have to let the tears out because otherwise my skin will pop like a fat, pus-filled blister.

And then the house phone rings.

I hope it's not what I think it is. I hear Mom pick up down-stairs and say, "Hello?"

Then a long pause. "What? Who are you? Why are you calling here? How did you get this number?"

I run out of my room, out to the railing over the landing. Mom puts the phone down and looks up at me.

"Who was it?" I call down to her, my voice flayed.

She shakes her head. "Nobody, Sam."

"*Who was it?*" I am shouting.

"A prank caller!" She breathes hard, trying not to cry. "It's fine, Sam."

The phone rings again.

This time Mom picks up the receiver and slams it down. She unplugs the phone after that.

i think u should do us all a favor and just kill yourself,
u meaty lizard.

Hey, I have an idea . . . why don't I come over and rape
you again? Since you seem to be into that kind of role play.

you're such a stupid little ugly fuckin liar I cant
believe he would touch you

I can't stop reading them, even though each one makes it all worse. A lot of people from Edwards resort to name-calling. *Meaty lizard* is the most popular one, though I don't know what it means.

By midnight I am made of stone, clicking through each one like they have some kind of answer to offer me. Maybe if I can find the words hidden between lines, I'll understand why no one could consider that maybe, just maybe, I'm telling the truth.

I stay up reading until I'm tired down to the black pit in my stomach. This is good data to send to Harper. I tally the threats until the early hours.

Kill, rape, suffocate, rape.

Rape, kill, rape.

CHAPTER NINETEEN

HARPER

The Inspector's been inundated since press time. This story has more hits than anything they've published since that piece in 2015 on fame ruining the lives of child stars.

Harper calls Sam the day after the story drops to set up another meeting, but it goes to voicemail.

No big deal. Sam's on vacation in Philadelphia blowing off steam.

But Harper does need to know how the pre-trial hearing went for Mark's next article. And she's got to stay Sam's friend to keep getting what she needs.

She's thankful to spend her week thinking about something else, churning out other pieces for Mark. Still, she leaps to check her inbox whenever she gets a new email.

Then it comes.

TO: Harper Brooks (hbrooks@nyinspector.com)
FROM: Sam Barker (sbterrier@shmail.com)
SUBJECT: Sorry

Scully's requested a judge, instead of a jury. Melissa says that's pretty unusual in criminal cases. They must think this guy will be nice to Scully—that has to be the reason.

Anyway, I wanted to write sooner, but it's been hectic. I know you tried to hide identifying details and stuff, but that blog was out there for a while before we took it down, and someone at school figured out it was me. Now everyone knows.

People are calling my parents' house all the time. I get several dozen hate emails a day, and I had to shut down my Facebook and Instagram accounts.

I don't really know why, but I started counting them.

Death threats: 7
Rape threats: 12
General threats of violence: 18

Maybe this would be interesting for your next article, since you're planning to write another one? I know that's why you still want to buy me lunch and stuff. It's fine. I like free food.

bye,
Sam.

Seven death threats. Why would someone send a death threat to a fifteen-year-old girl?

Lord. And she read through all of those so she could categorize and tally them? Sam must have guts of steel. How does a girl who wanted so badly to be part of the in-crowd just a few months ago handle this kind of abuse?

Harper doesn't reply right away. Those last few lines keep making her pause.

Maybe this would be interesting for your next article.

She's so casual—almost eager. Everything about how Sam has behaved since Harper called her father has been . . . strange. That day at the Juice Bar, it felt like Sam wasn't even really mad about Harper going over her head—just pretending to be mad.

If it had been Harper on the receiving end, she'd be furious. They'd have never talked again.

What did it mean? Harper turns it over in her mind. Clearly Sam had wanted this story. She'd swallowed a lot of tough pills to make it happen. But then, why had she fought Harper so bitterly at first about coming forward, when that was the last barrier to making it a reality?

Harper pulls up the digital version of the article. The linchpin of the piece? Where Sam's parents find out what's happened to their daughter, and demand that she go to the police despite her fears. It paints a picture of a girl who was victimized twice over, first by her rapist, then by the school's oppressive honor code.

Harper chokes on her coffee.

This was what Sam wanted all along. She pulled Harper in, got her invested, made her realize this was a big story. Forced her to act and go to the father.

Harper got played. Pretty smooth move for a teenager.

She opens up a new document on her computer and starts writing the lede of her next article.

Abandon any expectations you might have had that "coming forward" is all women need to do to be believed. This is the fallout in our society of reporting your own rape.

SAM

We get a short break after Philly Weekend, which is really just more time for me to skim my hate mail and flinch whenever the phone rings.

The new semester starts Wednesday. The drive back to Edwards on Tuesday night is long, and I spend the entire time imagining my reception back at school.

Whatever it is—I will endure it. I just have to get through the next few months. Eventually, people will forget about me. Some other drama will stir them all up and the spotlight will move on.

I'll pull through. I'll show everyone.

Taking my seat inside the massive stone cathedral, I plan to doodle in my sketchbook until Morning Prayer starts. But some girls in front of me keep sneaking peeks, giggling, whispering to each other. I focus on my sketch of Huge Condescending Jesus in Stained Glass, but all the snickering makes it hard to keep my eyes down. The rattle gets inside me.

Can't look up. Can't let them know they get to me.

I put my bag on Gracie's seat and imagine her sitting next to me. *They've just bought into it. It's like* The Matrix. *Once you're outside it, everyone still inside seems stupid.* That's what she'd say.

In Hamilton Hall, I've got a full tray of food in my hands when I find our usual table's empty. Bex is laughing at another table, way on the other side of the cafeteria. That table is full— no room for me.

Whatever. I sit in the same spot by myself and eat my breakfast. I can feel eyes everywhere, burning holes in my clothes, but I ignore them.

Probably the only person who isn't looking at me is Scully. Joking about something, he and Cal get up early and leave. Even if I can't escape seeing him, at least that No Contact order's working.

When I'm done, I dump my tray like usual and leave. As I'm pushing open the heavy door out of Hamilton, pain explodes across my shoulder blade.

What the fuck?

Lying on the floor is a half-smashed apple. Nobody has moved, and everyone turns away as I look around for whoever threw it.

On my way out, I rub the spot where it hit me, and my skin screams. There will be a bruise.

Should I text Melissa and tell her?

No. That would just give Mom more reason to pull me out of Edwards.

But everywhere I go on campus that day, it feels like there's a target painted on my back.

Every turn I take, there's Scully's mop of blond hair, or his stupid friend Cal. It was hard enough getting to class on time before I had to take all these U-turns to avoid them. I feel like a rabbit navigating a maze full of foxes.

In American Government, Mr. Jordan assigns us to groups to debate prayer in schools. Every time I try to talk, someone interrupts me.

"Considering that schools are government institutions—" I begin.

"Not all schools," one of the guys who used to invite me to

his study group says. "Only public ones."

"Right, but—"

"And students can opt out," someone else jumps in. "It's not required, so it's not a violation."

I close my mouth and stop talking. The debate goes on without me.

Tennis is just as bad. After Gracie left, Bex or Eliza or Lilian would pick me as a partner for doubles out of pity. Now nobody will take me. I'm forced to play with Coach, until she gets fed up and starts assigning me teammates. The first time, my new teammate stands on the edge of the court and simply watches as green tennis balls fly by. I spend the entire practice running across the court just so we don't lose every single game, and by the end, my lungs and calves are shredded meat.

At least in Drawing Club, we don't have to talk—but people stare. I skip it whenever Scully comes in to model.

I don't know how much longer I can do this. The coal of anger inside me grows hotter and redder every day. I could breathe smoke.

HARPER

"Can we do that lunch?" Sam asks when she calls.

Harper hadn't expected to hear from her so soon. "Sure. How do I check you out of school?"

"I just have to tell Jean I'm leaving for something court-related and she doesn't even bother."

Once they sit down for lunch at the place Sam picked out, not far from campus, she doesn't stop talking.

"The DA offered him a plea bargain with a smaller sentence if he pleaded guilty," Sam says. Harper has seen her experience a lot of emotions, but never has she been this righteously riled up. "The bargain was for a year in jail! That's it. Just a year for what he did. But his lawyers laughed at her. They think they'll win without even trying."

"When does the trial start?" Harper asks.

"They won't know for at least another month." Sam sighs. "And who knows how long it'll last. I could be a grandma by the time there's a verdict, if Scully's lawyers drag it out."

One of the gifts of the privileged.

"What about the school's investigation?"

"They're doing it now, or so they say," Sam says. "They have to share whatever they find with the police."

"I don't want to scare you," Harper says, but this is half a lie, because Sam would do well to exercise some caution. "But once the trial starts, you'll be under the microscope. I'm sure the DA has told you this, too, but I want to be real with you so you can be prepared for what's next."

"After these last few weeks, nothing's too real," Sam says.

As if. Sometimes Sam seems almost like an adult, then reverts back to being fifteen.

"Once you go to court and we publish another story, all that hate you've gotten from your classmates will go wide."

"Good."

This is not the same Sam that sat across from Harper a month ago, giving her interview as quietly as she could, hoping that no one nearby would overhear.

This Sam has vengeance written into her skin. She wants to act.

"What if . . ." Sam begins, and Harper feels a shudder

run across her, like the feeling she gets when a storm is coming. "What if that's okay? I mean, if I'm going to get all the publicity anyway, like you said—what if I could do something with it?"

A nauseating discomfort settles in Harper's stomach. "Do what?" she asks.

"I mean, if they're going to take me apart in the media anyway—maybe I could use it."

Sam runs her hand over the long edge of the menu, thinking. "The news coverage, the death threats. If I'm already being publicized . . . what if I told them what to publicize, instead of letting them dig around?"

"I suppose," Harper says carefully. "I know you feel powerless right now, waiting for the trial to start—"

"I could seize the narrative, like you said."

"You have a right to free speech," Harper hedges. "There's nothing stopping you from using your voice." Should they even be talking about something like this, just the two of them? This is more than Harper signed up for.

"I could take the hate public. The way they're treating me at school. People are always like, *Why didn't you come forward sooner?* Well, here's why. Death threats. People calling my parents at all hours."

"Would that mess up the court case?" Harper asks. But she has to admit, she likes where Sam's going with this.

This is what got her into this job in the first place—why she decided to get her master's in journalism. *Because people should know the truth.* Sam wants the same thing.

"I don't know," Sam says, sipping her drink. "Melissa probably wouldn't like it." She looks up. "If I did do this—would it be in your next article?"

Harper gives a quick nod. "It would make an excellent story." A powerful story.

Then their lunch arrives and they don't talk for the ten minutes it takes for Sam to devour her sandwich and fries.

"Are you coming with me?" Sam asks suddenly, wiping barbecue sauce from her mouth.

"Where?"

"To court. You're going to be there, right?"

Harper couldn't have hoped for a better, more straightforward in.

"If you want me there," Harper says, "I'll be there."

SAM

Melissa calls my folks that week. We have a court date—almost three months away. I can't believe I have to wait that long. While I've got her, I ask what the downsides are to my idea—*to going public.*

"You lose your anonymity," she says, point blank. "Anonymity that everyone has worked hard to protect."

"I'm not anonymous at school," I say. "Where I live 24/7."

"Of course you can do what you like, Sam—you're entitled to say what you want. But remember what I said about factual admissions."

I know that line. *Anything you say or do could be used against you in a court of law.*

"The reporter thinks it could help the case," I say. "To take control of my own narrative. My own story."

"That's happened," Melissa says. "Having such a negative

story out there about Scully forces his lawyers onto the defensive. It could work for or against you. I can't really help you with decisions like this."

But the way she says it, it's clear what she thinks: I should stay quiet and let the court take care of things.

As if staying quiet has worked out all that well for me up to now.

I have to take back my power. People should know.

So I browse all my new hate mail, looking for the worst-best nuggets. I've learned how to read with just part of my brain—it's the only way I can keep it from getting inside me. Read, don't absorb. Let my eyes glide over the words but don't distill their meanings.

One message has a weird subject line.

TO: Samantha Barker (sbarker@edwardsacademy.org)
FROM: Mallory Raven (mraven@edwardsacademy.org)
SUBJECT: I'm a coward

Sam,

I'm not sure if you remember me, but I'm the one who brought that whiskey at the Mixer.

I just want to tell you . . . I believe you.

He did it to my roommate when we were First Years. She left.

I've never said anything. For fuck's sake, I still hang out with him.

I hope you get some kind of justice.

Mallory

Mallory.

The girl with her family's coat of arms engraved on a silver flask. She'd seemed nice—I guess she actually is.

I don't reply, but I forward it to Melissa in case she wants to follow up. After a few minutes, I also forward it to Gracie.

"Look," I write. "Some people believe. Always a couple roses among the thorns."

Gracie doesn't reply.

———————————

Mallory's email sticks with me. I can't stop thinking about her roommate, the girl who dropped out of school. Who is she? What if she testified in court? If someone could corroborate that Scully's a serial rapist, there's no way the judge could just gloss over it.

That night, I call up Mom.

"I want to go shopping downtown on Sunday. Can you take me?"

"Shopping? What for?"

"I want to replace that outfit. The one I threw away."

"Oh god, Sam, why?"

"I'll tell you about it when you pick me up."

When I get in the car with her on Sunday, I tell her about my idea—how I could use what's happening to me to turn the tide against Scully. How one girl already reached out to me, and if I revealed myself and came forward, maybe more girls would do the same.

"I don't know," she says as we park outside the mall. "Couldn't his lawyers use it against you, too? 'She's a loose cannon,' they could say."

"Sure, they could. But it might not matter if other girls step forward and testify. They can rule out just one girl as a 'loose cannon,' but not two or more."

"Fine," she says, giving a resigned sigh. "If this is what you want to do." And we head to H&M, where I bought the first blue skirt that ended up in the dumpster out behind Isabel House.

Leafing through clothes is comforting in a way I didn't expect. There are so many styles and colors, textures and fabrics. It's like a game, searching for just the right thing. When I find that same blue skirt, now on clearance, it shocks me with static. In the dressing room, I slide it on with the leggings and a similar black shirt and peer at myself in the mirror. I look the same as that night. I can almost see the rip in the side even though when I touch the skirt, it's whole. I swallow back some bile, remembering Scully's hand worming its way underneath it.

We buy the outfit and Mom drives me back to school. There's no way people on campus will be able to ignore this, brush me under the rug, keep me quiet. I'm going to fill the world with the sound of my voice.

The next morning I tear off the tags and put the clothes on, then scribble my message onto white foam board with sharpie. On my way to class I prop my phone on a ledge and set the photo timer, capturing the iconic Edwards clock tower in the background behind me and my sign. People stare as they walk by.

Fine. Look. Stare.

That night after Twilight Study, I upload the photo I took to Instagram and start writing a post.

This is the outfit I was raped in.

I go through my hate mail on my laptop and copy them into the post.

wanna go again? I won't be as nice to you

Hope u get herpes, slut

Why don't you do us all a favor and just die. I can come help. You'll be better off that way.

The last line of the post is the same text that I wrote on my sign:

I will not stop wearing these clothes until there is #JusticeatEdwards.

My hands are shaking as I touch SHARE. It's up. It's out there. My hands are tingling.

I send the link to everyone whom I can still call a friend: Mom, Dad, Harper, my friends from middle school. Dr. Winegard. Melissa. Mallory.

Gracie.

I turn off my phone before I can regret it, and pull out a textbook. Maybe my post will get a couple of likes by morning. If even one other girl like Mallory sees this, it'll be worth it.

CHAPTER TWENTY

SAM

First, only friends and family comment on my post. My uncle in Vermont shares it on Facebook. Some other reporters who must be friends of Harper's pick it up on Twitter.

Seven shares.

By morning, my old middle school friends have rallied and shared it.

> This is my friend, and she doesn't deserve this!!

> Sam is not a liar. What happened to her is horrible. Justice for Sam. #JusticeatEdwards!!

Fifteen shares.

Wow, I feel like an asshole for how I treated them over Home Weekend. Turns out they're still better friends than Bex and her troupe ever were.

I focus on my feet as I walk to class, keep my eyes on my notebook as I work, and pay close attention as my teachers lecture. It's all I can do not to think about what my post is doing, where it's going, and who's reading it while I'm here.

But everywhere I go on campus, wearing the same clothes as yesterday, an undercurrent travels with me. It's like electricity that runs through the whole school.

By lunch, Edwards kids have filled the Instagram post with comments. They share it everywhere.

haha look at this attention whore. so desperate

The bitch was bitter that nobody would climb on her pity wagon, so now she's begging!

Dragging Scully wasn't good enough? You're pathetic and so is this stunt.

Twenty shares. Forty shares.

After lunch, every person I pass on my way to class turns to stare at me. I want to avoid them, skip school, but I can't. I put myself out there. I took their hate into my hands and formed it into something new, better, fiercer. I have to carry it around in my arms or I shouldn't have made it at all.

The lake near Isabel House is frozen over and dark. I sit on one of the grimy, wet benches, looking down at it. Beneath the surface lie the silent, immobile bodies of koi. Hibernating for better weather.

I will not hibernate.

I pull out my old sketchbook. In December, I ripped out and destroyed all my sketches of Scully and stopped using this book at all. But I remember the Drawing Club instructor complimenting my doodle of Gracie's fake smile, so I flip to that page.

I start redrawing it in my new sketchbook. That night, I finish the drawing and pin it to my wall.

When I open my laptop to check up on my post, I find a local DJ has shared my post to her Facebook fan page.

> This is privilege in action. Men like Mr. Chapman get a pass no matter what, while women are shamed and tormented.
> This is rape culture.

Three hundred shares.

I grip the sides of my laptop. My head swims as I read through all the shares, all the comments.

Somebody has asked, "How do we keep letting this happen?"

"This has to stop," someone else writes. "We complain that girls stay silent, but they only suffer more when they speak up."

My blood feels heavy and thick, viscous inside my veins.

Five hundred shares.

It goes on growing like that all night. I finally go to bed at midnight. It's been shared over a thousand times.

At Morning Prayer the next day, the provost walks up to the podium, his face completely red, as if he's just learned of a death in his family.

"There will be repercussions for harassment," he says breathlessly into the mic. "Anyone we discover doing it will be immediately suspended. I am deadly serious about this, everyone."

It feels like the entire student body turns to look at me at once. The provost making an announcement isn't going to make a difference.

I wear the same clothes every day and change into sweatpants twice a week to wash them. And thanks to my #JusticeatEdwards post, word about my assault has spread rapidly.

Twenty-five hundred shares.

Six thousand shares.

Fifteen thousand shares.

Now the comments on my original post come from everywhere.

> scum. wrecking this good dude just because you're mad. you're ruining his life. how do you feel about that, bitch?

I screenshot that one and post it to my Instagram.

"Poor Scully," I write. "He gets to come to school every day and everybody loves him. Worships him. Must be hard. #JusticeatEdwards."

Fifty-six thousand shares. Eighty thousand shares.

On my way back from the bathroom the next morning, I find someone has spray-painted SLUT in enormous white letters across my door. I feel hot all over. I glance down the hall to see if I can catch whoever did it, but it probably happened while I slept last night.

I snap a photo.

"This is the price for speaking up," I write. "This is why we so often stay quiet. Who would willingly bring this into their life? #JusticeatEdwards!"

I take my usual back route to class to avoid as many people as possible, the one that winds down the tiny alley between the art building and the medical museum. I'm busy pressing SHARE on my phone when I notice the way ahead is blocked by two tall guys leaning against the side of the museum. The tang of tobacco smoke wafts toward me, and I stop mid-stride.

I know that slouching silhouette from my nightmares.

Scully exhales a huge drag, the cigarette smoke spiraling up into the air. Panic washes over me. My legs are lead. I guess he smokes more regularly than he let me believe.

He and Cal are talking about something, but I'm too far away to hear. I take a few quiet steps back, so they won't notice me. Pleading to old Dr. Morgan Edwards himself that they don't. Why can't I ever get away? He's like a disease—everywhere all at once.

Scully's phlegmy, ugly laugh fills up the alley as I back up to my escape route. How did I ever like him? One of his eyes is shaped funny. He always poses, as if some invisible photographer is shooting him for a *GQ* cover.

Sliding back the way I came, I turn and run as fast as I can in the opposite direction. I don't care if I'm late to class.

I hate him—in a way that I've never hated anyone before. It's heavy and sharp and consuming, like gut-twisting hunger after a day when you forgot to eat.

And there's only one thing that will ever make me feel full again: seeing him led away in a jumpsuit.

A week before the trial starts, it seems like people have finally started to forget. There's a big to-do over some lewd graffiti that, thankfully, steals some of my spotlight.

One afternoon, I send Gracie an email with the first court date, time, and location.

"It's open to anyone," I write. "In case you want to be there."

I get no response—not like I expected one.

The whole week, I can barely eat. Everything tastes like cardboard, and as soon as I swallow it, I want to heave it back up. Drinking water is like swallowing ash. What will they ask me? How am I going to answer without crying?

Then, two days before it starts, Gracie emails me.

I am trembling with excitement as I open the message. It has no subject.

As if I would support this performance theater.
I thought you knew that grandstanding isn't my thing.

My throat closes, and my face feels like someone has poured hot oil into my ears. What happened to all those nights we stayed up late and days we drew pictures on the quad? This was supposed to bring her back to me, to erase Scully from the space between us. Not push her farther away. The tears come fast and thick, and it's as if my body has given up, deciding every agony must escape right now.

I climb onto my bed, where I become a thousand tiny, broken pieces of Sam.

━━━━━━━━━

"You don't have to go to this," Dad says as we drive to the courthouse early Friday morning.

I've told myself this a thousand times, too. "I want to hear the statements." Even though, the whole car ride so far, I've felt like puking out the window.

Mom just shakes her head. She has given up trying to change my mind about things.

The courthouse is a boring white building with dead grass and five short steps out front. After we pass through the metal scanner, the hallways are claustrophobic, and the fluorescent lights flicker as we walk under them.

Inside the courtroom, I search for Harper among the long, bench-like seats in the gallery. They remind me of finding my seat next to Gracie in Cath that very first day of school.

There she is—Harper's curly black hair is pulled back with a band, and she's wearing a sharp blazer and skirt. Just seeing her, I feel calmer, and we slide in next to her.

Soon the judge enters in silky black robes and climbs into his seat at the bench as we all stand up. He looks in his mid-fifties, with jowls like Provost Portsmouth and salt-and-pepper hair.

This is happening *right now*, and I can't stop what I've started. The room swells and then deflates, the walls swimming and stretching like the inside of a funhouse. I hope I don't get sick.

Where is Scully? He's almost late.

As soon as I think it, the doors open again. A team of two men and one woman in tapered, tailored suits walk to the other counsel table.

Then Scully comes in. A hush spreads over the courtroom. In another life, I would leap over the seats at him, claw him, tear at that horrid black suit, rip at his eyes.

Someone has slashed his too-long surfer hair into a neat, short, military cut. And he's wearing a pair of sleek, black-rimmed glasses.

"Harper," I hiss at her, "he doesn't wear glasses."

"Dressing him up for the judge." Harper makes a note. "Going for the geeky and wholesome look."

God. I'm so screwed. No one would rule to put that kid in jail.

Scully straightens the lapels of his suit as he takes a seat amid his counselors. Even my skin is filled with hate. Scully's dad, Mike, sits with his arms crossed over his chest. From this angle I can just make out his big mouth, which is exactly like Scully's.

The judge delivers the rules. It's time.

HARPER

The DA's assistant stands up at the front of the room.

"Anastasia Weber," she says. "Appearing for the prosecution."

A great name for a stony, sharp-edged woman like her.

Anastasia sails through her opening statement, presenting Sam as the perfect scholarship student: great grades, sharp mind, set on law school. Despite the mortifying hazing rituals on the first day of school, she dove in headfirst trying to make friends and fit in.

And then Scully happened.

"Mr. Chapman's modus operandi?" she says. "Scour every new class of freshmen for targets—young women with the lowest self-esteem, as determined by the prefects who conduct the 'body survey.' Once he's selected one from the survey results, he develops a relationship with the young woman. As he did with Miss Barker."

This was new. What else has Anastasia learned that Harper didn't know?

Once he had his prey in the crosshairs, Anastasia says, Scully went after her. Lured her to his room, closed the door, and made his move. And the honor code supported him the whole way.

Anastasia pulls a piece of paper out of her pocket and begins to read:

> *There are no secrets among us, as secrets are the barriers that keep us apart.*
>
> *We will confront each other directly when we have problems. We will respect each other even when we cannot agree.*
>
> *We will stand by each other. We will be our own wall, our own defense.*

"This, Your Honor," she says, holding out the paper to the judge, "is the Edwards Academy 'honor code.' Every student signs it at the beginning of the year, agreeing to live by it. Anyone who violates it . . ."

The clerk takes the paper and places it in front of the judge. He puts on his glasses and glances over it.

Anastasia finishes by detailing how Sam's parents were forced to step forward for her, because the honor code made her too scared to do it herself.

Short and sweet.

At his counsel table, Scully is twisting his hands under the table, wringing them out. His face looks impassive. Those glasses are too much.

The defense's head lawyer, a big man with a cue-ball head, rises from his seat.

"James Turnquist, appearing for the defense," he says, approaching the bar. "This isn't about a good, hard-working girl pulling herself up by her bootstraps."

He lays it out quickly: Scully was targeted. After doing nothing but helping his fellow students, after taking pity on Sam, she turned on him.

"When my client refused to have a relationship with Ms. Barker," Turnquist says, "she decided to attack his character. To drag his reputation through the mud. To destroy his future."

Destroyed his future? What about Sam's future?

Harper's been squeezing her pen so hard that it rips a hole in her notepad.

Looking pleased with himself, Turnquist sits down.

———

SAM

I glare at the shiny back of Turnquist's ugly, bald head as he takes his seat at the defense table.

The way he talked about me—as if he knows me.

I'll enjoy watching his face as the evidence mounts against Scully. As the judge reads his sentence, and Scully is condemned to an orange jumpsuit and a tiny room, and Turnquist realizes he's lost. To me. To a teenage girl he so obviously loathes.

I hope it really hurts.

The gallery around me is silent as the judge calls the prosecution's first witness.

"Hayden Kent."

Hayden? I glance at Harper, who's scribbling notes as fast as she can. But Hayden and Scully are friends. Why would Tasia call her?

Hayden enters the courtroom and approaches the witness stand, dressed in sharp, clean, flattering clothes. As she swears her oath, I remember that first day of school as she gave me that pitying look and said, *Hmmm, I give her a "Needs Improvement."*

Anastasia starts off asking easy, seemingly unrelated questions. Her name, age, position in the school. How she became Head Girl. How she knows Scully and me.

"Do you like Mr. Chapman?" Tasia asks.

"As my friend," Hayden says, crossing her arms.

"What about romantically? You're under oath."

Hayden purses her lips and turns her head away. "Sure, a little. Everyone does."

Tasia goes on to ask about the body survey. Annoyed, Hayden says, "I've already gone over this with the provost half a dozen times. I even got suspended because of that stupid story." She throws me a dirty look.

"Fine," Tasia says. "So what do you do with your survey results?"

Hayden frowns. "I pin them on my corkboard to track improvement, check in on the girls, give encouragement."

"Do you share the survey results with anyone outside Isabel House?"

"Just some of my friends." But Hayden's face is so red it's almost purple, like a pickled beet.

"Is Scully Chapman in that group of friends?"

"Uh . . ." She swallows. "Yeah."

"Can you tell us about the match-ups you organize for your house?"

Hayden breathes a sigh of relief. This is easy for her. She describes it like a harmless mentorship program between First Year girls and upperclassman boys.

"Why did you match up Scully and Samantha?"

"He asked for her," Hayden says.

"Do you know why?"

"He liked her art. And she was having a hard time fitting in."

"Was this before or after he saw the survey results?"

Hayden is silent for a long time.

"Miss Kent?" Tasia asks. "Please answer the question."

"After." She has a hand on her forehead, like she's trying to cover her face. "He asked about Sam after he saw the survey results."

"Thank you," Anastasia says. "That's all, Your Honor."

I am speechless at what she just pulled out of the Head Girl.

Hayden made this happen? She sold me off her list to Scully like . . . like I was a prize cow.

When Turnquist gets up to cross-examine, Hayden watches him approach her suspiciously.

"Can you tell me about your relationship with Scully? How long have you known each other?"

"We met as First Years."

"And have you ever seen him display aggressive behavior toward a girl?"

She scoffs. "Scully? No. The exact opposite. Everything he does, he does to help other people."

"Has he ever come on to you or someone you know?"

"No. And if he did, I don't think a girl at our school would object."

"Have you ever heard of him assaulting someone?"

"Never." Hayden makes her distaste clear. "He's gone out

with girls occasionally, and . . . I'm pretty sure he's had sex. But from everything I've heard and seen, it's completely consensual."

After grilling her about Scully's character, Turnquist presses her about my behavior—was I a drinker?

Hayden looks affronted. "Nobody in my House drinks, thank you."

"Does she smoke? Has she dated other boys?"

"My Firsties don't smoke, either. And I don't care who she dates, as long as she's safe."

How about my grades?

"I was never worried," Hayden says. She scrunches up her nose, like she wants to say something bad about me but can't come up with anything. "Sam's a decent student."

Turnquist tries a few more questions, but Hayden gives him flat, boring answers.

When Turnquist finally gives up and Hayden gets off the stand, she has a look on her face like she wants to slap someone. She stalks out of the courtroom, and the door slams behind her.

I feel sick.

I'm next.

HARPER

After the judge calls an adjournment for the day, Harper waits to leave the courtroom. It's hard to tell who's from Edwards and who isn't—until she spots two plain-looking white girls, one in a black polo that says BADGERS TENNIS. Maybe one of Sam's teammates.

When the two girls get up to leave, Harper follows them out. They take a right outside the courtroom. One ducks into the restroom, leaving the girl in the TENNIS shirt drinking out of a water fountain.

"Hi," Harper says, smiling brightly. "Do you go to Edwards?"

The girl stands up and wipes her mouth. "Yeah, I do."

"Are you friends with Samantha?"

The girl gives a little snort. "Sam doesn't have friends anymore."

"Do you play tennis?" asks Harper, pointing at the shirt slogan.

"Yeah, I'm on Edwards's team."

"You play together?"

The shift from casual to suspect is immediate. The girl's eyes narrow. "Yeah, when she shows up. But she's been absent a lot lately. A flake, just like her best friend who ditched the team last semester and dropped out or whatever."

"Best friend? I thought she didn't have any friends."

"Girl named Gracie. They were roommates. Did everything together, totally inseparable. It was so pathetic."

Sam had given Harper the impression that she and Gracie lived together but didn't really have anything to do with each other.

The TENNIS girl's friend returns from the bathroom, saying, "Jeez, Lilian, these bathrooms are pretty gross." She stops and stares at Harper. "Who are you?"

Harper offers her hand. "Harper Brooks."

She ignores it. "You're that reporter who tricked Bex into talking, then wrote that horrible story for *The Inspector.*" She grabs her friend's arm. "Don't talk to this bitch, Lilian. She's the one pushing Sam's agenda."

"I just report the facts," Harper says, keeping her voice level.

"Sure you do," the older girl says, rolling her eyes. "And you trick people into telling you stuff." Lilian gives her the bird before they stalk off down the hall.

Oh, well. People have called her worse things than *bitch*.

She makes a note to reread her transcription, because she hadn't thought Sam and Gracie were all that close.

They did everything together.

Lord, this thing is such a mess.

CHAPTER TWENTY-ONE

HARPER

That night, Harper rereads the transcript of her interview with Sam. But, like she'd thought, there's not much about Gracie. They both had crushes on Scully and did the same activities. They got into a fight at the big dance and stopped talking.

Then Gracie left Edwards. Sam made it sound like the academic rigor had just been too much for her.

None of it's enough to warrant the word *inseparable*.

As she's reading, an email comes from Mark.

> The trial's hot. I need that second piece from you.
> How's it coming?

Harper bites her lip and closes the email without responding. He's right. Even NBC did a short segment on Sam's #JusticeatEdwards campaign, flashing the photo of Sam in her black blouse and blue skirt and marked-up sign.

The picture's been shared almost 400,000 times on Facebook. Each of Sam's Instagram posts gets hundreds of comments.

But something's missing. And bad reporting on a story this fragile—the fallout could be a lot worse than finding her ass on the curb.

She tries to find out anything she can about Gracie, but it's like she doesn't exist. No social media under her name. The best she gets is a Facebook photo of a middle school debate team with a tall, slender, dark-haired girl standing on the edge. She's tagged GRACIE CALEZA, but her name is grayed out— and her profile's deleted.

Harper picks up her phone and dials a number scribbled on a piece of paper. Her last resort.

"It's Waldo," a bored voice answers.

"Waldo, it's Harper Brooks. From *The*—"

"*The Inspector*, I know. I remember. Wasn't that long ago you jumped me at the Juice Bar."

Jumped is a strong word.

"I have a follow-up question I'm hoping you can answer."

"I get to be in another article?" Waldo asks. "Cool. My quotes in that last one got Mike and Scully real pissed. Maybe this will give old Mike cardiac arrest. One can only hope."

"Do you know Gracie Caleza?" Harper asks.

"Who?"

"Skinny, tall, long black hair with bangs. She was friends with Sam. Transferred out over winter break."

"Why are you asking me?" Waldo laughs. "Shouldn't you ask your girl?"

"Just answer the question."

"Skinny, black hair, bummed around with the loser." He goes quiet for a moment. "Kind of a weird goth?"

"That's her."

"Caleza. Sounds familiar. I think they were friends of ours, long time ago. Long Island people. But," Waldo adds before Harper can speak, "I've never talked to her at Edwards."

"Do you maintain any connection with her?" Harper asks. "Are you Snapchat friends?"

"As if I screw around with that stuff," he says, laughing at her.

Waldo has no more information, so she hangs up.

Gracie was out of the picture in Sam's life midway through last semester. Sam had even said, *I knew nothing about her life after we stopped talking.* But according to TENNIS girl, they had been best friends.

What is she missing?

———————————

SAM

We get a brief respite from court for the weekend. On Sunday morning, I sit alone in the cafeteria—as usual—and still in the same clothes as always, dreading my testimony tomorrow.

Ding! New email. I take out my phone with a sigh.

I usually don't read hate mail during the day, but the subject line intrigues me.

> TO: Sam Barker (sbarker@edwardsacademy.org)
> FROM: Olivia Lauren Crosswell (o.l.cross@shmail.com)
> SUBJECT: You're not alone
>
> I wish I had half the guts you do.

Scully was a Second Year when I was a Firstie. And he liked me. He took me on a date to the Roast. It was a huge compliment.

You know what that's like.

Afterwards we snuck into Cath to make out. He started feeling me up, and I decided I wanted to call it good. I mean, my parents would have freaked just knowing I was kissing boys. And I didn't want people to think I was a prude.

But he wouldn't stop. And he did the same thing to me that he did to you.

I had an abortion my first year in high school. And I had to ask my parents to help me get it.

I almost dropped out. I only stayed because my parents made me. It was the trade-off for the abortion. They didn't even ask who did it. They wanted to pretend like it never happened.

I'm sorry everyone is treating you like this. Whatever you need, let me know.

I can write a statement.

I can write a letter.

I can share your post a million times.

I want to see Scully smashed into tiny pieces just as much as I'm sure you do.

With all the love in the world,
—O. L. C.

I have to pause my reading to breathe three times before I can finish. By the end, my hands shake so much I have to shove them under my legs to make them stop.

There were more. There *are* more.

Zzzzzt.

I'm having trouble breathing as I forward it to Harper. My eyes are blurry.

"What should I do with this?" I ask.

I've never met Olivia Lauren. Facebook says she's a Third Year, swimming team MVP, and the student in charge of Edwards's small, student-run Women's Center.

I want to go find her right away, hug her, tell her we can beat this together. But what if word got back to Scully? His lawyers can't know we've connected, or they'll anticipate Olivia's testimony. Better to catch them off guard.

Harper emails me back.

> Get her to testify. Tell Anastasia right away. This is exactly what you need.

The night before my testimony, I take down the drawing of Gracie I'd pinned on my wall—the one with her real smile— and slide it inside a folder that'll go home with me.

Even though Gracie's last email was hostile, I still find myself writing back.

> I'm going up on the stand to testify tomorrow.
> Gracie, I'm terrified. Please come.

I'll sleep at home tonight, and the stylist will meet me there in the morning. Clean me up, put me in a demure dress, make me look younger than I am, and parade me out to the witness stand.

Dad and I don't talk much on the drive home because there isn't much left to say. But he does let me put on whatever music I want.

That's how I know he's afraid.

———————————

I stare at myself in the mirror as the makeup artist props me on a stool and heats up the flatiron. The slight smell of burning hair as she works on me reminds me of that afternoon makeover Gracie gave me before the Inaugural Mixer.

After my hair's tamed, she covers my imperfections with light foundation. No makeup around the eyes except some mascara and eyebrow definition.

I look wholesome, like the girl Tasia described. The most innocent kind of victim I can be.

I remember Scully's new haircut, the glasses he doesn't need to wear. We are just actors being dressed up, given lines to say, and paraded out on stage.

Gracie was right. It's all theater.

When we get in the car, my stomach's sour. A wadded-up copy of a local newspaper sits in the back seat of the station wagon. The headline's about the trial. I don't look at it.

We find Harper in the long pew seats of the courtroom and slide in next to her. Then Tasia calls my name. I'm light-headed as I stand up.

Every pair of eyes in the courtroom follows me to the bench, where I place my hand on a Bible and repeat some words I don't remember.

The judge's eyes are flint as I climb onto the witness stand.

"Thank you for being here, Samantha," Tasia says, offering me an encouraging smile. "I know this was tough for you."

I nod. I can't speak or butterflies will fly out of my mouth.

"Can you tell me about that?" asks Tasia. "Why coming forward has been so difficult?"

"I was scared," I say. My gaze darts to Scully. To his dad, sitting with his arms crossed over his chest. To the three lawyers flanking them like a battalion of bodyguards.

"Why are you scared?"

"I was scared for my family, what they would think," I say. "I was scared about how I would be treated at school when I broke the honor code by coming forward."

"What's school been like since then, Samantha?"

"Everyone at school loves Scully," I say. I tell her about the kids with painted faces at the polo game, howling every time Scully scored. I tell her about the hate mail, and Tasia produces some printed copies.

"How'd the police get involved?"

"My parents found out, and I didn't have a choice."

"Your parents told the police?"

"I was all messed up over break, so they went fishing around. Then they found my blog, and it was all over."

This is the story we're sticking with—Mom, Dad, Harper, and I.

Tasia produces printed copies of the blog for the judge, who barely looks at it.

"Can you tell us what happened between you and Scully?" Anastasia asks. "What you wrote on your blog that your parents found?"

I rehash the same story—this time, with my parents in the room. I hate that they have to hear all this. Everyone in the courtroom is staring at me. My voice echoes. It's crackly, and sounds pathetic.

I feel my tear ducts filling as I talk. The judge's face is impassive—sometimes he doesn't even look at me as I describe how Scully tore into me. I don't know how I manage to get the words out, but each one rips itself from my lips until they are all gone.

Scully's shaking his head, glaring daggers at me, when one of his lawyers taps his shoulder and whispers in his ear.

I have never hated someone like I hate him. I want to get off this witness stand, walk over, and slam his face into that table.

"Thank you," Anastasia says, her eyes soft. "That's all, Your Honor."

We take a recess so I can recover before the defense interrogates me. I feel hollow as we sit outside, not talking.

Then it's Turnquist's turn.

He gets up, flattens the lapels of his black suit, and runs a hand over his bald head as he approaches me at the stand.

He grills me about every detail. Dates, times, what happened when and where and with whom. He asks if I've had boyfriends. How many times I've kissed. I know he's leading me somewhere, but where?

"When Mr. Chapman said he'd tutor you in his room alone, did you feel excited about that?"

"Yes," I say, "but I really thought we'd just—"

"So you went to his room specifically knowing, intending, to be alone together." Turnquist gets an ugly smirk on his face as he says, "And you and Mr. Chapman had kissed before."

"Just because I was okay with kissing doesn't at all mean I wanted more," I say, my voice cracking. "As soon as he started touching me, I was incredibly uncomfortable. I wasn't ready."

"But you would have been ready later? If this alleged rape really did happen, as you say it did, how is a teenage boy supposed to know these fine-point differences?"

"Kissing and sex are totally different!" I find my voice climbing, and the judge shoots me a look. "I tried to push him off me and make him stop—"

"I read the account in your blog." Turnquist's demeanor and voice are as placid as a glacial lake. "Did you ever actually say 'No'?"

My head is pounding. "I think that me begging him not to do it, pushing him away, counts as a 'no'—" I begin.

"Did you ever," Turnquist says slowly, crossing his arms behind his back and staring me straight in the eye, "actually. Say. No?"

My mouth is dry as ash. I didn't think I had to. I thought not saying yes would be enough.

"No," I whisper. "But I—"

Turnquist doesn't let me finish.

"No further questions, Your Honor."

———

I wish I could die.

Tasia comes back with redirect questioning to try and undo the damage Turnquist has done, but it's futile.

"You didn't agree to have sex, did you?" she asks me gently.

I blink tears back hard. "No. I pushed him off. I did everything I could to get away."

The judge listens with his lips set in a flat, heavy line.

I crawl off the witness stand and scurry back to the seats where Mom, Dad, and Harper are sitting. I fly into my mother's arms.

I have never felt so small, ashamed, helpless.

"You did great up there," Mom says, smoothing my hair. "You did so good."

"I did terrible," I moan into her shirt. The tears finally rush full and fast down my face, into my mouth, tasting like the ocean. "I did absolutely terrible."

I let that asshole Turnquist walk all over me.

Thank god we're done for the day. All I want to do is go to sleep and never wake up again. Once we're finally free of that suffocating courthouse, I think I might collapse into a puddle on the cement outside.

"I can't believe I let him get me like that," I say to Harper, covering my face.

"He skewed your testimony and put words into your mouth," she says. "Don't worry, it's all going in the story. The world will see how Turnquist bullied you and the judge let him do it."

Good. Maybe it'll be okay if my pain can create something, if that grilling becomes the clay for a beautiful story that Harper will make.

While Harper and Mom talk about my testimony, and the calls Mom's been getting at the house at all hours, I start drafting an email to Gracie on my phone.

I testified today.
Scully's lawyer is a real piece of work. But I survived, Gracie. One step closer.
Don't worry, if you're worrying. I'm going to win this.

I send it, knowing I won't hear back. But I hope she at least reads it.

HARPER

Reporting has brought Harper into many ugly, uncomfortable situations. But never has she felt like she did watching Turnquist interrogate Sam like a bear tearing into salmon.

Still, Sam's testimony was underscored by something—a gut feeling that Harper wished she could banish.

Gracie, that dangling thread, wouldn't leave her alone. So as soon as Harper's home, she writes an email.

> TO: Gracie Grace (graciegrace12@shmail.com)
> FROM: Harper B. (harperbb@shmail.com)
> SUBJECT: A quick quote from you
>
> Hello Gracie,
>
> Thank you for replying to my last email. I understand your hesitance. Reporting rape can be messy and painful for everyone involved.
>
> Sam testified today, and the Chapmans' lawyer attacked her relentlessly.
>
> I'm writing an article about this. The world needs to know how girls who come forward are treated. But I can't publish the story without speaking to you first. You were Sam's roommate. You must have noticed something.
>
> Let's talk, please.

Harper presses SEND, then spends the rest of the night typing up a draft of her next story while she waits for an email back.

Nothing comes.

CHAPTER TWENTY-TWO

SAM

I climb into my own bed at home that night and stay awake for hours, replaying everything I could have said differently.

Next morning, I'm drained and heavy the whole drive back to the courthouse. I have to remember that I'm the one who chose to be here today.

Tasia addresses the judge, saying, "I want to call Olivia Lauren Crosswell to the stand as a character witness."

Olivia!

A tall, slender girl stands up in the back of the courtroom. She has pale skin and white-blonde hair, like someone has sucked all the color out of her. She nods to me as she walks up the aisle to the witness stand.

I wish I could see Scully's face right now while Olivia gives her oath, but I can only see the back of his head.

"How do you know Scully Chapman?" Tasia asks.

"We both go to Edwards Academy. I'm a Third Year."

"Another witness told the court that he's never been aggressive toward women. What are your experiences interacting with him?"

Olivia takes a deep breath and closes her eyes.

"That's false," Olivia says

"Can you tell us how you know this?"

"Because he raped me."

The gallery murmurs. Anastasia asks her to describe her experience.

"I'm on swim team, and we share the pool with the polo team. Scully and I became friends three years ago. After some flirting, he asked me on a date. We walked around campus for hours, just talking, until we ended up at Cath. I thought it was weird that he had a key, but he's buddy-buddy with the provost. He locked the door so nobody would, in his words, 'bother us.'"

"What happened in Cath?"

"We made out for a while. I kept thinking how mad my parents would be if they knew I was even kissing a boy. But then he started putting his hand under my shirt, and I told him I wasn't ready."

"What did he do?"

"He didn't care. He pushed me down behind the podium. I told him no over and over again, but he just covered my mouth. I ripped his shirt trying to push him off me."

"You definitely said 'No'?" Tasia asks.

"Multiple times."

"What happened after that?"

"He left me there. A few weeks later I missed my period. I went home for the weekend, took a pregnancy test, and found out I was pregnant."

I press thumbs into my eye sockets so I don't cry.

"Did you tell anyone?" Tasia asks.

Olivia shakes her head. "No. The honor code is pretty clear: *We will stand by each other. We will be our own wall, our own defense.*

I had four years left, and I didn't want to ruin it. And my parents would freak if they found out I'd had sex with someone. But eventually I had to tell them."

"What did they do?"

"They were pissed. Said something like, *This is where kissing boys will get you.* They didn't want to go to the police. I think they thought people would accuse them of bad parenting. But they helped me get an abortion."

"And you never told anyone at school."

"Never. Then it came out that Scully had raped Sam, too—"

"Allegedly," Anastasia says.

"That Scully had *allegedly* raped Sam. I realized I wasn't the only one. And I had to come forward to stop this from happening to even more girls."

Olivia gets it. She understands.

"That's all, Your Honor," Tasia says.

Turnquist stands up slowly, like a guard dog who's just noticed you on his property.

"It seems odd to me that your parents never asked who got you pregnant, Ms. Crosswell," he says, crossing his arms behind his back. "Maybe it was someone else?"

"I'd never had sex before Scully raped me," Olivia says. She is steel as she stares back at Turnquist. "And I haven't since. So, no, it couldn't have been anyone else."

"How come you didn't tell a friend?" Turnquist asks. "Anyone? It sounds like you came forward now because this was a convenient time to get your fifteen minutes of fame."

"Fame?" asks Olivia. "If I'd come forward three years ago, I'd be the one getting death threats right now. I mean, I had to have my parents' help getting an abortion. I felt ashamed enough."

"Do you have any proof of this?" asks Turnquist.

"Look at my medical records. My abortion is on there, and so are the hundred hours of therapy. Ask my therapist. She'd love to tell you all about it, I'm sure."

Turnquist huffs. "No further questions, Your Honor."

Olivia is shaking when she gets off the stand. She gives me a tiny nod before she stalks from the courtroom. I wish I could follow her out, hug her, share all our tears together—but it will have to wait.

She did a big thing today. Together, we're going to get what we came for.

HARPER

When court's adjourned for the day, Harper stuffs her notes into her bag and rushes outside to check her email on her phone.

A reply from Gracie.

> I don't talk to people on the phone. I don't like it.

That's all it says. Harper's heart starts beating faster as she writes a response.

Something is wrong.

> You don't even need to talk to me, if you don't want.
> You could answer the questions over email?

Back at home, Harper waits and waits. She fiddles with the draft of the article she's written, but it's not ready to go to Mark yet, not without this last piece about Gracie. Her gut is telling

her that something's off, and she won't publish anything feeling that way.

Time for bed—there's more testimony tomorrow. She'll
just check again in the morning. As she's crawling into her soft,
warm bed, her phone lets out a *ding*.

> This was her choice, not mine. I didn't tell her to do
> this for me. I want no part in Sam's revenge quest.
> Don't email me anymore.

What is Sam doing for Gracie?
Harper responds to the email anyway.

> If you testified and verified Sam's claims from that
> night, she could win. She could put Scully away for
> everything he's done.

As expected, there's no reply.
Another dead end, but a dozen more questions.

SAM

I've hardly been at school. My room doesn't look lived-in—my
things always spilling out of my duffel bag onto the floor, desk
covered in dusty papers. At least I graduated from Level One
after break, so no more inspections. One of my few things to
be thankful for right now. But now it feels like not even my
room is mine anymore. Like I don't belong, even among my
own things.

Sun spills in my window early, and it's the only thing that gets me out of bed. I feel like I'm full of water—sniffling, groggy, heavy. I've been up past midnight every night this week downloading class PowerPoints and finishing my assignments. Even after I send them in, I'm awake for another few hours obsessing over the trial.

I drag myself to Morning Prayer, then breakfast—to my table where I used to sit with Bex, Eliza, Lilian, and Gracie. I have earbuds in like always, poring over research for my next Art History essay, when a tray lands on the table across from me.

Olivia Lauren has three whole plates full of food, which makes no sense to me, given she's tall, lanky, and made of all lean muscle.

"Hey," she says, and starts in on her breakfast immediately. I can't look away from her shoveling food in her mouth at maximum speed. It's amazing.

But Olivia Lauren is the ideal Edwards student. Perfect platinum hair, an amazing figure, not a bit of excess body fat on her. How does she look like that and still eat like this?

"Swimming," she says, not looking up. "I have to gag down five thousand calories a day or else I crap out halfway through practice."

I forgot how nice it was to eat with someone else. With Olivia sitting across from me, I feel better about the school hearing coming up on Monday. Scully's at his usual table with Cal, Sloane, Mallory, and everyone else across the cafeteria—for once, they aren't laughing. Maybe Scully knows it doesn't look good for him. That no matter what else happened, the honor code was violated when he closed that door and we kissed. I just hope it spells more than a few days of suspension for him.

I spend the weekend at Edwards, catching up on work I missed during the week. I hang out with Olivia at the library, and she helps me study because she took all my classes last year.

Before I can blink, it's Monday. The school hearing will be in one of the small rooms in the student union, with the low, graphite ceilings. All morning my hands are shaking, so I can't write straight.

The provost loves Scully. He'll fight hard for him. What if I'm the one who gets suspended? I went to the cops. I broke the honor code.

I'm the one everybody hates.

As soon as I walk in, I spot Dr. Winegard sitting behind the table on the far side of the room. As much as I want to, I don't wave at her. I don't want everyone to know that we have any particular relationship. Mom's sitting in one of the chairs set up on the other side of the room—confined to just watching and listening, as much as she probably wants to get up and shout on my behalf.

Here there are no bailiffs, clerks, recorders, or judge. Just a panel of teachers and administrators with stacks of paper in front of them in a silent classroom.

When I walk in, Scully's sitting on the left side of the room. He looks small and weak without his fake court glasses, his fancy court suit. Turnquist's not here to protect him.

I'm not scared anymore.

Dr. Winegard gestures for me to sit in a chair on the right. Scully stares at me, radiating something ugly and angry. Those stormy eyes that I used to think were so gorgeous are hard and flat. He can think all the bad thoughts he wants.

The questioning starts.

"Where did it happen?" Dr. Winegard asks me. "When?"

They have all the check-in and check-out records. I can see the teachers nod when everything I say matches up.

"What did you say to Mr. Chapman when he touched you?" the provost asks.

As I speak, describing everything I've described before, Dr. Winegard's face grows more and more drawn. Eventually, she stops me and says, "Thank you, that's enough."

After that, Scully's allowed to respond.

"I didn't touch her," he says, proud and clear. "It's a lie."

Ugh. He's such a giant asshole.

"What were you doing that night when your House Father let you and Sam go back to your room together, alone?" asks Dr. Winegard. "With the door closed."

"Studying."

"You told your House Father it was a one-hour tutoring session," she says. There is a touch of vindictiveness in her voice. "But Sam was checked out only half an hour later."

"We covered the material quickly."

"Hmm. So no kissing, touching, nothing?"

"No."

He's a really bad liar. And like that, the hearing is over.

"We'll call you back in when we've made a decision," Provost Portsmouth tells both of us. "In the meantime, Mr. Chapman—" his face twists as he says this— "you're off the polo team."

Scully scowls, and stalks out of the room. No state championship for him and Frank. I could laugh at them.

The staff close the doors behind us, and I find Olivia waiting on a bench in the hall.

"Dinner?" she asks. It'll be nice to have someone to talk to while the teachers debate—it'll distract me from obsessing about it while I wait. I say goodbye to Mom, and Olivia and I walk to Hamilton together.

On my way back to Isabel House that night, Dr. Winegard catches me outside the door. She gives me a hug.

"Don't worry too much," she says in a whisper. "Olivia gave her testimony to us yesterday, and I think it looks good for you. I want this campus to be a safe place. So do the other teachers."

"Are you going to fire Jean?" I ask.

She shakes her head. "I don't know. After that *Inspector* article, we might have to. Parents are furious that we let this happen. And they're right to be."

I thought it would be at least a week before I knew, but then Dr. Winegard stops me after class the very next day to deliver the news: the school ruled to expel Scully.

I have to sit down on a bench by the side of the main path because the bones in my legs have become jelly. Dr. Winegard asks if I'm all right, and I wheeze out, "I'm just surprised, thank you." She leaves me alone to call Mom and tell her the news.

"At least one good thing," Mom says over the phone. "I won't feel so horrible about letting you go to that awful school now that he's not around."

Walking back to Isabel House, it's like the saturation on the world has been turned up to 100. The bright green leaves glow with moisture, the blue sky radiates, the edges of the buildings shimmer.

I can be here again without looking over my shoulder. I can exist without taking alleys and side paths, without guessing where Scully will be.

Gracie needs to know about this.

I curl up in bed and dial her number, but it only rings once before going to an automated message. Still blocked. And she'll just delete my emails.

How do I get through to her?

I pull out the notebook that Gracie left behind. Inside the front cover is inscribed:

IF FOUND, PLEASE RETURN TO:
Gracie Isabel Caleza
1093 Hudson Ln
Rosland, NY

I get on my laptop and pull up the New York bus system. If I take the school shuttle downtown and pick up a Greyhound to Long Island, I should be able to get on a city bus that will take me pretty close to Gracie's house. I plot out my course on Google Maps, scribble each step in a notebook, and I'm all set.

But getting to Long Island by myself will take the whole day. I'll leave tomorrow. The school will think I'm doing a court thing. Which I should be—Waldo will be testifying. But this is more important.

I got Scully expelled. Gracie has to know Edwards Academy is safe again. Then she'll come back and everything will return to the way it used to be.

She *has* to. It was the whole reason for everything.

———————

As I'm working on my homework due tomorrow, there's a commotion outside. It reminds me of the night Scully was arrested and everyone ran to the windows, hoping to get a good look.

I follow the group into the lounge to peer outside. Something is happening over at Thomas House.

"Scully's leaving!" a girl shouts.

"He got expelled today," someone else says.

So that's it. Hayden lets out a cry and makes a run for the stairs, followed by a few other prefects. Everyone else stays looking out the window, muttering.

"I knew that would happen," my next-door neighbor says.

"About time," says someone else.

While Hayden sails out the front door, I take the side stairs and run out the heavy back one that nobody uses. It dumps me onto the tiny rear path, overgrown by bushes and small trees. Everything is alive and green, thanks to all the sun and rain we've been getting the last few weeks.

I can see Hayden and her posse through the trees, lining up to say goodbye to King Scully. I slide between a tree and a lamppost to get a good view, my shirt catching on the tree bark. I hear it tear but don't bother to check out the damage.

Scully's leaving Thomas House, wheeling a suitcase. His dad and Cal walk alongside him, carrying more luggage, heading out to the curb where their enormous, pearly-white Escalade is parked.

Other people have lined up, too—but not everyone seems sad to see Scully go. They look varying shades of disinterested, like his exit is just another spectacle to observe.

Scully exchanges promises to hang out over the summer with Hayden's small group of loyalists. Hayden herself is openly crying. God, I can't stand seeing her. After everything she's done, and she has the nerve to cry?

I can't let it end like this. I can't give her the last word.

I want to see Scully's face now that he's lost.

I walk out from the trees onto the sidewalk—right in front of everyone. I find myself standing directly between Scully and the parking lot.

Cal goes around me, as if I'm not there. Mike shakes his head and scowls as he waits for his son. No way he's letting us speak without being in earshot.

But Scully stops in front of me, letting his suitcase stand up.

"If you think this is over, you're wrong," he says. "You're a little liar, and someday, someone's going to find you out."

"Scully," calls Mike, "don't bother. Don't give her anything to use against you."

"Whatever," Scully says, grabbing his suitcase again and barreling past me. "You were always pathetic, Sam. I can't believe I ever felt bad for you."

He's rattled. That unflappable, cool mask he wears is cracked, falling off.

I don't need to say anything. He's the one being expelled from school. The bright, white edge of the clock tower glints in the late afternoon sun as Scully and his dad climb into their SUV and drive away.

People are staring at me, but I'm used to it now. Since I'm already out, I think I'll go for a walk in the graveyard.

CHAPTER TWENTY-THREE

HARPER

It's back to Pennsylvania again the next day. The drive has become as familiar to Harper as her commute to work in the morning.

Anastasia's planning to call Waldo, and she doesn't want to miss what he has to say. But when she gets to court, Sam's not here. How could she miss this?

On the stand, Waldo acts like he's about to get on stage for his solo show. He settles into the witness chair, testing the arm rests, wiggling the microphone around so that it sits perfectly at mouth level. He leans in and says, "Test? Test?"

"Everyone can hear you," the judge says, letting out a sigh.

"Waldo, can you tell me how you know Scully?" Anastasia asks.

Waldo leans back in his chair and explains all about Ron, Mike, and Provost Portsmouth going to Edwards together in high school. Partway through, he stops and says, "By the way, Mr. Judge, as Scully's childhood BFF, he doesn't really wear glasses. Those are fake. He's dressing up for you."

Harper covers her mouth. Waldo has no fear—or sense of decorum.

"Please address me," Anastasia says, "Are you and Mr. Chapman still friends?"

Waldo scoffs. He repeats the line he gave Harper: "I'm not friends with rapists."

"Why do you say that?" Anastasia asks.

"He's told me many times about his 'conquests.' Nonconsensual conquests—I'd like to make that clear, for the record?" He glances at the court reporter, who gives him a confused look back. "He does it to piss me off. All the upperclassmen at Edwards know that Scully loves to screw Firstie girls. It's a joke, like, *What fresh meat do you think he's going to take home after tomorrow's game?*"

"Other people know about this?"

"Sure. Just like everyone knows about that body survey. That's where you find the girls with really shit self-esteem, the new ones who want to fit in. And the best way to do that is to sleep with the hot polo captain, am I right?"

Anastasia ignores the question. "Why didn't you tell the administration about this practice?"

"Why would I? There will always be some provost's favorite snooping around for prey. The school would find a way to make it disappear, like they do with everything else."

She asks him how he knows Samantha, and Waldo rattles off every time he saw her with Scully. It's a long list. He yawns then, and Harper cannot believe his gumption—to sit in front of all these people, in front of a judge, and yawn. Only a rich white kid could get away with that.

"It's too bad more girls haven't come forward," he says. "I know there are more."

And then it's the defense's turn. Turnquist smiles as he approaches the stand.

"Mr. Wilson," he says, "you expressed in your deposition an interest in taking over your dad's half of Blue Crescent, yes?"

Waldo gives the same story as before: He might be young, but he's ready to step up. Except that the Chapmans seem set on pushing him and his dad out.

"Interesting," says Turnquist. "If Scully is convicted, that would look bad for the Chapmans. You and Ron might get the whole company for yourselves."

"There are plenty of criminals on Wall Street." Waldo laughs in Turnquist's face. "Having a rapist for a kid won't make a difference. I just want Scully to pay for what he's done—that's all."

"Why are you so intent on making him, quote, *pay?* Are you jealous that Mr. Chapman has an easier time with women?"

Anastasia stands up. "Objection—leading question."

"I'll allow it," the judge says.

Waldo grins at Turnquist. "By *an easier time with women*, you mean raping them, right?"

Turnquist is trying hard, but smart as he is, I can't help feeling that Waldo's a little bit smarter. He bounces back the lawyer's questions with monosyllabic answers, and Turnquist complains to the judge.

"He's still answering," the judge says.

"Fine." Turnquist crosses his arms. "The defense rests."

When Waldo gets off the stand and heads out of the courtroom, he stops halfway. He turns, yells, "Hey, asshole!" When Scully turns around, Waldo flips him off.

A bailiff comes to escort him out. "Fine, it's fine," Waldo says. "I'll stop."

He leaves the courtroom, the bailiff following him out.

Maybe he's not Sam's friend, but he did what nobody else was willing to do—stand up to the Chapmans.

So where was Sam?

SAM

I've never taken a Greyhound before. The seats are starchy and hard. The guy sitting next to me smells like body odor, and his jacket reeks of cigarette smoke. He's eating pepperoni sticks from a bag, occasionally trying to talk to me. I just stare out the window, ignoring him.

I visited New York City once with my dad, when I was in middle school. But even that didn't prepare me for the sheer chaos of arriving at the Port Authority Bus Terminal. It's like fighting an oncoming river current just trying to get off my Greyhound and find the bus number I wrote on my sheet of paper.

The ride to Rosland, out on Long Island, is tedious. I have to switch buses again somewhere in the middle, and even then, it's a mile from the final bus stop to Gracie's address in the middle of a rich suburb. It's late afternoon by the time I'm walking down block after block of sprawling green lawns, stone cherub fountains, and high, wrought iron gates.

I stop outside a massive, three-story Tudor with a stone façade, the number "1093" mounted on a huge slab of flagstone in white calligraphy. The property extends into the woods, wrapped in a white picket fence with a pretty red barn in the far back. But there are no horses that I can see as I walk up the long path. I plant both feet on the front step of the porch, next to the big wooden swing, and ring the doorbell.

It takes almost a minute for someone to answer the door. It's a young, blonde woman in a black dress and apron.

"Hello?" she says, like a question.

"Hi." I offer her my hand. Who is this? Gracie's white, blonde sister? Some friend I don't know about? "I'm a friend of Gracie's."

Perplexed at first by me asking to shake her hand, the woman smiles politely and takes it.

"Gracie doesn't want visitors," she says.

"I know," I say, as if I am perfectly aware of Gracie's situation. "That's why I'm here. I'm Sam Barker—we were best friends at Edwards. And I have something really important to tell her, but I can't get through to her phone."

"She probably won't want to talk to you," she says. She looks like she feels sorry for me.

"That would be okay." Even though it would cut me to my core. "I'm not here to make trouble. This is just something she really needs to know about, and then I'll leave."

The woman glances into the house like she's about to call for someone, then thinks again.

Oh. She must be the housekeeper.

"I'm really not supposed to let anyone in to see her." She keeps her voice low, like she's worried someone will overhear. "But it's not healthy for her to be alone all the time. Lately it seems like she's getting better."

"I'm so glad to hear that." And I am. I think about her all the time in her house, alone, not talking to anyone, and probably replaying everything on an endless loop the way I have been.

"She did say something about you over Home Weekend," the housekeeper says. She looks like she's leaning toward breaking the rules for me. I just have to tip her over the edge. "Before she dropped out."

"I was her roommate there." I put on a wistful smile. "We did pretty much everything together. I miss her a ton."

"Right." She nods. "I remember." After one more look over her shoulder, the housekeeper gestures for me to come in.

One step closer.

"Okay, follow me," she says. "But don't go anywhere except where I tell you."

She closes the front door, cutting off the afternoon sunlight. Without it, the high-ceilinged entryway is all shadows. The dark wood used for all the embellishments makes the house feel like a medieval castle. Small bits of sun seep through windows in the neighboring rooms, painting long, orange rectangles on the wood floors.

The housekeeper takes off at a brisk walk up the wide stairs just ahead. The whole house is silent, and every creak of the floor feels like it will wake up some sleeping monster. Ahead of me, she rounds the stairs at the second floor, checking down the hallway before we keep going. I get a sense deep in my gut that I'm not the only one who's not supposed to be here.

That no one is supposed to be here.

She stops at the third floor and glances up and down this hallway, too, before ushering me to follow her. There are so many doors—dark wood, like the rest of the house, and closed. Even though the doorknobs are all bright, polished, and spotless, it feels like no one has actually used them in ages. Which one is Gracie's? It's like I'm in a funhouse.

As we walk down the long hallway, it seems like it's narrowing. I feel suffocated. The scratchy sound of a television turned way down trickles toward us. At the end of the hall, the housekeeper stops and gently raps her knuckles on the last door.

"Sorry, Gracie," she says. "But you have a visitor."

"A visitor?" a voice on the other side asks.

I'm flying. It's her—it's really her. Her actual voice. I missed it so much.

"I don't want visitors," Gracie says. "You know that, Rachel."

I can feel the pounding of my heart in my toes.

"But, Gracie," Rachel says with an encouraging voice, as if she has said it many times before.

Footsteps echo on the other side of the door. It opens five inches, revealing one shoulder and half of a face. "I don't want to talk to—"

When she sees me, Gracie stops mid-sentence. I expect her to run back inside and slam the door.

"What are you doing here?" she snarls.

"I have something to tell you."

"She says it's important," Rachel says in a placating tone. "Why don't you just talk for a few minutes? You haven't seen any of your friends in months."

Gracie eyeballs me, sucking on her lower lip. The skin under the one eye I can see is dark and thin. She opens the door just wide enough for me to slide in sideways and then closes it again. "You have five minutes."

It's dim inside Gracie's bedroom, only a few scraps of light slipping through the slats in the blinds. Clothes litter the floor. A TV in the corner plays an old movie on low volume with the closed captioning on.

She is still my favorite person in the whole world. I want to throw my arms around her, but I don't.

"How are you?" I blurt.

She just crosses her arms, staring at me.

This wasn't at all how I had imagined this going. I stumble for something to say, something to fill the space.

"I've really missed you," I say. "It's been horrible at Edwards. Everyone hates me." Her expression darkens. "There's so much you need to know. So many things happened. It's really lonely there without you."

She stands there, closed up. I can feel the anger radiating off her like steam.

"Please say something."

"Four minutes," she says.

"Why did you leave?" Maybe a question will elicit a response. "You didn't have to leave me."

Gracie's face shifts from irritation, to disbelief, to . . . anger? She finally turns to look at me, and her voice is dead flat. "Why are you here, Sam?"

Everything I'd come here to say withers in my throat.

She hates me, too.

I glue my eyes to the floor. This is worse than the hate mail, the apple—worse than everyone at Edwards shutting me out.

"First you wouldn't shut up," Gracie says, and I can feel her gaze burning into me. "And now you won't talk?"

"Scully got expelled." I finally look up. "I got him kicked out. For you."

"What?" Her face contorts. "You did *what?*"

Why is she so mad? "He came after me, too!" I cry. "He pushed me down, too. He ripped my skirt open! But he knocked over that boiling tea—"

Gracie's eyes narrow into slits. "Don't you dare compare what we went through."

"He had to be punished." My face feels bloated with tears. "I did it for us."

She lunges at me, her fists clenched. I fall back against the closed door. She jabs her finger in my chest. "For us?" I think the room might explode—if Gracie doesn't incinerate me first. "For *us*?!" She repeats, so loud my eardrums vibrate. "Scully didn't rape you, Sam. Maybe he tried, but you didn't suffer at all like I did. He raped *me*."

My blood is roaring, filling my head. The tears break free.

Her face hardens as I start to cry. "You read my blog," she says, her voice sounding dangerous. "As if you could just . . . learn my lines and pretend to be me." She's shouting now. "You stole my story. You stole *me*."

My legs are shaking. Without the door holding me up, I would fall. "I was just trying to help," I manage to get out. "What happened to you . . . it was my fault. I had to fix it—"

"So what if it was your fault?" she says. "Maybe you should have warned me. But you didn't. In the end, I went over the next night having no idea—and Scully raped me." I want to evaporate, because she's right. "But that's not where you fucked up. Instead of letting me deal with it the way I needed to, you had to go all vigilante. I didn't ask you to be my white knight, Sam."

I'm too stunned to say anything. Not that she gives me the chance.

"Just because *you* felt like you had to do something doesn't mean that *I* did. All those emails and calls, over and over, telling me—do this, do that, come forward—you know why I didn't answer?"

I stay silent. I don't want to hear what's next.

"Because I didn't want to! It would fuck up everything in my life. But that must not have been the answer you wanted, was it?"

"I—"

"How do you think it's been for me?" she demands. "Your face all over the internet, with *my* words. And then, *him*, on every TV station, every newspaper. Every time I see his face I feel sick. What did you want? A cheerleading section for your big show?"

"But, Gracie," I say through the tears flowing down my lips, "I just wanted you to be happy again." That charcoal drawing of my friend with her real smile, the one that's been pinned to my wall day in and day out . . . "Scully's gone. We can start over now."

"Wow." Gracie shakes her head slowly. "Do you live in some kind of alternate dimension? Don't pretend like you did this for me. You *liked* the attention. That's why you made that hashtag."

I gape at her. No. That's not true. I thought only of her, of what Scully deserved.

"You wanna know something?" she says, coldly searching my face. "I left because I didn't want to sit through your guilt. That's your problem, not mine. What *was* my problem? My trauma. But you couldn't let it be. You couldn't let me deal with it the way I needed to."

"You could have told someone," I whisper. "The police. Like I did. Or your parents—they could have helped you. You wouldn't have had to drop out."

Gracie looks at me like I'm stupid. "Yeah, right, *keep this community sacred* and all that. Come on, Sam. We both know the problem isn't who to tell. It's the fallout for telling."

"But, Gracie—"

"And I did tell my parents. They tried to help. I've seen therapists, got drugs. But the Chapmans are top shit around

291

here. My parents knew making a big deal out of it would just draw out my pain. That would make it all worse."

The energy drains out of her, and Gracie sits down on her bed.

Snot is running from my nose. "What about justice?" I demand.

Gracie is emotionless. "You're obsessed."

"I . . . I thought it was the right thing to do."

"I don't care what you thought was the right thing," she says. "What you did? Instead of supporting me, and what *I* wanted to do, you made it all about yourself."

I have no tears left. My eyes are full of sand and my cheeks feel too tight. I thought getting rid of Scully, getting justice, would fix everything.

I was so wrong.

Gracie sighs. "You need to go."

Her tone is final.

I leave her in the dark room with the muffled, flickering TV.

CHAPTER TWENTY-FOUR

HARPER

As soon as she exits the courthouse, Harper checks her phone.

Sam missed everything today. What could possibly be her reason? She's dutifully showed up to see every testimony until now, even though she's not obligated to.

No new texts. No email, no voicemail, no calls.

Something is wrong. Harper can feel it in her gut.

In the car on her drive home, her phone suddenly buzzes. She glances down at it, even though she knows she shouldn't.

A new email. And it's from Gracie.

She'd wanted this reply so much, but now that it's here, she feels bile boiling up. She has to drive another few miles until she can get off the road. Parked at a rest stop, her hands shaking, she pulls up the email.

> TO: Harper Brooks (hbrooks@nyinspector.com)
> FROM: Gracie Grace (graciegrace12@shmail.com)
> SUBJECT: collect your girl

I've tried to ignore this, to keep it out of my life, but you and Sam just won't let it drop. You won't let me be.

So fine. Here it is—that reply you've wanted so bad.

Sam wasn't the one who was raped by Scully Chapman.

It was me.

I wrote that blog. I know you've seen it, the one Sam's claiming is hers. But it's not.

The story she told you is my story. She wanted to take down Scully, so she lied to you. She lied to everyone.

Now please—**please**—stop emailing me.

Gracie

"Oh my fucking god," Harper says aloud. She tosses her phone into the passenger seat like it's diseased. She presses her face to the steering wheel, wishing she could unread it.

Sam used her. This entire time, Sam had been using her. Everything Harper wrote was a lie.

She should have known better. She *did* know better—her instincts had been telling her at every step not to get involved, that this story was full of landmines, and she ignored it.

The whole drive home, Harper wishes she could take it back. But it's out there now, with her byline all over it.

SAM

After a bus ride and another Greyhound home from Long Island, the taxi to Edwards costs me every last dollar I have.

I don't get to school until one in the morning, and the door to Isabel House is locked. I end up sleeping on a couch in the student union until people are up and moving about, and I scuttle back to my dorm room before a teacher notices.

When Mom and Dad pick me up, we're all exhausted. Thinking about yesterday keeps me silent, squashed into the back seat of the station wagon, all the way to the courthouse.

A few minutes before testimony is supposed to start, Harper slides into the courtroom. She has circles under her eyes, and heads to the other end of the gallery to sit down. She pulls out her notebook and folds her hands on her lap. As I stare at the side of her face, she starts to turn around. Her dark brown eyes lock on mine.

She knows.

She knows.

She knows.

I jerk my head back to face front, not able to look her in the eyes anymore.

This is bad. Gracie must have told her last night. What will Harper do with it? Somewhere online I read that journalists issue retractions when they get something wrong. Will she take it all back? Surely that would look bad for her, too. And it would ruin any chance I have to put Scully in jail. It would wreck everything I've done.

It's hard for me to pay attention as Turnquist trots out a whole host of witnesses to vouch for Scully's character. His friend Cal goes on and on about how generous his pal Scully is with other students. One of Scully's teammates from the polo team gets on the stand and laments how the team's suffered without him. Even his dad testifies about how the Berkeley administration read the *Inspector* article and immediately revoked Scully's admission.

I want to feel victory, but I can only think about how everything is unraveling.

Then Turnquist says, "Gracie Caleza to the stand, please."

Gracie?

I sit up and spin around as the doors open. And sure enough—in walks Gracie.

She's dressed up in a black pencil skirt and gray button-down—exactly her style. She looks wonderful.

"That's your friend from school, right?" Mom asks.

I nod.

"Why is she here?"

"I don't know," I lie. But I do.

Gracie is here to tell the truth. It will all come crumbling down, right here, right now.

She strides up to the stand, swears her oath, and lands in the chair still warm from Mike Chapman. She stares straight ahead.

I am a house made of glued-together popsicle sticks, about to fall to pieces. Everyone will see me for what I am.

But if she's the one bringing it to the ground, I almost don't mind. I probably deserve it.

Turnquist approaches her, his shiny head reflecting the fluorescent lights. "Can you tell us how you know Samantha Barker?"

"We were roommates at Edwards," Gracie says. "But I transferred out."

"What was she like, when you lived together?"

"Smart. She got good grades. Great artist, too—we did Drawing Club together. She got me into playing tennis."

"If she's so smart, and has such good grades, do you know why she got tutoring that night?"

Gracie shrugs. "Dunno. Maybe she was falling behind."

"Don't you find that strange?" asks Turnquist. "That she went in for tutoring when she didn't need it?"

"No. Scully and she were friends. They went on dates or whatever. She probably just wanted to hang out with him."

Turnquist *hmms.*

"Did you notice anything strange after Sam's tutoring session with Scully?" he asks.

"No," says Gracie. "Everything seemed normal. But I was very stressed out at the time."

"I see." Turnquist can't help the smile that bites at his lips. He turns to the judge. "Everything seemed normal, huh? You must have been close, doing all those activities together, living in the same room. But nothing seemed off? She said nothing about Scully?"

Gracie's not fazed by the way Turnquist talks down to her. "No."

"Thank you," Turnquist says, waving a hand. "The witness is—"

"I didn't notice because I was pretty preoccupied," Gracie interrupts. "Considering he had tried to rape me the night before."

I'm frozen to my seat as the courtroom explodes into noise.

This is the last thing I expected her to say after last night. What is she doing?

The judge lays into his gavel. "Order, please!"

"Can you repeat that?" says the floundering Turnquist.

Gracie is the only one in the courtroom who's holding it together. "It wasn't just Sam," she says. "Scully Chapman tried to rape me, too."

"Your Honor," says Turnquist. "Hostile witness."

"She's your witness," the judge says. Turnquist searches for something to say, and the judge asks, "Are you done, defense?"

"No, not at all." He exhales. "How come you told no one about this before now? It seems very calculated."

Gracie snorts in derision. "You're the one who contacted me."

Turnquist, speechless, waves a hand at the judge and walks back to his table. Scully has sunk deep into his chair, one of his hands over his face.

I can't believe her. Gracie. She is just as amazing as I've always known.

"Your witness, prosecution."

Tasia comes up to the bench. She and Gracie seem to exchange some silent words with their eyes. "Can you describe to the court what happened the night of the seventh?"

"I asked Scully for help, and went to his room for tutoring."

She recounts exactly what happened to me.

"He . . . he tried it out on me first. I asked for tutoring, and he took advantage of the situation by inviting me up to his room. He shut the door. Forced me down and pulled up my skirt and—" She covers her face with her hands. "He made a mistake. You know how he makes the tea?"

"You mean the way he made tea for Sam?"

"Yes, exactly. He put in the teabags and set the mugs next to the couch. When he was trying to pull off my underwear . . . he hit a mug with his arm, knocked it over. Got boiling water all over himself. He fell off the couch just long enough for me to run."

It's my story. Coming from her . . . does this mean she believes in what I'm doing? Does she finally want to see him put away, too?

298

"Harrowing," says Anastasia. "Why did you never come forward before?"

"I was terrified. Embarrassed. I didn't even tell Sam because I was so ashamed that he'd almost gotten away with it."

Anastasia nods. "No more questions," she says, and returns to her counsel table. Turnquist is given a chance to re-examine, but there aren't any holes to poke in her story.

I glance over at Harper, and find her looking back at me. Will she write about this? She can't possibly print a retraction now —not after Gracie's testimony. She'd be throwing both of us under the bus for perjury.

She just shakes her head and looks away.

I spend the whole night and next day obsessing over what Harper might do. I don't know which testimonies we can expect next—until early the next morning, when my victim advocate calls.

"The defense won't bring Scully to testify," Melissa says. "There's so much out there already, they're letting his original statement stand."

"The one where he says he never touched me?" I ask, filling the words with as much derision as they can hold.

"Yep, that one. Think about it this way, Sam: It's over. You don't have to go anymore."

"The whole trial is over?"

I hear a breath of air hit her microphone. "No. There's closing statements, character reference letters, all that. But no more testimony."

"Do you know how long until a verdict?"

"No idea. But I'll call you as soon as I do know. In the meantime, you can write a letter of impact, if you want."

"A what?"

"A letter about how this has all negatively affected your life. Changed your relationships, your parents, school—anything you'd like. And the judge will take it into consideration when he makes his ruling."

Sure he will.

"I'll think about it," I tell her.

But I immediately send Gracie a text. It doesn't bounce back—I must not be blocked anymore.

Small steps.

> You were amazing yesterday.

I don't get a response, so I send another one.

> The trial is going to be over soon. They've asked me for a victim impact statement. I think it should come from you.

I expect not to hear back—or at least, for her to wait a while. But her reply comes immediately.

> What's that?

> You tell the judge how what happened changed your life. Or messed it up. How you feel. Whatever you want. Do you want to write it?

There's no response for a long time. I go back to watching a show on my computer, keeping an eye on the space on my phone screen where her text will appear. Finally, I see that she's typing a reply.

Okay. I'll email it to you.

Melissa wasn't kidding about the defense dragging things out. In April, I go to the courthouse one last time to read the statement that Gracie prepared. Harper's not here today. We agreed I'd just send her a copy of it so she wouldn't have to drive out here for the millionth time.

Gracie said to read it straight to the judge. It was meant for him.

"Your Honor," I begin, my voice shaking, "I address this to you instead of to the defendant, because nothing I say has ever mattered to him anyway. No amount of *no, please don't, please stop* has made a difference. So maybe instead, you will listen.

"I don't know if you know what it's like to have your voice stolen. When you have no voice, you stop speaking. You stop trying. I was used and discarded, and then robbed of my ability to talk about it. And then I was told by a lawyer in this very room that what happened to me was my fault. That the reality I experienced wasn't real. But the desolation, the isolation, the inability to exist inside my own skin without chafing—that is still very real. What Scully Chapman has done to me can never be undone. His father said that his life is over. But what about mine? I would like what he did to my life to matter to someone."

I shut my eyes and fold up the paper. "That's all. Thank you." I return to my seat in the gallery with my parents, my hands trembling. Scully stares at me as I walk by.

He must know those are Gracie's words. I hope he does.

I've been the worst friend ever. I took her voice, too. Giving some of it back is one very small thing I can do.

———————

Since Scully's expulsion, the school has slowly started to forget about me. By May, the fact that Scully ever attended Edwards Academy, that I ever accused him of rape, is forgotten. The soccer captain caught two of her players making out in the dressing room, and it's all anyone can talk about until school gets out.

Gracie doesn't come back to school. After she raked me over the coals in her bedroom that day, I didn't expect her to. She still isn't ready to talk to me, and I'm giving her the space she wanted all along. I'll wait forever if I have to.

Word got out that Olivia had testified, and she gets special permission to change rooms. It's unorthodox for a First and Third Year to live together, but it works.

I don't miss having that big, two-person room to myself. I way prefer sharing it with Olivia. She's so much more awkward than the cool, collected girl she seems like—all she ever talks about is swimming. She wants to go to the Olympics.

I make it all the way through finals, to the end of the year, before the judge reaches a verdict. I move out of Edwards for the summer the same day we're scheduled to go hear the judge's decision.

I could have waited for a news report, or Harper's article—if she's going to write one—but I want to hear it for myself.

Gracie's waiting when we arrive at court. It's incredible to see her.

"You're here!" I say, charging up to her, but not throwing my arms around her.

"Hey," she says. She looks . . . fantastic. Her eyes are bright, and she seems strong.

"Have you been working out?" I ask.

"Yeah, actually. I play tennis at the rec center."

"It shows. I bet you could beat me at a game now."

Mom waves at me as she and Dad find their way to a group of open seats.

"Want to sit with us?" I ask Gracie. "It's about to start."

"Sure." I know she hasn't forgiven me, so it's the best gift she could give me.

I notice Harper arrive behind us, too. She takes a seat on the other side of the courtroom.

The judge picks up his glasses and balances them precariously on his nose as he reads the verdict. He glances at Scully and Mike just before he begins. Scully has his hands clasped in front of him like a prayer.

Bullshit.

"Due to a lack of substantial evidence that, beyond a reasonable doubt, the alleged crime has occurred, I am forced to strike down the charge of statutory rape in the first degree," the judge says, but he doesn't sound the least bit repentant.

I have to cover my mouth to hold in a cry. How could he do this? After Olivia and Gracie testifying, after the statement I read?

"I do, however, believe that sexual contact occurred between the defendant and the victim, and thus charge Scully Chapman with the felony of sexual exploitation of a minor. I sentence Mr. Chapman to thirty days in minimum-security detention and an addition of his name to the Sexual Offender Registry."

A month.

That's it. That's all he gets for what he did to us.

"What the fuck?" Dad hisses, and I've never, ever heard him curse like that.

I squash my eyes closed to stop tears. I did everything I could—everything within my power. Next to me, Gracie is already crying.

HARPER

Thirty days. Just one month in low-security detention for raping two girls and trying to rape another. White men are still great at protecting other white men in power.

Still, a misdemeanor. It's something. The registry—that's also something that will follow Scully for a long time. He's branded now, so at least any school he tries to attend will know what he's done. He's been expelled from Edwards, and won't be going to Berkeley.

Harper flips on the TV when she gets home. They're running a story about the trial. It's a sanitized interview room with soft lighting—and in it is Mr. Chapman.

The interviewer starts by asking, "As his father, what do you think of this case getting such wide national attention?"

"Scully is sick to his stomach constantly," Mike says on the TV. "Filled with anxiety and worry. Just because of some high school drama, he has started obsessing about what prison will be like—"

She shuts off the TV as quickly as she turned it on.

Just some high school drama. That's all it is to them.

What about Gracie's months and months of anxiety?

It feels like an open wound in Harper's chest left to bleed. If only she'd listened to her instincts and just said, *This story's too fragile*, and refused Mark's push to go after it, she wouldn't feel like this.

She wouldn't yet again be seeing the cracks in the system, the gaping holes. Why did she think it would work? How did she get suckered into believing it would serve any kind of justice, when it never does? The court failed Sam, Gracie, and Olivia, just as Sam had once predicted it would.

Harper shouldn't be surprised. The system is doing exactly what it was designed to do: protecting people like Scully, at the expense of everyone else.

She wants to write that piece—an incisive study of the failure of the court to find truth, to mete out justice, to protect the people who are the most at risk. But writing that piece would be untruthful, too.

Harper starts typing.

Stick to the facts. Cover the official statement from the school. Leave the opinions to the readers.

If only she could headline it:

WELL, WHATEVER. IT'S SOMETHING.

The next day, Mark's not the happiest with what she's written.

"Where are all the interviews you did with the victim?" he asks, face red. "You mentioned the hashtag once. I thought you were going to do a whole insider exposé."

That would've been the story Sam wanted. And probably the story the world needed.

But Harper can't put her name on that piece.

The sanitized result ends up on Page 3D. An emotionless follow-up with no conclusions about truth or guilt—simply what the judge ruled.

At least it's over.

The story prints the next day. Harper calls Sam to let her know. At the end of the call Sam says, "I'm sorry it happened this way."

Harper doesn't respond for a while. Is she apologizing for using Harper? For lying? Or for everything?

"Thank you," Harper says, not sure that she wants to know. She just wants to rinse her hands of this and be done. Sam says goodbye, and they hang up.

At least now she can move on.

---

http://girloficeandspice.tumblr.com
June 22, 2018

Hello.

This is my second blog on here, because my first one had to be deactivated. It's . . . it's a long story.

I'm an aspiring artist living in Long Island. I'm posting my pictures here to hopefully build up a portfolio and get into art school in the city in a few years. Please feel free to share things I post, but don't repost without giving credit!

It was a long, hard school year this year, but finally, school is out. Even my online school lets us go for a month, though I'll have to be back at it in August.

I like online school, but let's face it—sitting at home on your computer all day is lonely, and makes you feel like a loser. The worst part is my only friend lives, like, hours away, so we hardly get to see each other. I can't wait to go off to college. Meet people like me. Actually get professional training in my art.

Maybe by the time college rolls around, I'll be able to handle dorm life again. Anyway, that's enough about me. I'm just a girl with some scars. I may not always like the marks they've left on me, but they make me the artist I am now.

Since this is supposed to be an art blog, here's a drawing of my friend. You might recognize her. She has scars, too.

Don't we all.

ACKNOWLEDGMENTS

I have to start by thanking my incredible partner and husband, Dan, for walking this long, hard road with me. *Honor Code* was a difficult book to write, a difficult book to revise, and a difficult book to edit—you sustained, supported, and loved me through all of it. Thank you for those many trips to the corner store at midnight, and hand-washing all my dirty dishes because we didn't own a dishwasher then. (How things have changed.)

Huge thanks to my agent Fiona Kenshole, with Transatlantic Agency, who's believed in me as a writer from the very beginning. You've helped me out of so many fixes and worked so hard to make my dreams come true—I look forward to whatever comes next for us!

This whole project was possible because of Alix Reid—my talented editor with a brilliant idea and a heart of gold. How many conversations about this book started with us celebrating some new life event? What a journey we've had together creating this challenging, wonderful story.

I couldn't have written about the courthouse as truthfully or realistically without my two on-call lawyers: my life-long friend Tim Kelly and the incredible Tracy. Thank you so much for all of your fast reads, knowledgeable advice, and steady encouragement—this last year and all the years before it.

And of course, all the thanks in the world to Kate Brauning, writer/editor extraordinaire—my friend, champion, and confidante. I couldn't have done this without your expert guidance.

I must thank the gifted team at Carolrhoda Lab and Lerner Books for all the hard work they've put in to make this book a reality. And a big shout-out to our expertise and sensitivity readers, Sarah Corsa and Kelsey Keimig. And finally, Heidi Mann, for taking my rough words and making them shine like diamonds.

Sending enormous thank-yous to my two best friends in the world: Meredith Feiertag and Sione Aeschliman. Meredith, for the many, many hours we've spent on the phone discussing this book—your wisdom is everything to me. And Sione—you always seem to magically conjure up an hour to soothe my troubled soul. I would move continents for you.

Finally, Amber—who dropped everything and anything at a moment's notice to help me untangle a plot problem, or rip apart and rewrite a major scene, or even read the whole manuscript in a matter of days. This book wouldn't exist if I hadn't met you.

TOPICS FOR DISCUSSION

1. Why is the Edwards Academy honor code so important? How does it affect the ways in which students and faculty interact and behave with each other? How does it affect the ways in which students and faculty interact and behave with people outside of Edwards?

2. As the novel progresses, Sam and Gracie find themselves in complicated situations facing difficult decisions. Discuss some decisions the two characters make, such as leaving school or contacting Harper. Which decisions would you classify as "right" or "wrong" and why?

3. What does Sam want to do for a career? Why, and who does she specifically want to help? How does this play out in the second half of the book?

4. What does the Isabel House hazing entail? Would Hayden consider it hazing? Why or why not? Why do you think Sam and Gracie have a tacit agreement to never talk about it?

5. Hayden talks about the need to "get it." What does Sam come to realize "getting it" means, and how does it relate to the honor code?

6. What roles do students like Hayden, Mallory, and Waldo, who are aware of Scully's pattern of illegal behavior, play in Scully's assaults? Would you consider them partially responsible for what happens? Why or why not?

7. Sam wonders, "Did I do something really catastrophically stupid by taking this on?" and "Is she right, that it's foolish for me to be talking to Harper? Was the article a bad idea?" How did you originally interpret these statements, and how does your comprehension of them change at the end of the novel?

8. Why does Harper persevere in writing the articles? How could she potentially benefit from them?

9. Why does Gracie drop out of Edwards Academy? Does she get what she wants by dropping out?

10. Compare and contrast how Gracie's and Sam's parents react to what their daughters tell them. How do Gracie and Sam feel and what do they do after talking with their parents?

11. When Scully assaults girls, he asks, "Isn't this what you wanted?" What does this suggest about what Scully thinks of his behavior? Do you agree with Sam when she says, "He'll never admit to anything, because he doesn't believe he's done anything wrong"?

12. What happens to Sam's and Gracie's friendship following the rape, and why do you think it happens?

13. Do you think that what Gracie calls Sam's "revenge quest" is more about punishing Scully, fighting for Gracie, or something else? Which of Sam's actions do you think are or are not justified?

14. What effect does the Tumblr blog have with the main narrative of the story? Could the novel have made sense without it? How does your interpretation of the blog change in the last chapters of *Honor Code*?

15. How does the honor code influence the events of *Honor Code*? What are some other possible titles of the book?